STAR TREK

VOLUME 5

STAR TREK®

VOLUME 5

Collection Cover by Tim Bradstreet, Colors by Grant Goleash
Collection Edits by Justin Eisinger and Alonzo Simon
Production by Tom B. Long

Star Trek created by Gene Roddenberry.
Special thanks to Risa Kessler and John Van Citters of CBS Consumer Products for their invaluable assistance.

IDW founded by Ted Adams, Alex Garner, Kris Oprisko, and Robbie Robbins

ISBN: 978-1-61377-687-2

16 15 14 13 1 2 3 4

IDW®

Ted Adams, CEO & Publisher
Greg Goldstein, President & COO
Robbie Robbins, EVP/Sr. Graphic Artist
Chris Ryall, Chief Creative Officer/Editor-in-Chief
Matthew Ruzicka, CPA, Chief Financial Officer
Alan Payne, VP of Sales
Dirk Wood, VP of Marketing
Lorelei Bunjes, VP of Digital Services

Become our fan on Facebook facebook.com/idwpublishing
Follow us on Twitter @idwpublishing
Check us out on YouTube youtube.com/idwpublishing
www.IDWPUBLISHING.com

Originally published as STAR TREK Issues #17–20.

Written by
MIKE JOHNSON, F. LEONARD JOHNSON,
and **RYAN PARROTT**

Art by
CLAUDIA BALBONI

Additional Art by
LUCA LAMBERTI

Inks by
Erica Durante

Colors by
CLAUDIA SGC and **ARIANNA FLOREAN**

Letters by
**CHRIS MOWRY, SHAWN LEE,
NEIL UYETAKE,** and **TOM B. LONG**

Creative Consultant
ROBERTO ORCI

Series Edits by
SCOTT DUNBIER

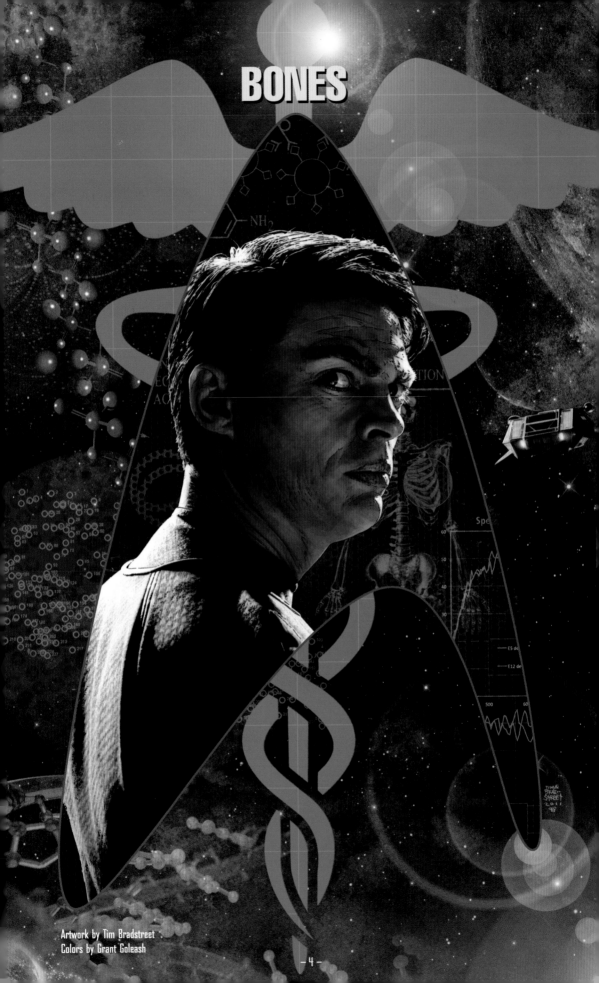

BONES

Artwork by Tim Bradstreet
Colors by Grant Goleash

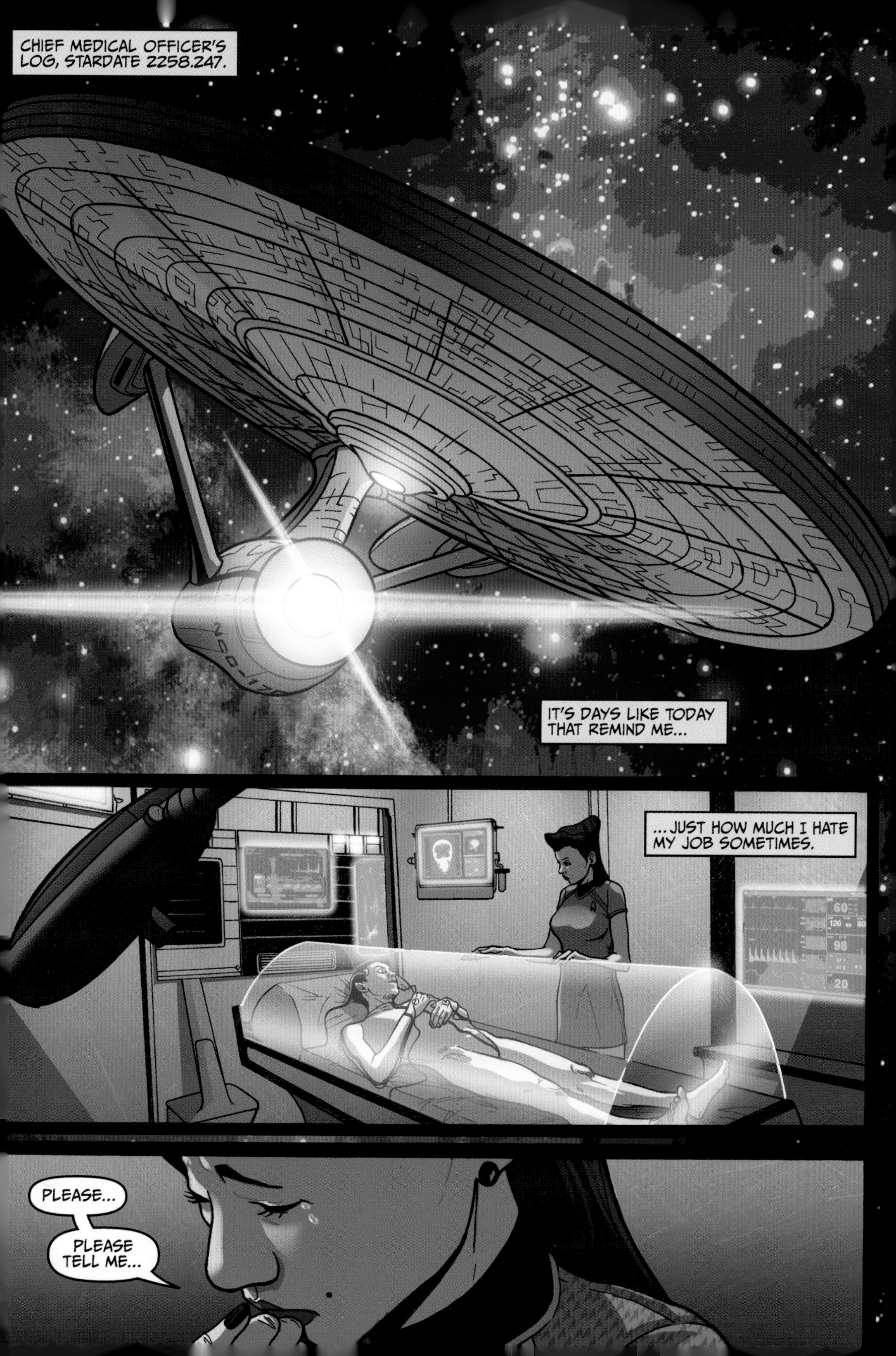
CHIEF MEDICAL OFFICER'S LOG, STARDATE 2258.247.
IT'S DAYS LIKE TODAY THAT REMIND ME...
...JUST HOW MUCH I HATE MY JOB SOMETIMES.
PLEASE...
PLEASE TELL ME...

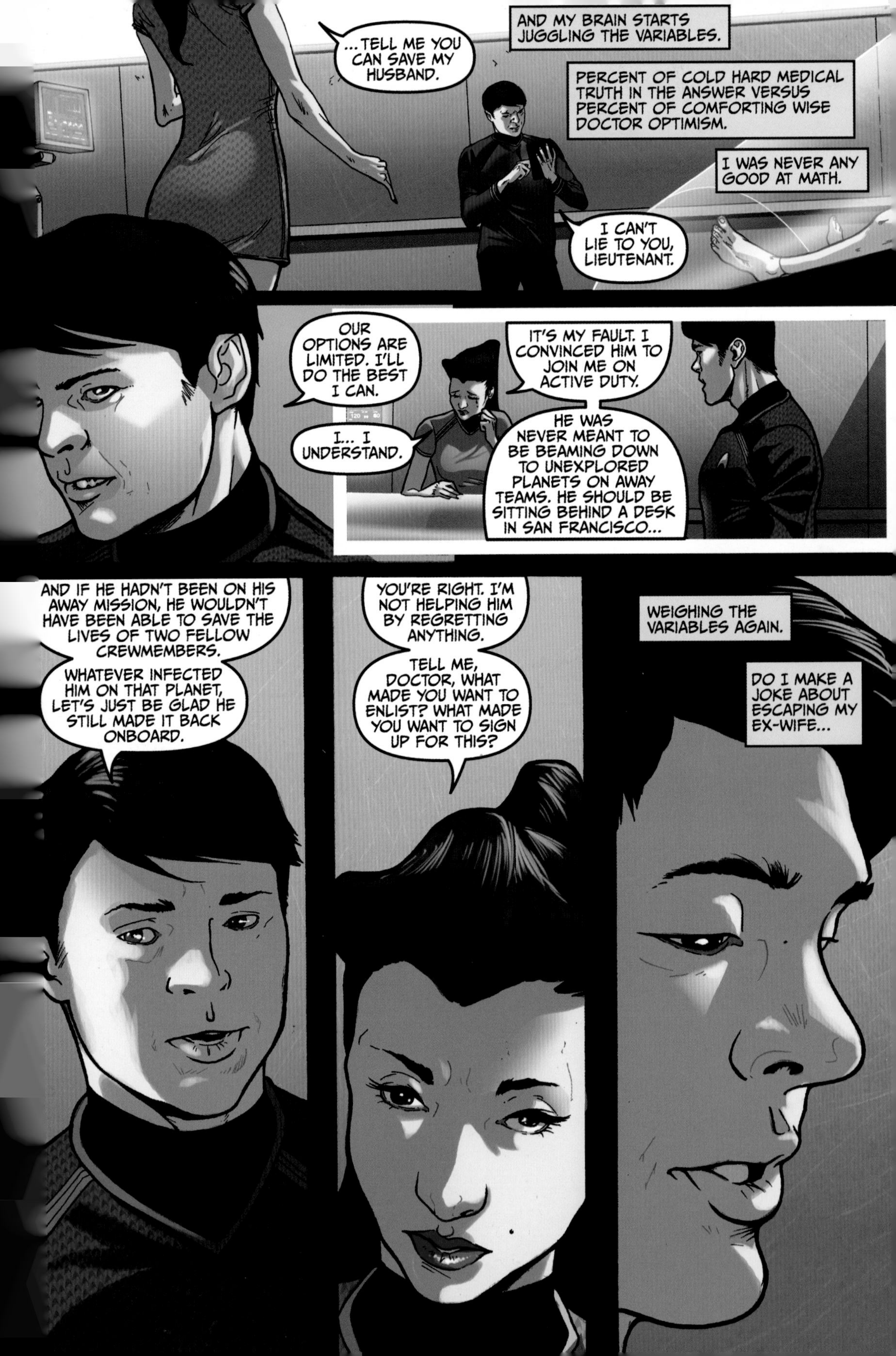
...TELL ME YOU CAN SAVE MY HUSBAND.
AND MY BRAIN STARTS JUGGLING THE VARIABLES.
PERCENT OF COLD HARD MEDICAL TRUTH IN THE ANSWER VERSUS PERCENT OF COMFORTING WISE DOCTOR OPTIMISM.
I WAS NEVER ANY GOOD AT MATH.
I CAN'T LIE TO YOU, LIEUTENANT.
OUR OPTIONS ARE LIMITED. I'LL DO THE BEST I CAN.
I... I UNDERSTAND.
IT'S MY FAULT. I CONVINCED HIM TO JOIN ME ON ACTIVE DUTY.
HE WAS NEVER MEANT TO BE BEAMING DOWN TO UNEXPLORED PLANETS ON AWAY TEAMS. HE SHOULD BE SITTING BEHIND A DESK IN SAN FRANCISCO...
AND IF HE HADN'T BEEN ON HIS AWAY MISSION, HE WOULDN'T HAVE BEEN ABLE TO SAVE THE LIVES OF TWO FELLOW CREWMEMBERS.
WHATEVER INFECTED HIM ON THAT PLANET, LET'S JUST BE GLAD HE STILL MADE IT BACK ONBOARD.
YOU'RE RIGHT. I'M NOT HELPING HIM BY REGRETTING ANYTHING.
TELL ME, DOCTOR, WHAT MADE YOU WANT TO ENLIST? WHAT MADE YOU WANT TO SIGN UP FOR THIS?
WEIGHING THE VARIABLES AGAIN.
DO I MAKE A JOKE ABOUT ESCAPING MY EX-WIFE...

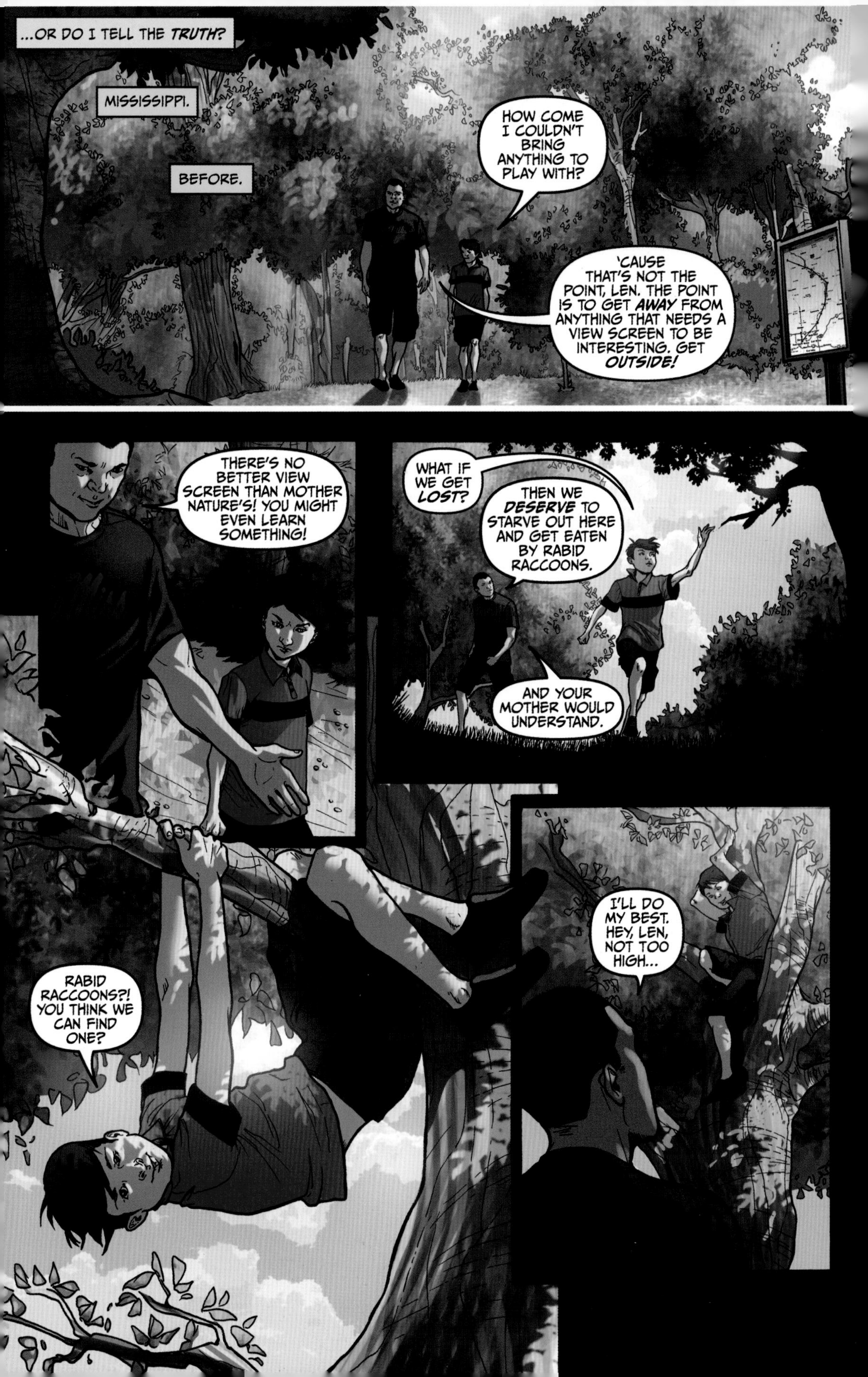
...OR DO I TELL THE TRUTH?
MISSISSIPPI.
BEFORE.
HOW COME I COULDN'T BRING ANYTHING TO PLAY WITH?
'CAUSE THAT'S NOT THE POINT, LEN. THE POINT IS TO GET AWAY FROM ANYTHING THAT NEEDS A VIEW SCREEN TO BE INTERESTING. GET OUTSIDE!
THERE'S NO BETTER VIEW SCREEN THAN MOTHER NATURE'S! YOU MIGHT EVEN LEARN SOMETHING!
WHAT IF WE GET LOST?
THEN WE DESERVE TO STARVE OUT HERE AND GET EATEN BY RABID RACCOONS.
AND YOUR MOTHER WOULD UNDERSTAND.
RABID RACCOONS?! YOU THINK WE CAN FIND ONE?
I'LL DO MY BEST. HEY, LEN, NOT TOO HIGH...

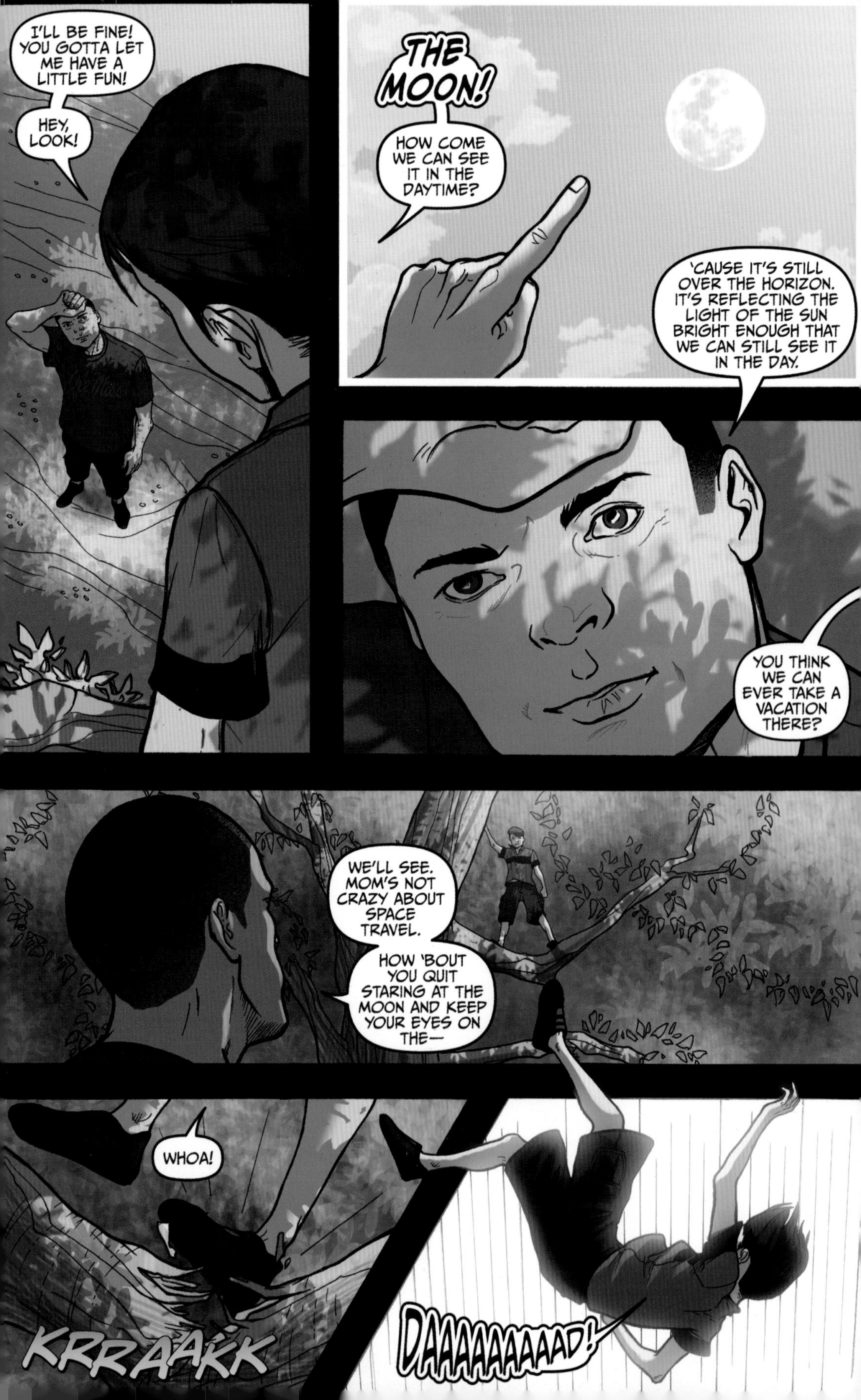
I'LL BE FINE! YOU GOTTA LET ME HAVE A LITTLE FUN!
HEY, LOOK!
THE MOON!
HOW COME WE CAN SEE IT IN THE DAYTIME?
'CAUSE IT'S STILL OVER THE HORIZON. IT'S REFLECTING THE LIGHT OF THE SUN BRIGHT ENOUGH THAT WE CAN STILL SEE IT IN THE DAY.
YOU THINK WE CAN EVER TAKE A VACATION THERE?
WE'LL SEE. MOM'S NOT CRAZY ABOUT SPACE TRAVEL.
HOW 'BOUT YOU QUIT STARING AT THE MOON AND KEEP YOUR EYES ON THE—
WHOA!
KRRAAKK
DAAAAAAAAAD!

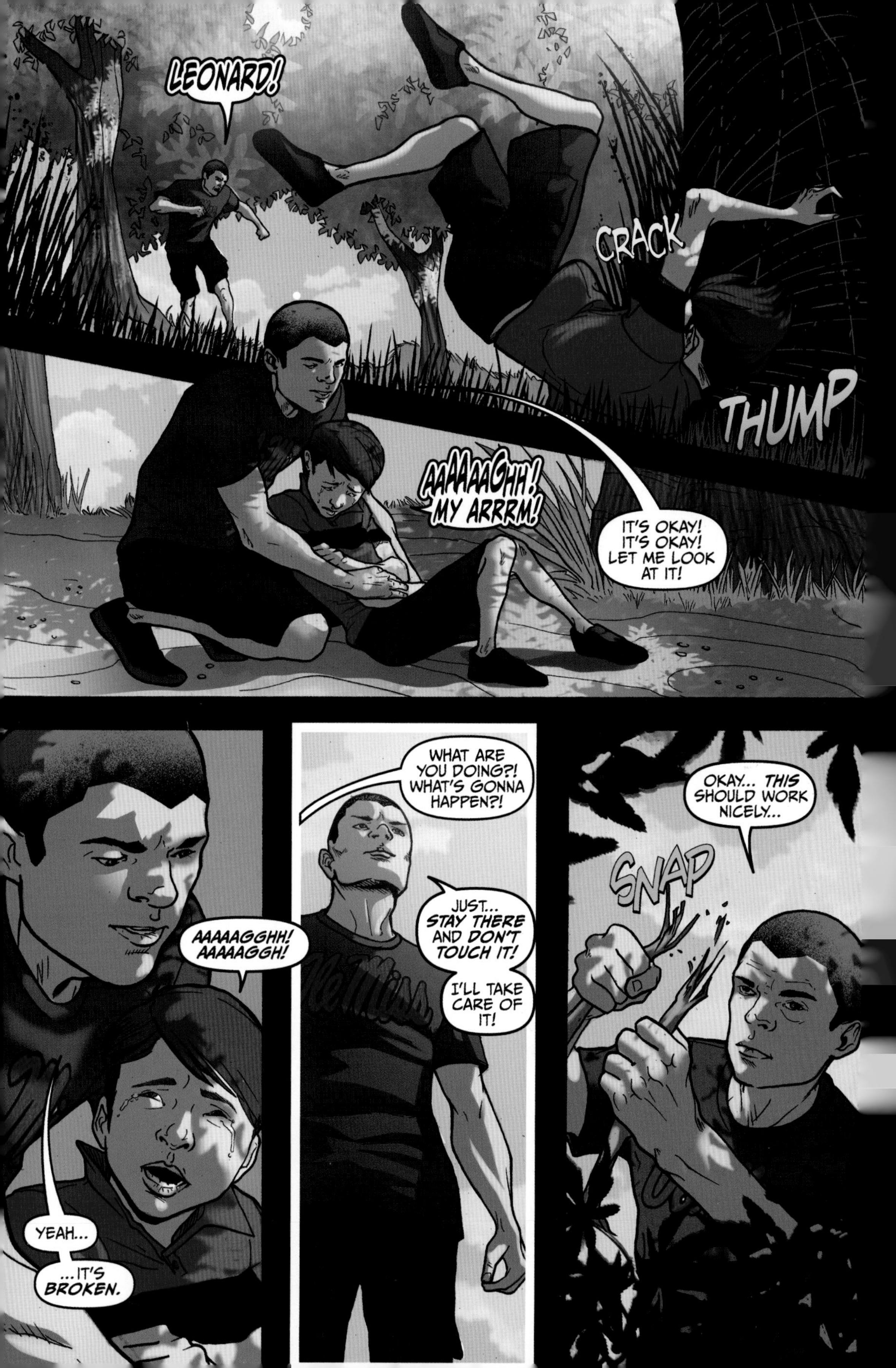
LEONARD!
CRACK
THUMP
AAAAAAGHH! MY ARRRM!
IT'S OKAY! IT'S OKAY! LET ME LOOK AT IT!
AAAAAGGHH! AAAAAGGH!
YEAH...
...IT'S BROKEN.
WHAT ARE YOU DOING?! WHAT'S GONNA HAPPEN?!
JUST... STAY THERE AND DON'T TOUCH IT!
I'LL TAKE CARE OF IT!
OKAY... THIS SHOULD WORK NICELY...
SNAP

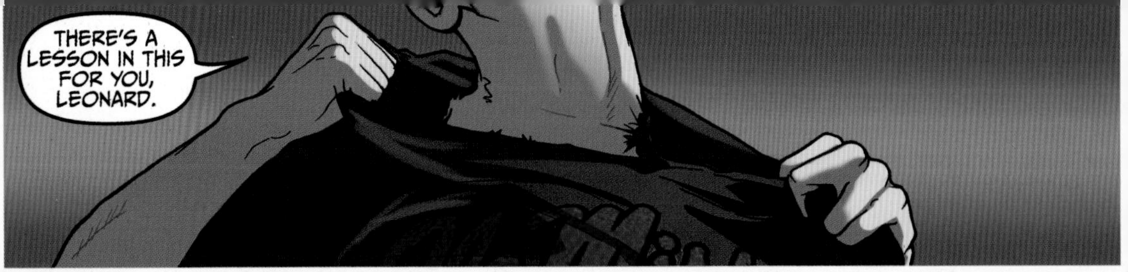
THERE'S A LESSON IN THIS FOR YOU, LEONARD.

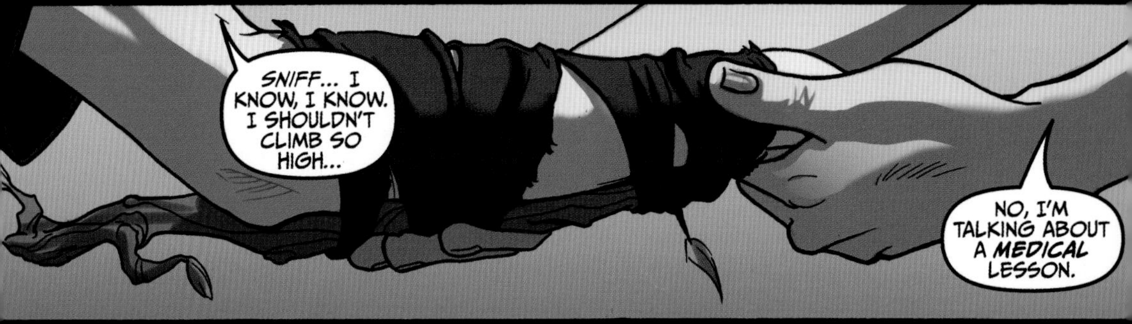
SNIFF... I KNOW, I KNOW. I SHOULDN'T CLIMB SO HIGH...
NO, I'M TALKING ABOUT A MEDICAL LESSON.

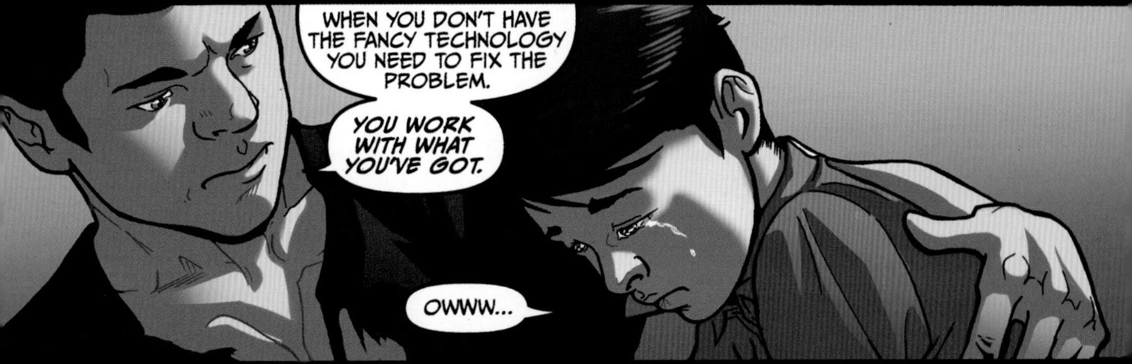
WHEN YOU DON'T HAVE THE FANCY TECHNOLOGY YOU NEED TO FIX THE PROBLEM.
YOU WORK WITH WHAT YOU'VE GOT.
OWWW...

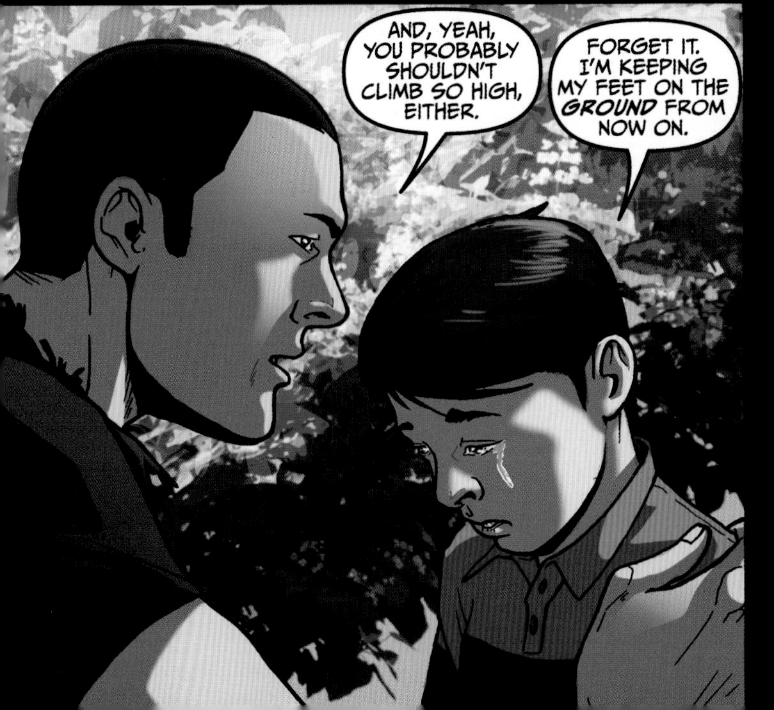
AND, YEAH, YOU PROBABLY SHOULDN'T CLIMB SO HIGH, EITHER.
FORGET IT. I'M KEEPING MY FEET ON THE GROUND FROM NOW ON.

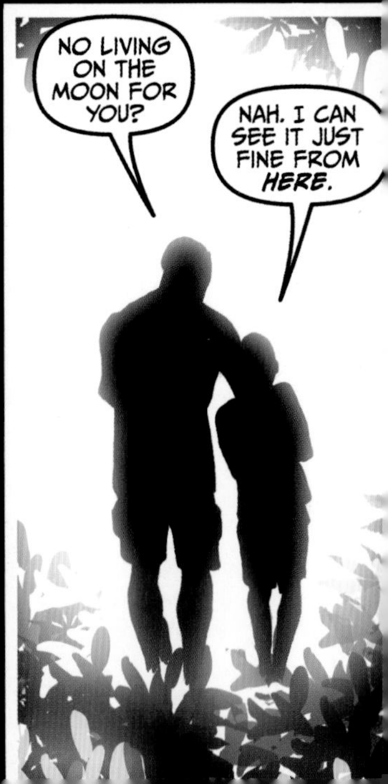
NO LIVING ON THE MOON FOR YOU?
NAH. I CAN SEE IT JUST FINE FROM HERE.

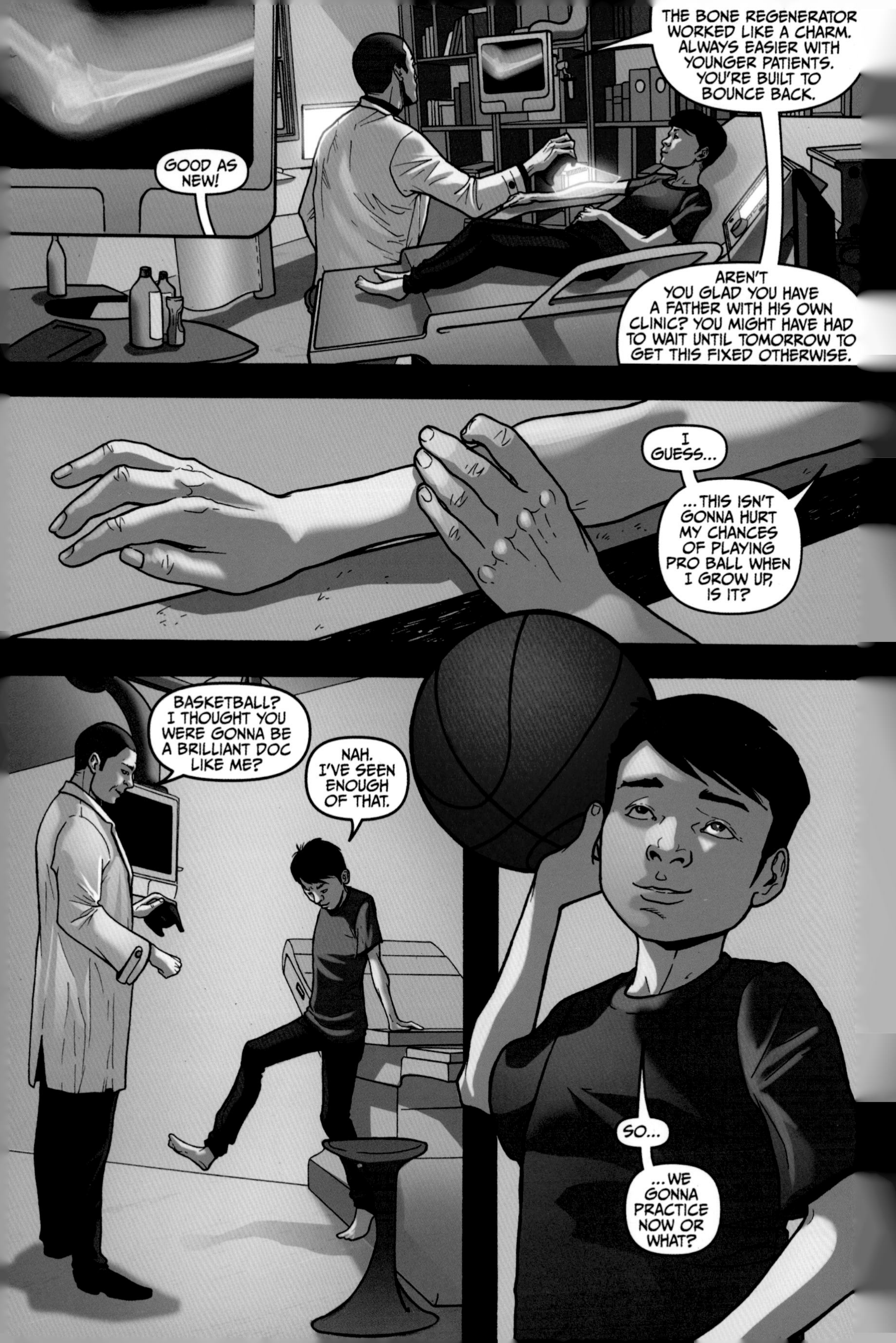
GOOD AS NEW!
THE BONE REGENERATOR WORKED LIKE A CHARM. ALWAYS EASIER WITH YOUNGER PATIENTS. YOU'RE BUILT TO BOUNCE BACK.
AREN'T YOU GLAD YOU HAVE A FATHER WITH HIS OWN CLINIC? YOU MIGHT HAVE HAD TO WAIT UNTIL TOMORROW TO GET THIS FIXED OTHERWISE.
I GUESS...
...THIS ISN'T GONNA HURT MY CHANCES OF PLAYING PRO BALL WHEN I GROW UP, IS IT?
BASKETBALL? I THOUGHT YOU WERE GONNA BE A BRILLIANT DOC LIKE ME?
NAH. I'VE SEEN ENOUGH OF THAT.
SO...
...WE GONNA PRACTICE NOW OR WHAT?

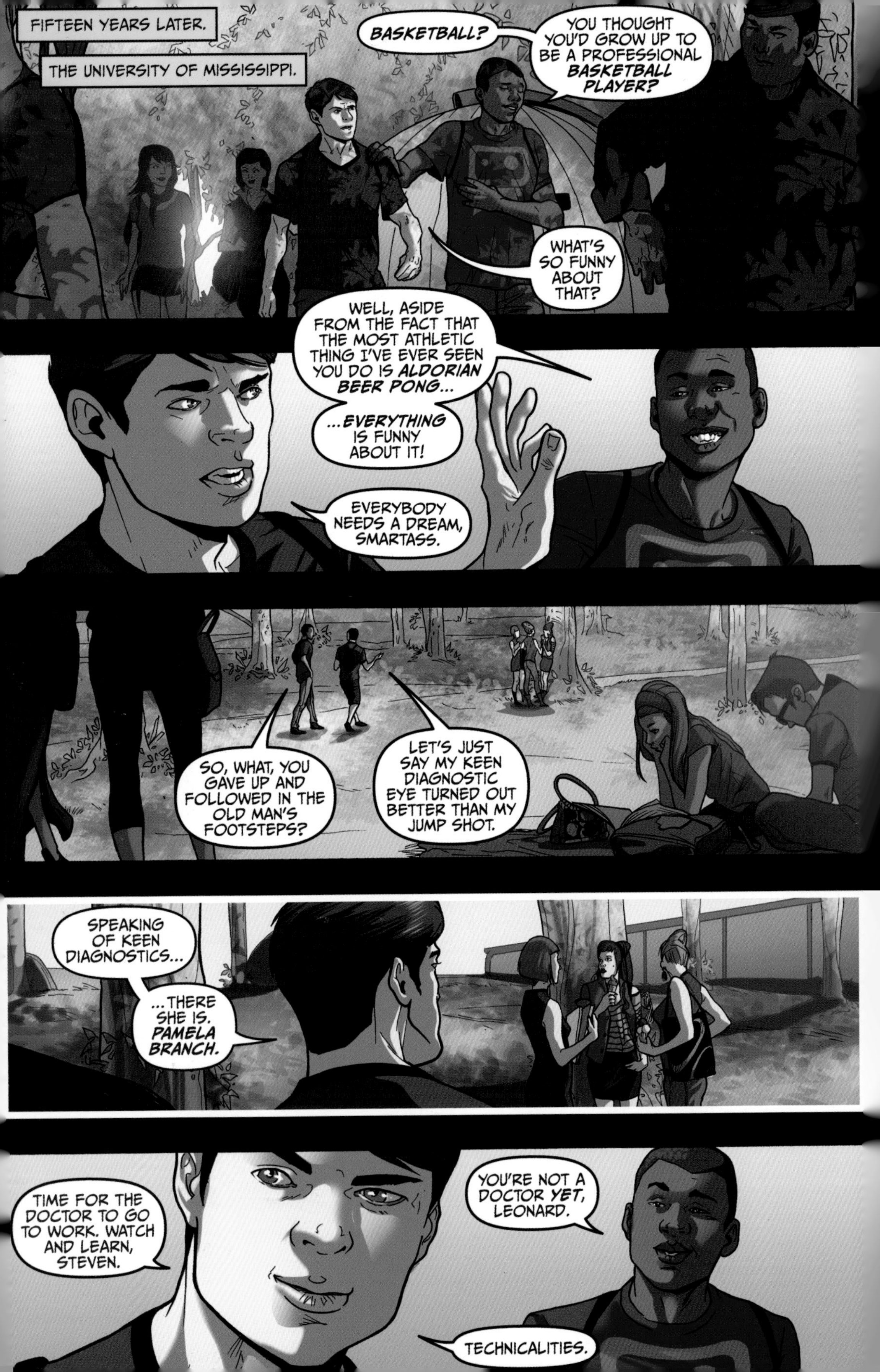
FIFTEEN YEARS LATER.
THE UNIVERSITY OF MISSISSIPPI.
BASKETBALL?
YOU THOUGHT YOU'D GROW UP TO BE A PROFESSIONAL BASKETBALL PLAYER?
WHAT'S SO FUNNY ABOUT THAT?
WELL, ASIDE FROM THE FACT THAT THE MOST ATHLETIC THING I'VE EVER SEEN YOU DO IS ALDORIAN BEER PONG...
...EVERYTHING IS FUNNY ABOUT IT!
EVERYBODY NEEDS A DREAM, SMARTASS.
SO, WHAT, YOU GAVE UP AND FOLLOWED IN THE OLD MAN'S FOOTSTEPS?
LET'S JUST SAY MY KEEN DIAGNOSTIC EYE TURNED OUT BETTER THAN MY JUMP SHOT.
SPEAKING OF KEEN DIAGNOSTICS...
...THERE SHE IS. PAMELA BRANCH.
TIME FOR THE DOCTOR TO GO TO WORK. WATCH AND LEARN, STEVEN.
YOU'RE NOT A DOCTOR YET, LEONARD.
TECHNICALITIES.

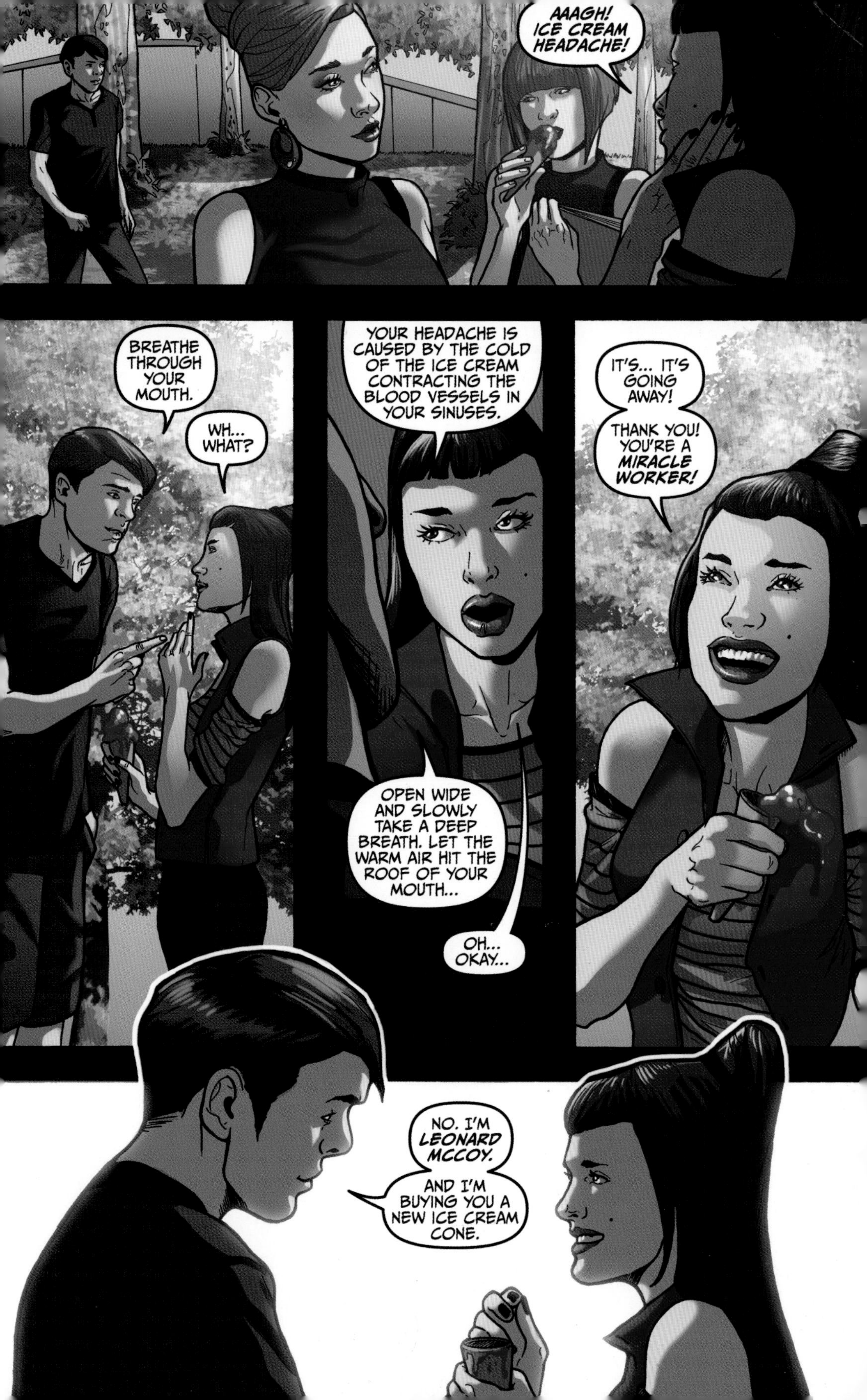
AAAGH! ICE CREAM HEADACHE!
BREATHE THROUGH YOUR MOUTH.
WH... WHAT?
YOUR HEADACHE IS CAUSED BY THE COLD OF THE ICE CREAM CONTRACTING THE BLOOD VESSELS IN YOUR SINUSES.
OPEN WIDE AND SLOWLY TAKE A DEEP BREATH. LET THE WARM AIR HIT THE ROOF OF YOUR MOUTH...
OH... OKAY...
IT'S... IT'S GOING AWAY!
THANK YOU! YOU'RE A MIRACLE WORKER!
NO. I'M LEONARD MCCOY.
AND I'M BUYING YOU A NEW ICE CREAM CONE.

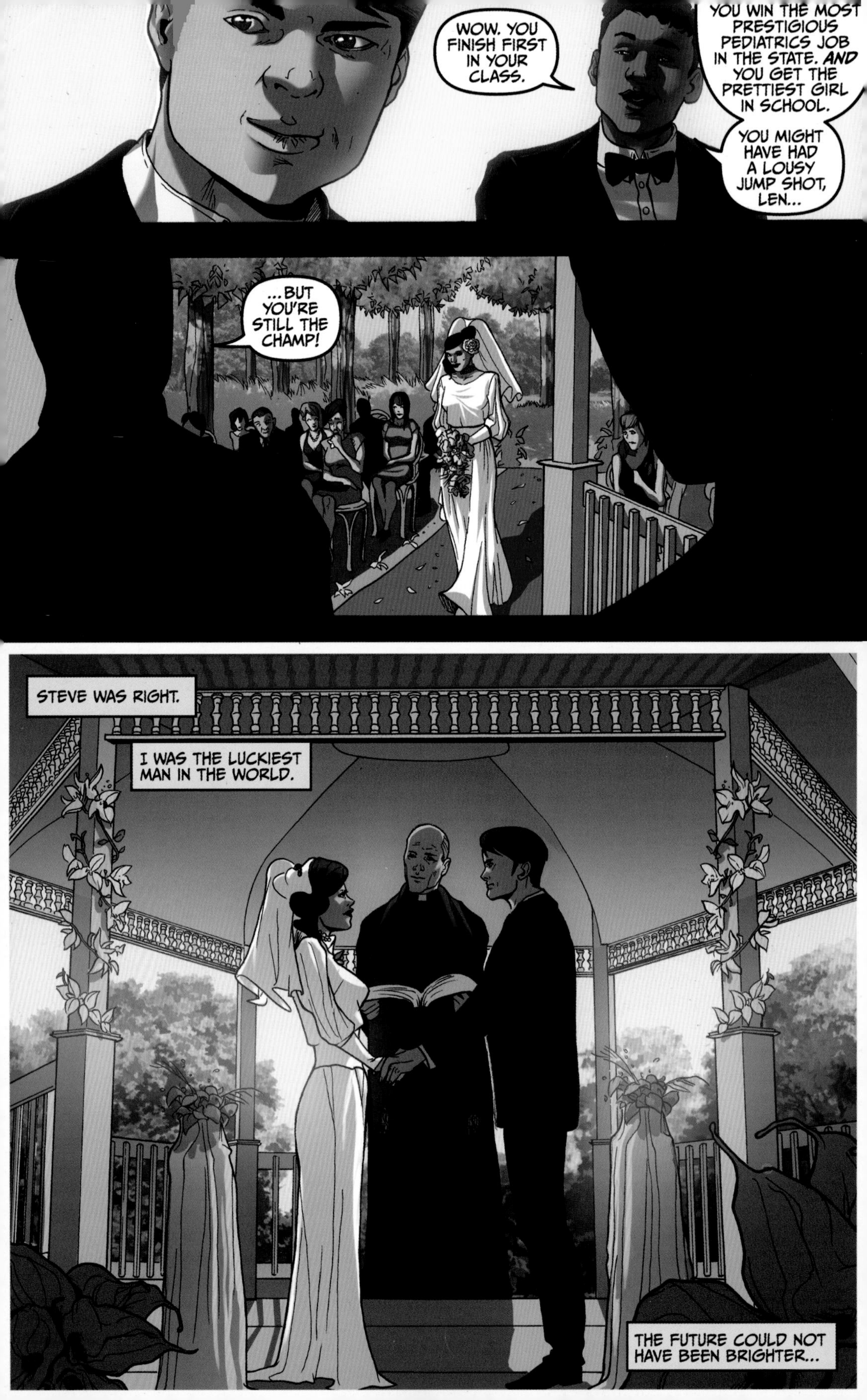
WOW. YOU FINISH FIRST IN YOUR CLASS.
YOU WIN THE MOST PRESTIGIOUS PEDIATRICS JOB IN THE STATE. AND YOU GET THE PRETTIEST GIRL IN SCHOOL.
YOU MIGHT HAVE HAD A LOUSY JUMP SHOT, LEN...
...BUT YOU'RE STILL THE CHAMP!
STEVE WAS RIGHT.
I WAS THE LUCKIEST MAN IN THE WORLD.
THE FUTURE COULD NOT HAVE BEEN BRIGHTER...

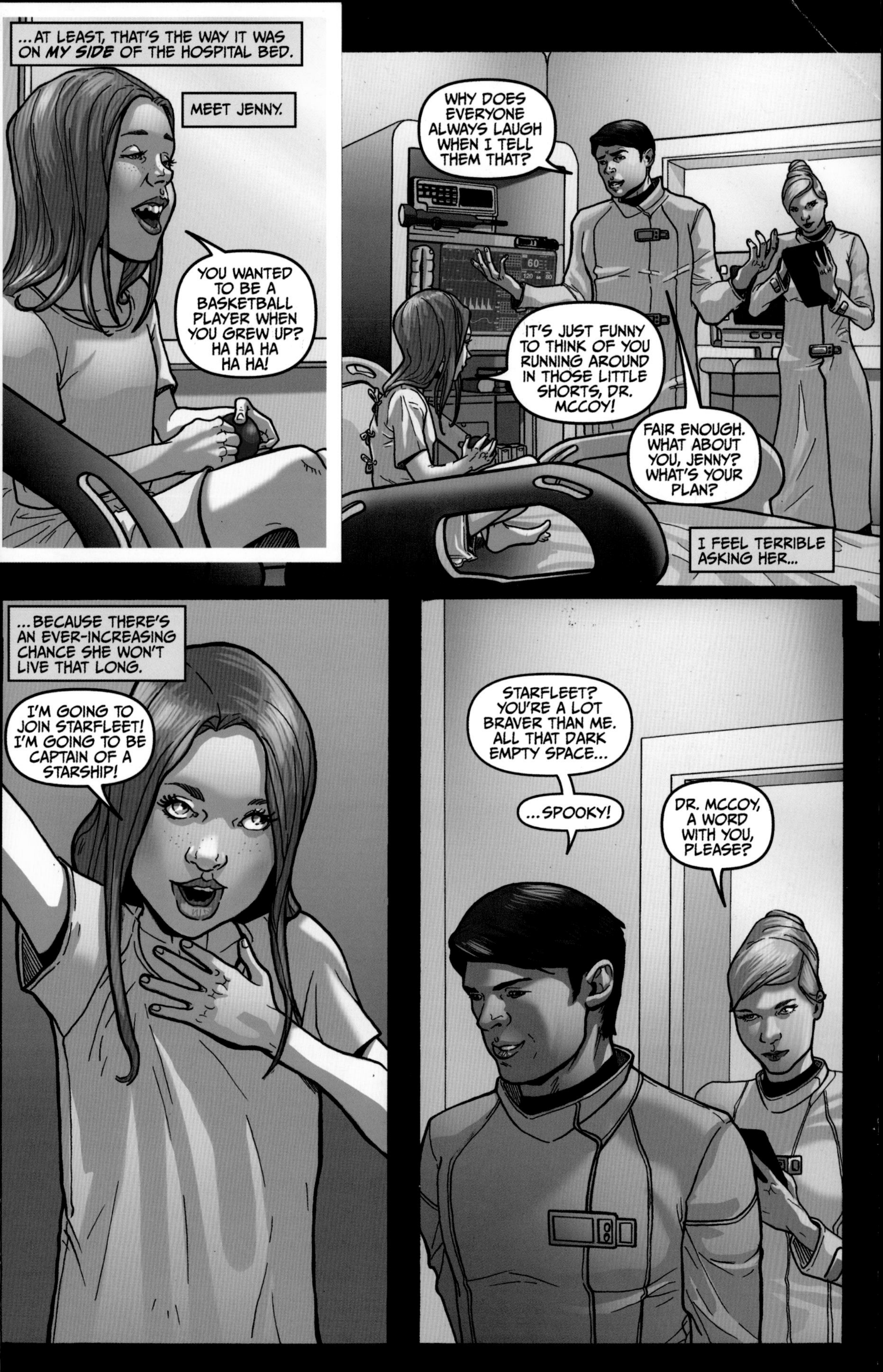
...AT LEAST, THAT'S THE WAY IT WAS ON MY SIDE OF THE HOSPITAL BED.
MEET JENNY.
YOU WANTED TO BE A BASKETBALL PLAYER WHEN YOU GREW UP? HA HA HA HA HA!
WHY DOES EVERYONE ALWAYS LAUGH WHEN I TELL THEM THAT?
IT'S JUST FUNNY TO THINK OF YOU RUNNING AROUND IN THOSE LITTLE SHORTS, DR. MCCOY!
FAIR ENOUGH. WHAT ABOUT YOU, JENNY? WHAT'S YOUR PLAN?
I FEEL TERRIBLE ASKING HER...
...BECAUSE THERE'S AN EVER-INCREASING CHANCE SHE WON'T LIVE THAT LONG.
I'M GOING TO JOIN STARFLEET! I'M GOING TO BE CAPTAIN OF A STARSHIP!
STARFLEET? YOU'RE A LOT BRAVER THAN ME. ALL THAT DARK EMPTY SPACE...
...SPOOKY!
DR. MCCOY, A WORD WITH YOU, PLEASE?

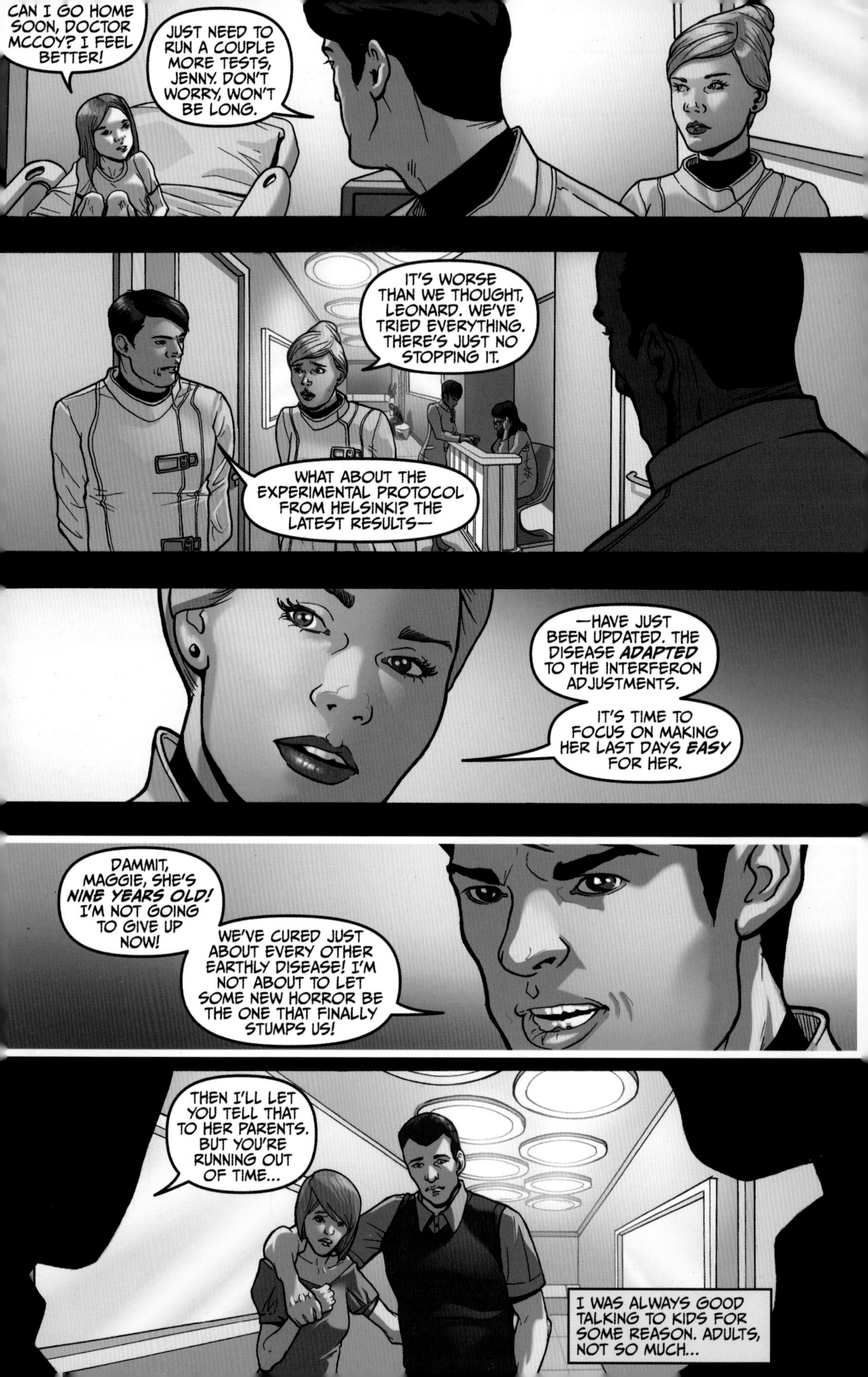
CAN I GO HOME SOON, DOCTOR MCCOY? I FEEL BETTER!
JUST NEED TO RUN A COUPLE MORE TESTS, JENNY. DON'T WORRY, WON'T BE LONG.
IT'S WORSE THAN WE THOUGHT, LEONARD. WE'VE TRIED EVERYTHING. THERE'S JUST NO STOPPING IT.
WHAT ABOUT THE EXPERIMENTAL PROTOCOL FROM HELSINKI? THE LATEST RESULTS—
—HAVE JUST BEEN UPDATED. THE DISEASE ADAPTED TO THE INTERFERON ADJUSTMENTS.
IT'S TIME TO FOCUS ON MAKING HER LAST DAYS EASY FOR HER.
DAMMIT, MAGGIE, SHE'S NINE YEARS OLD! I'M NOT GOING TO GIVE UP NOW!
WE'VE CURED JUST ABOUT EVERY OTHER EARTHLY DISEASE! I'M NOT ABOUT TO LET SOME NEW HORROR BE THE ONE THAT FINALLY STUMPS US!
THEN I'LL LET YOU TELL THAT TO HER PARENTS. BUT YOU'RE RUNNING OUT OF TIME...
I WAS ALWAYS GOOD TALKING TO KIDS FOR SOME REASON. ADULTS, NOT SO MUCH...

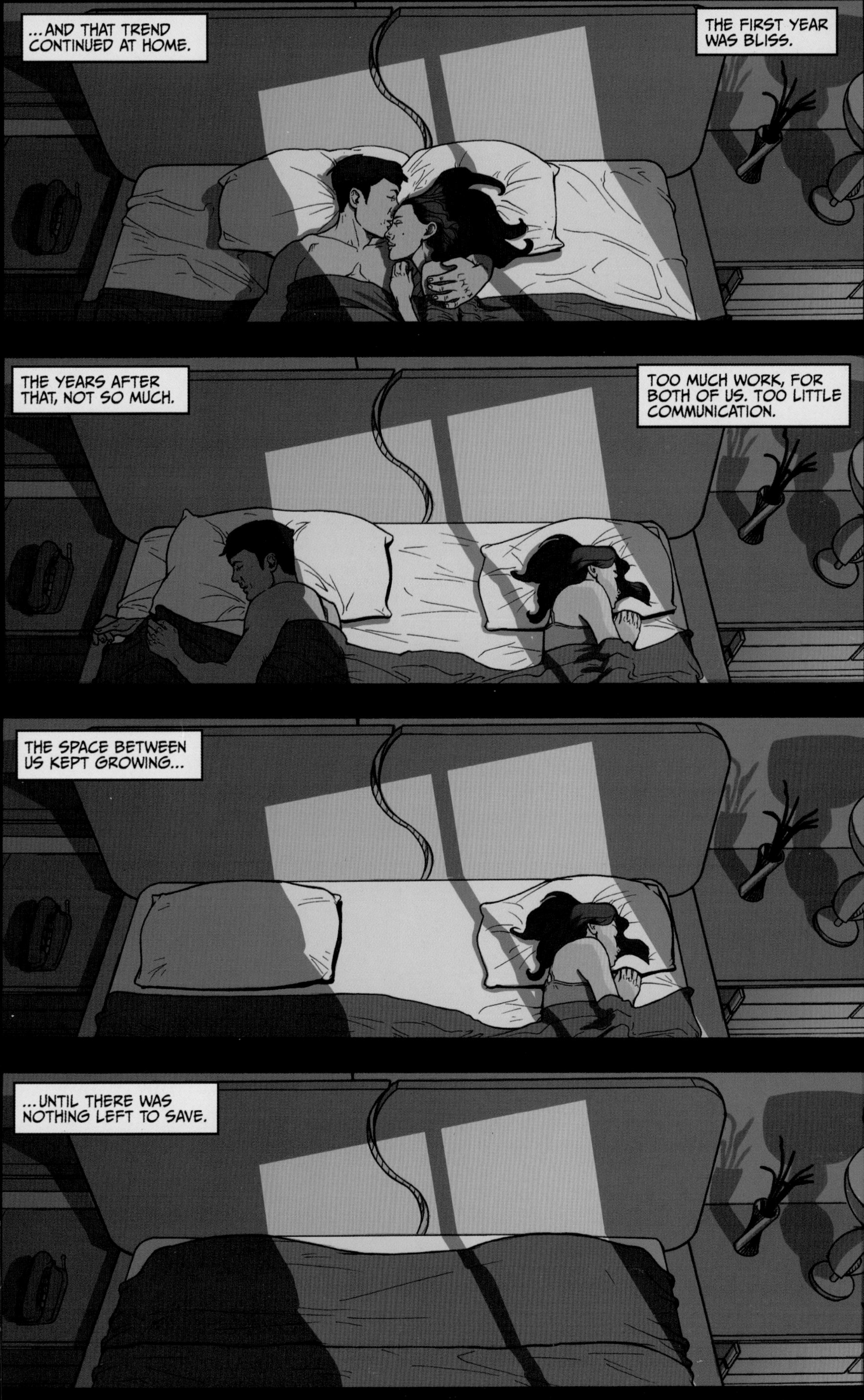
...AND THAT TREND CONTINUED AT HOME.
THE FIRST YEAR WAS BLISS.
THE YEARS AFTER THAT, NOT SO MUCH.
TOO MUCH WORK, FOR BOTH OF US. TOO LITTLE COMMUNICATION.
THE SPACE BETWEEN US KEPT GROWING...
...UNTIL THERE WAS NOTHING LEFT TO SAVE.

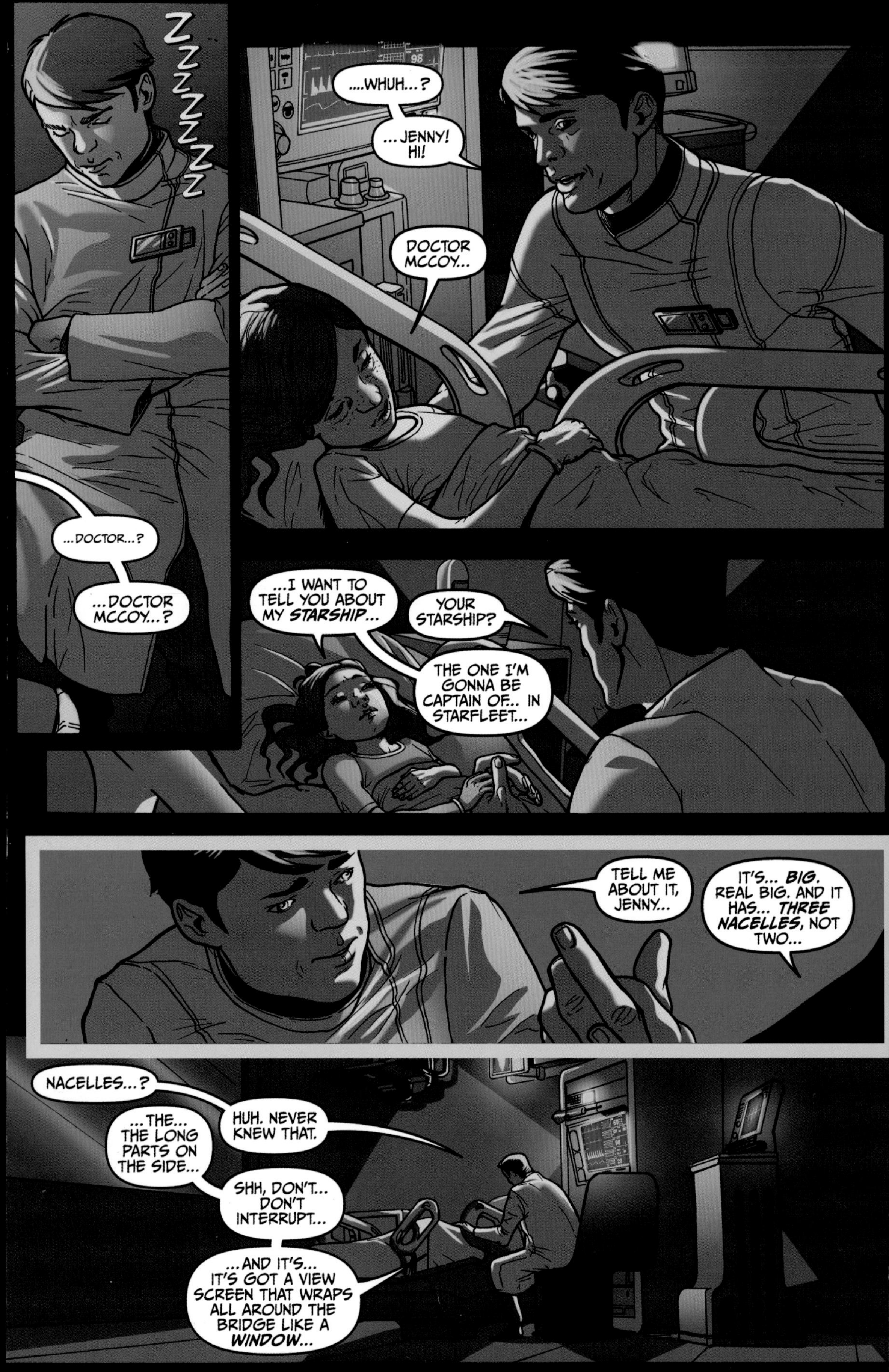
ZZZZZZZ
....WHUH...?
...JENNY! HI!
DOCTOR MCCOY...
...DOCTOR...?
...DOCTOR MCCOY...?
...I WANT TO TELL YOU ABOUT MY STARSHIP...
YOUR STARSHIP?
THE ONE I'M GONNA BE CAPTAIN OF... IN STARFLEET...
TELL ME ABOUT IT, JENNY...
IT'S... BIG. REAL BIG. AND IT HAS... THREE NACELLES, NOT TWO...
NACELLES...?
...THE... THE LONG PARTS ON THE SIDE...
HUH. NEVER KNEW THAT.
SHH, DON'T... DON'T INTERRUPT...
...AND IT'S... IT'S GOT A VIEW SCREEN THAT WRAPS ALL AROUND THE BRIDGE LIKE A WINDOW...

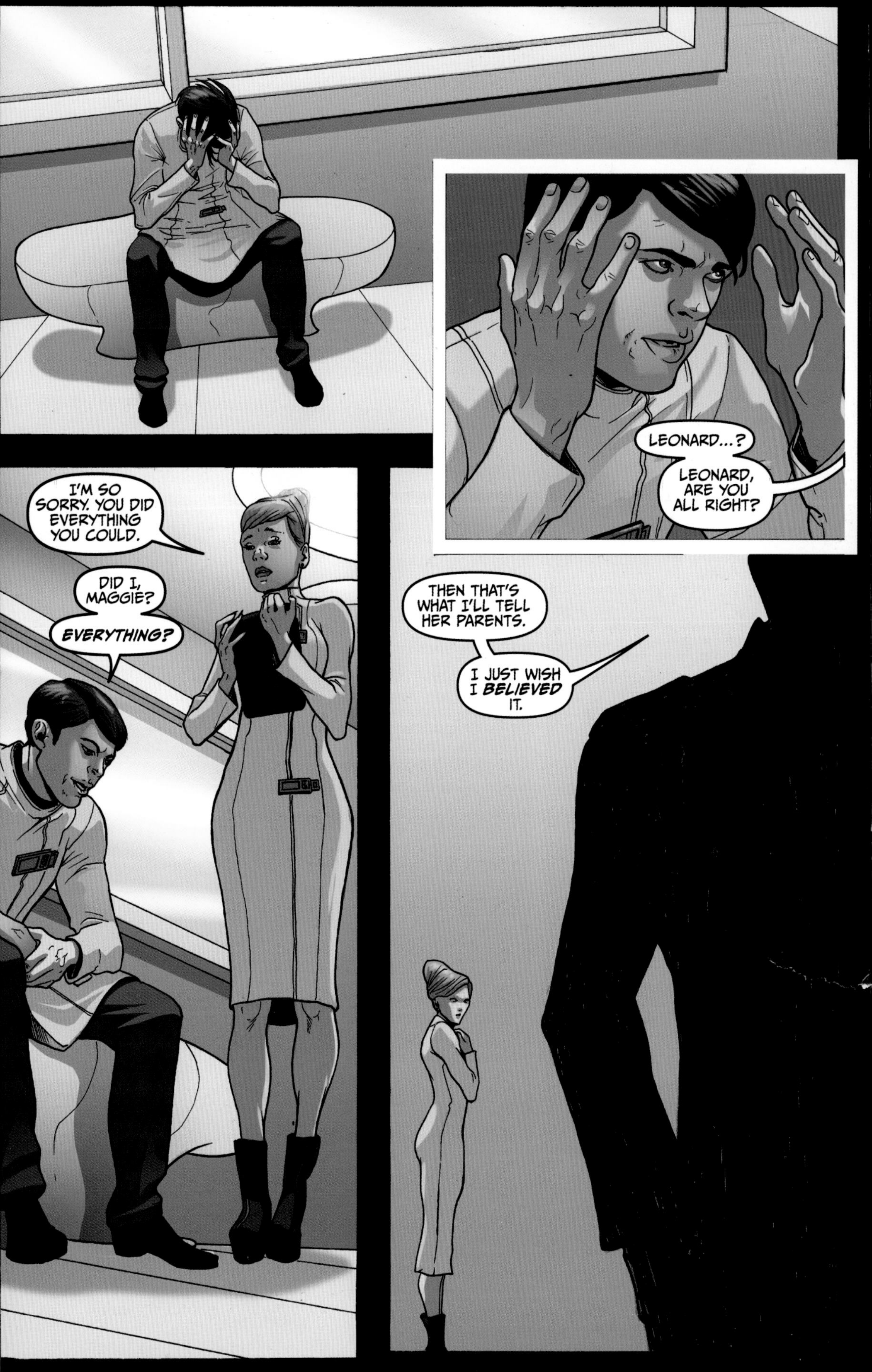
LEONARD...?
LEONARD, ARE YOU ALL RIGHT?
I'M SO SORRY. YOU DID EVERYTHING YOU COULD.
DID I, MAGGIE?
EVERYTHING?
THEN THAT'S WHAT I'LL TELL HER PARENTS.
I JUST WISH I BELIEVED IT.

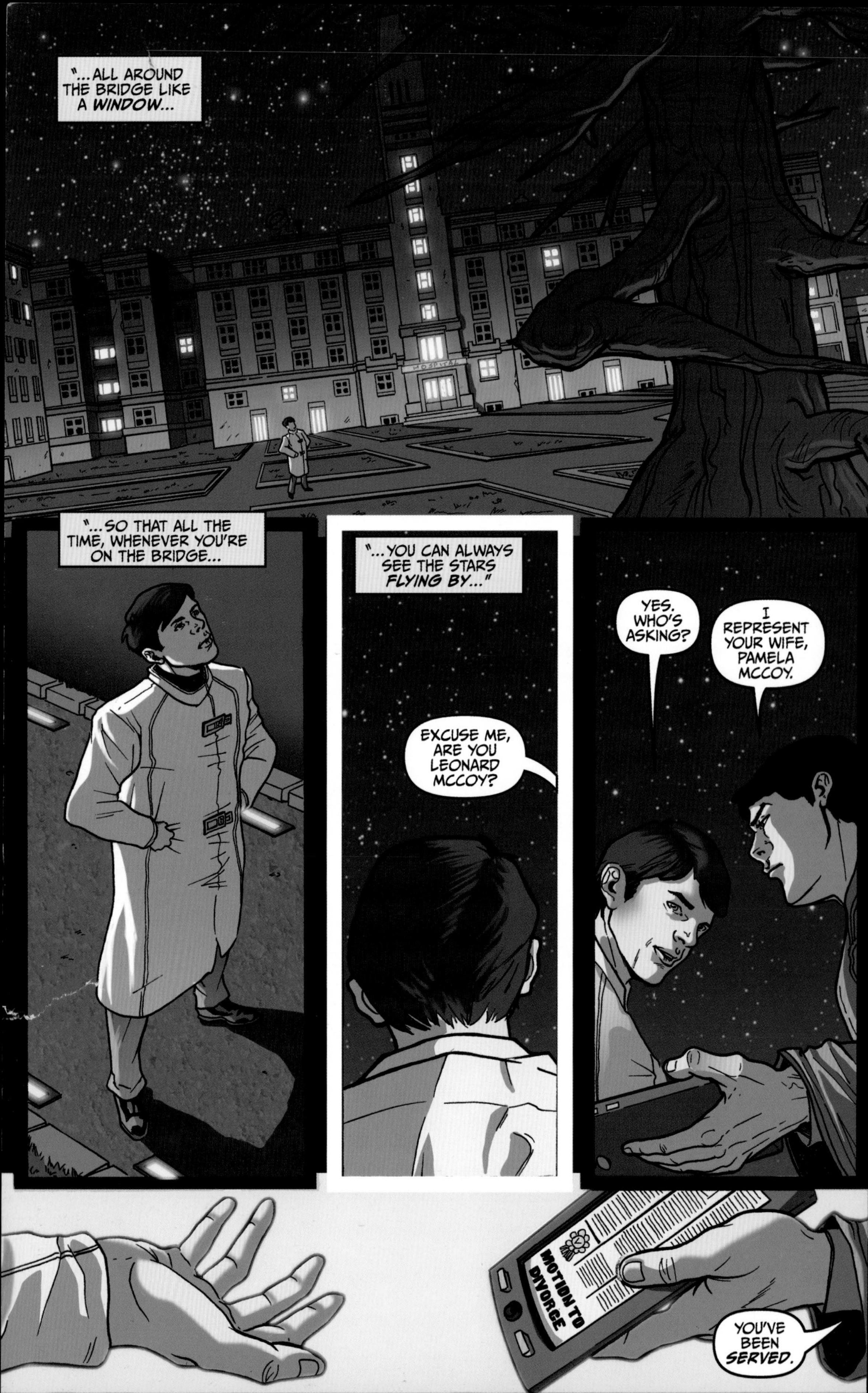
"...ALL AROUND THE BRIDGE LIKE A *WINDOW*...
"...SO THAT ALL THE TIME, WHENEVER YOU'RE ON THE BRIDGE...
"...YOU CAN ALWAYS SEE THE STARS *FLYING BY*..."
EXCUSE ME, ARE YOU LEONARD MCCOY?
YES. WHO'S ASKING?
I REPRESENT YOUR WIFE, PAMELA MCCOY.
MOTION TO DIVORCE
YOU'VE BEEN *SERVED*.

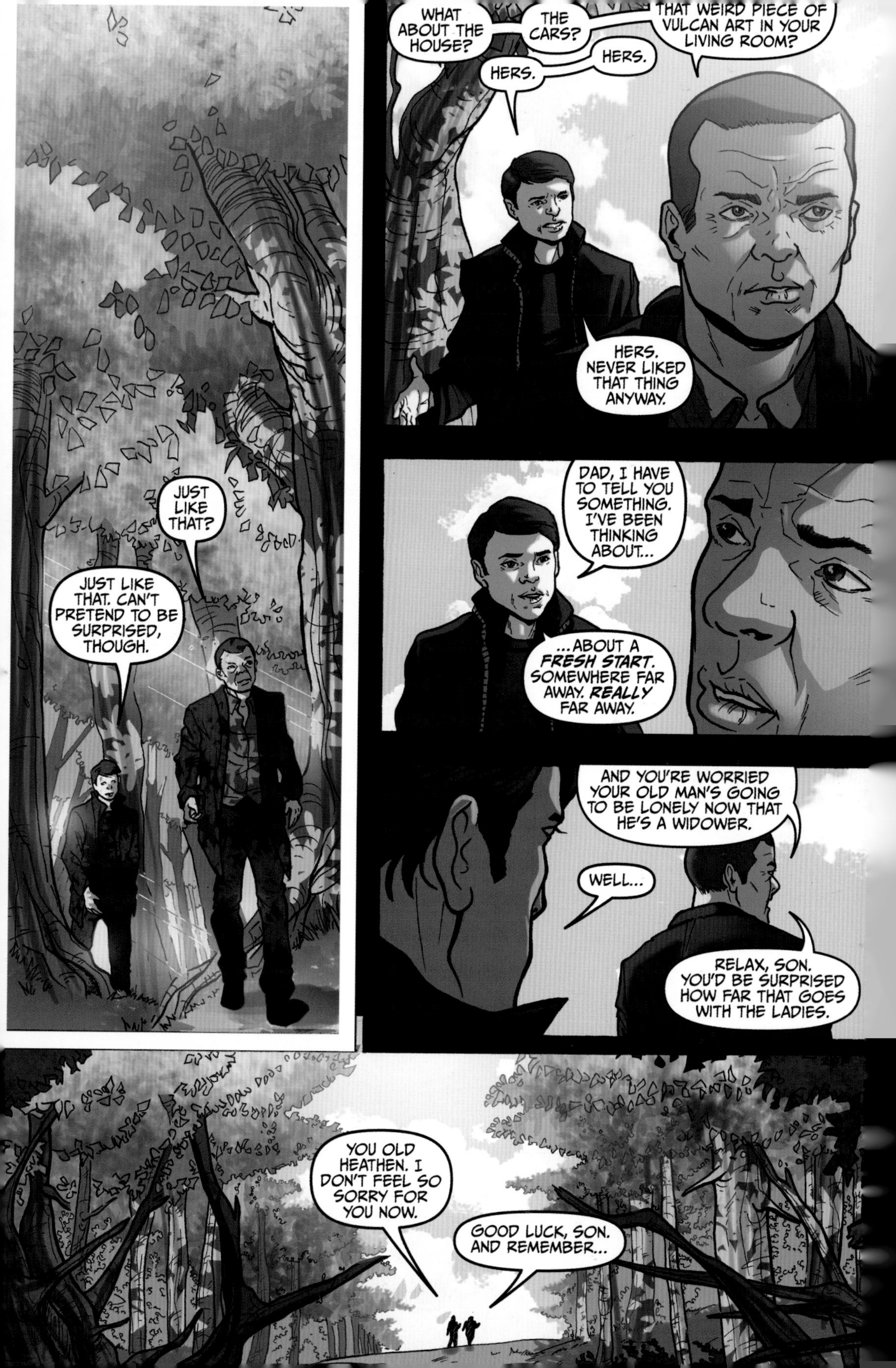
JUST LIKE THAT?
JUST LIKE THAT. CAN'T PRETEND TO BE SURPRISED, THOUGH.
WHAT ABOUT THE HOUSE?
HERS.
THE CARS?
HERS.
THAT WEIRD PIECE OF VULCAN ART IN YOUR LIVING ROOM?
HERS. NEVER LIKED THAT THING ANYWAY.
DAD, I HAVE TO TELL YOU SOMETHING. I'VE BEEN THINKING ABOUT...
...ABOUT A FRESH START. SOMEWHERE FAR AWAY. REALLY FAR AWAY.
AND YOU'RE WORRIED YOUR OLD MAN'S GOING TO BE LONELY NOW THAT HE'S A WIDOWER.
WELL...
RELAX, SON. YOU'D BE SURPRISED HOW FAR THAT GOES WITH THE LADIES.
YOU OLD HEATHEN. I DON'T FEEL SO SORRY FOR YOU NOW.
GOOD LUCK, SON. AND REMEMBER...

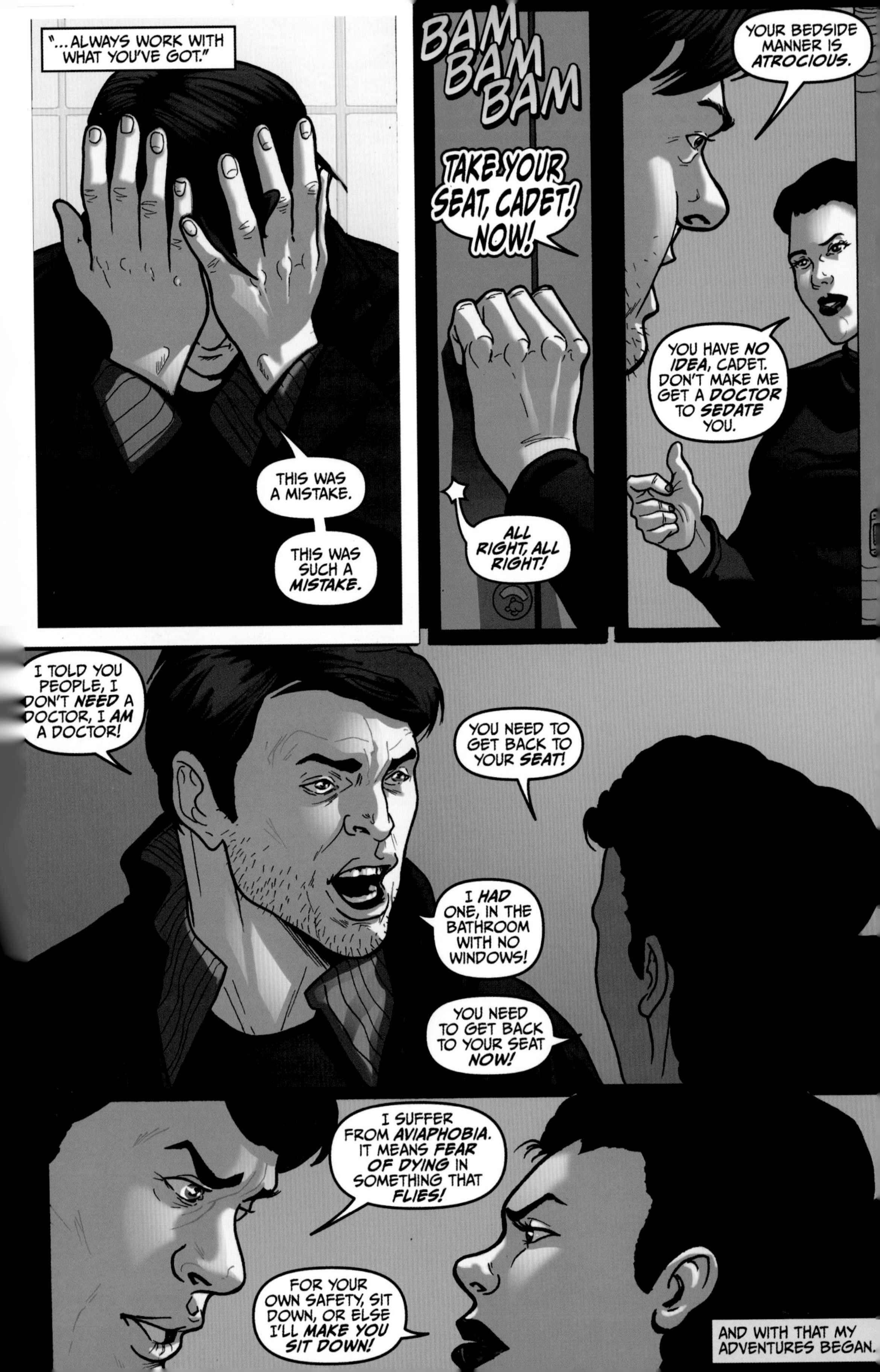

"...ALWAYS WORK WITH WHAT YOU'VE GOT."
THIS WAS A MISTAKE.
THIS WAS SUCH A MISTAKE.
BAM BAM BAM
TAKE YOUR SEAT, CADET! NOW!
ALL RIGHT, ALL RIGHT!
YOUR BEDSIDE MANNER IS ATROCIOUS.
YOU HAVE NO IDEA, CADET. DON'T MAKE ME GET A DOCTOR TO SEDATE YOU.
I TOLD YOU PEOPLE, I DON'T NEED A DOCTOR, I AM A DOCTOR!
YOU NEED TO GET BACK TO YOUR SEAT!
I HAD ONE, IN THE BATHROOM WITH NO WINDOWS!
YOU NEED TO GET BACK TO YOUR SEAT NOW!
I SUFFER FROM AVIAPHOBIA. IT MEANS FEAR OF DYING IN SOMETHING THAT FLIES!
FOR YOUR OWN SAFETY, SIT DOWN, OR ELSE I'LL MAKE YOU SIT DOWN!
AND WITH THAT MY ADVENTURES BEGAN.

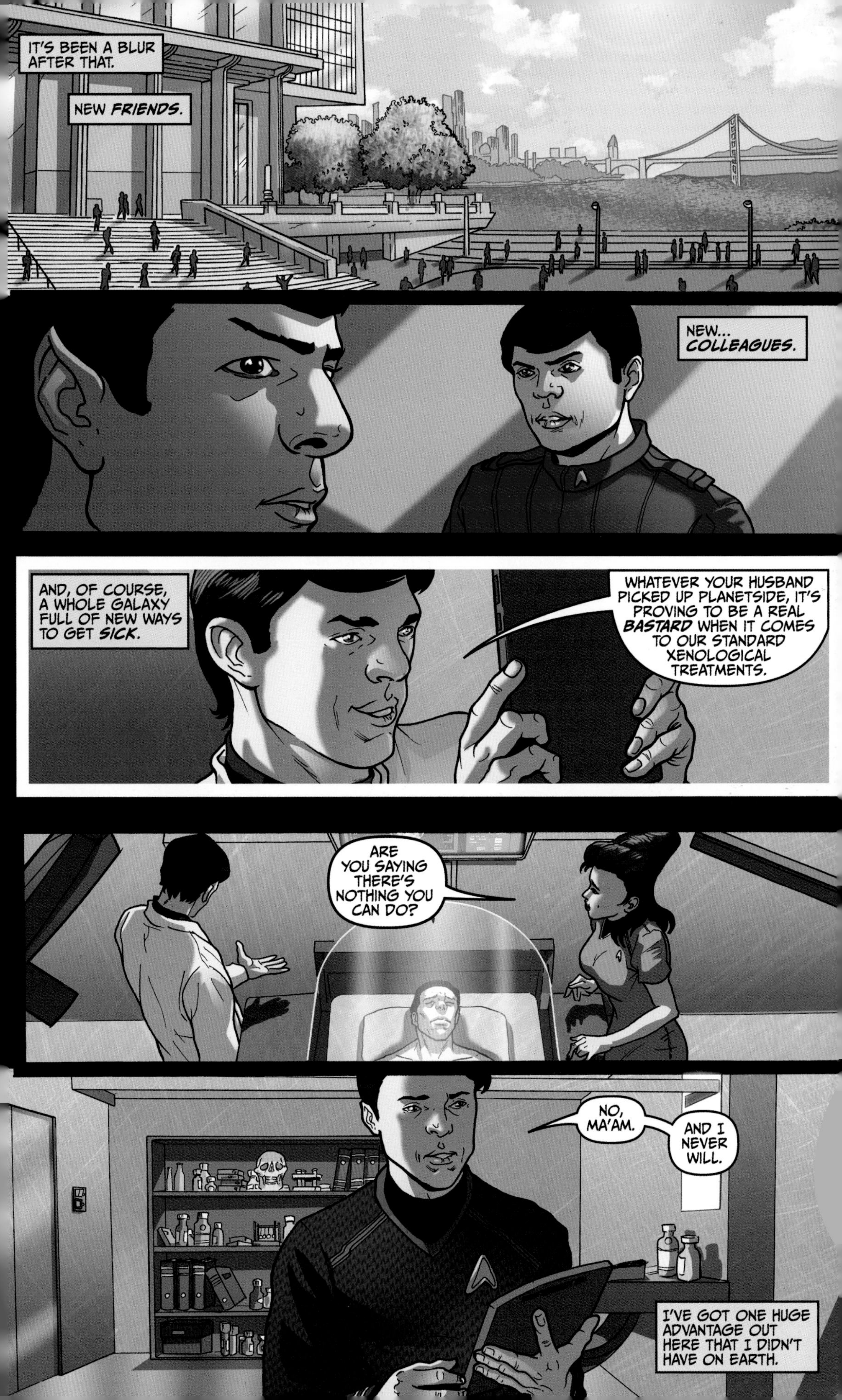

IT'S BEEN A BLUR AFTER THAT.
NEW FRIENDS.
NEW... COLLEAGUES.
AND, OF COURSE, A WHOLE GALAXY FULL OF NEW WAYS TO GET SICK.
WHATEVER YOUR HUSBAND PICKED UP PLANETSIDE, IT'S PROVING TO BE A REAL BASTARD WHEN IT COMES TO OUR STANDARD XENOLOGICAL TREATMENTS.
ARE YOU SAYING THERE'S NOTHING YOU CAN DO?
NO, MA'AM.
AND I NEVER WILL.
I'VE GOT ONE HUGE ADVANTAGE OUT HERE THAT I DIDN'T HAVE ON EARTH.

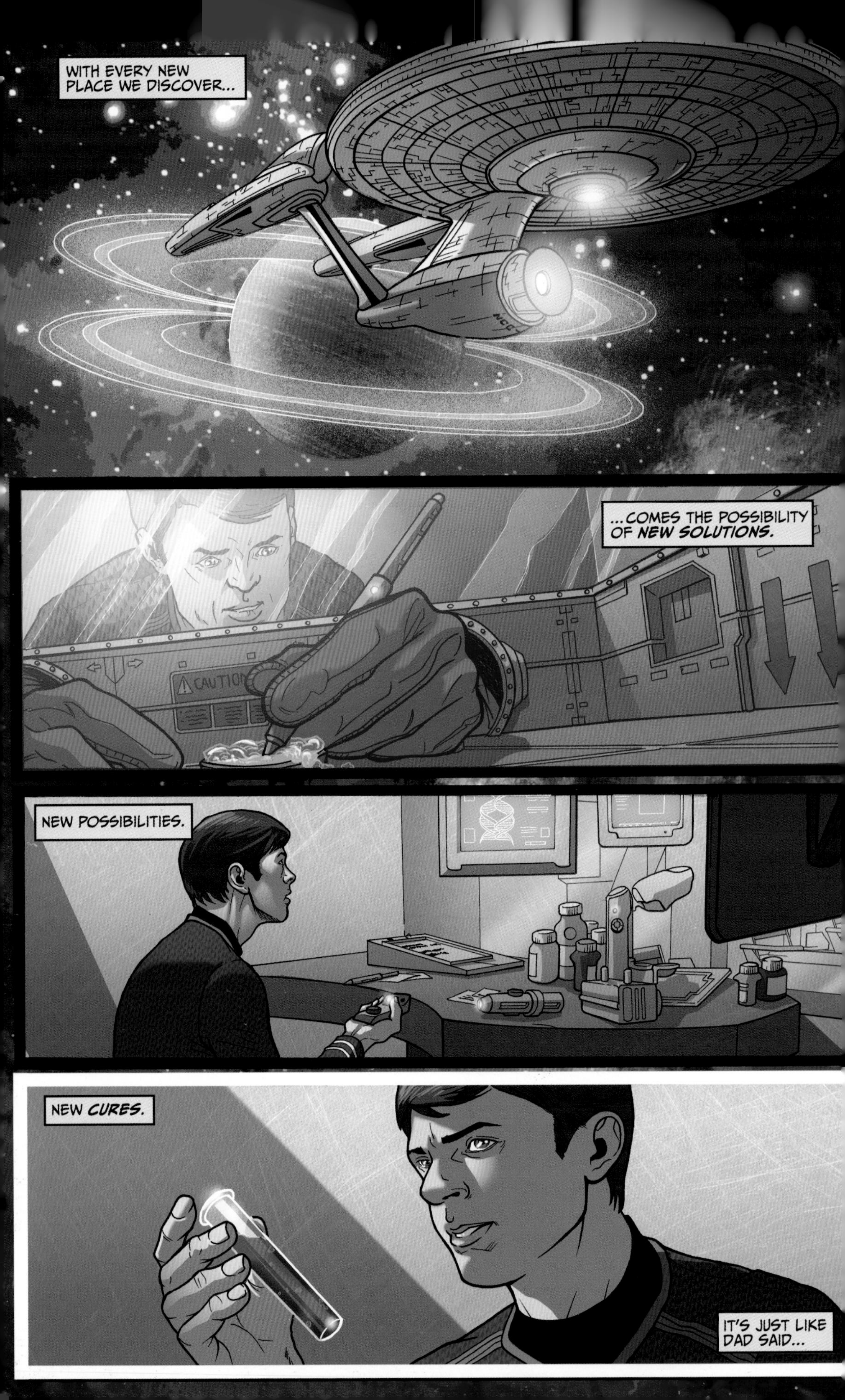
WITH EVERY NEW PLACE WE DISCOVER...
...COMES THE POSSIBILITY OF NEW SOLUTIONS.
CAUTION
NEW POSSIBILITIES.
NEW CURES.
IT'S JUST LIKE DAD SAID...

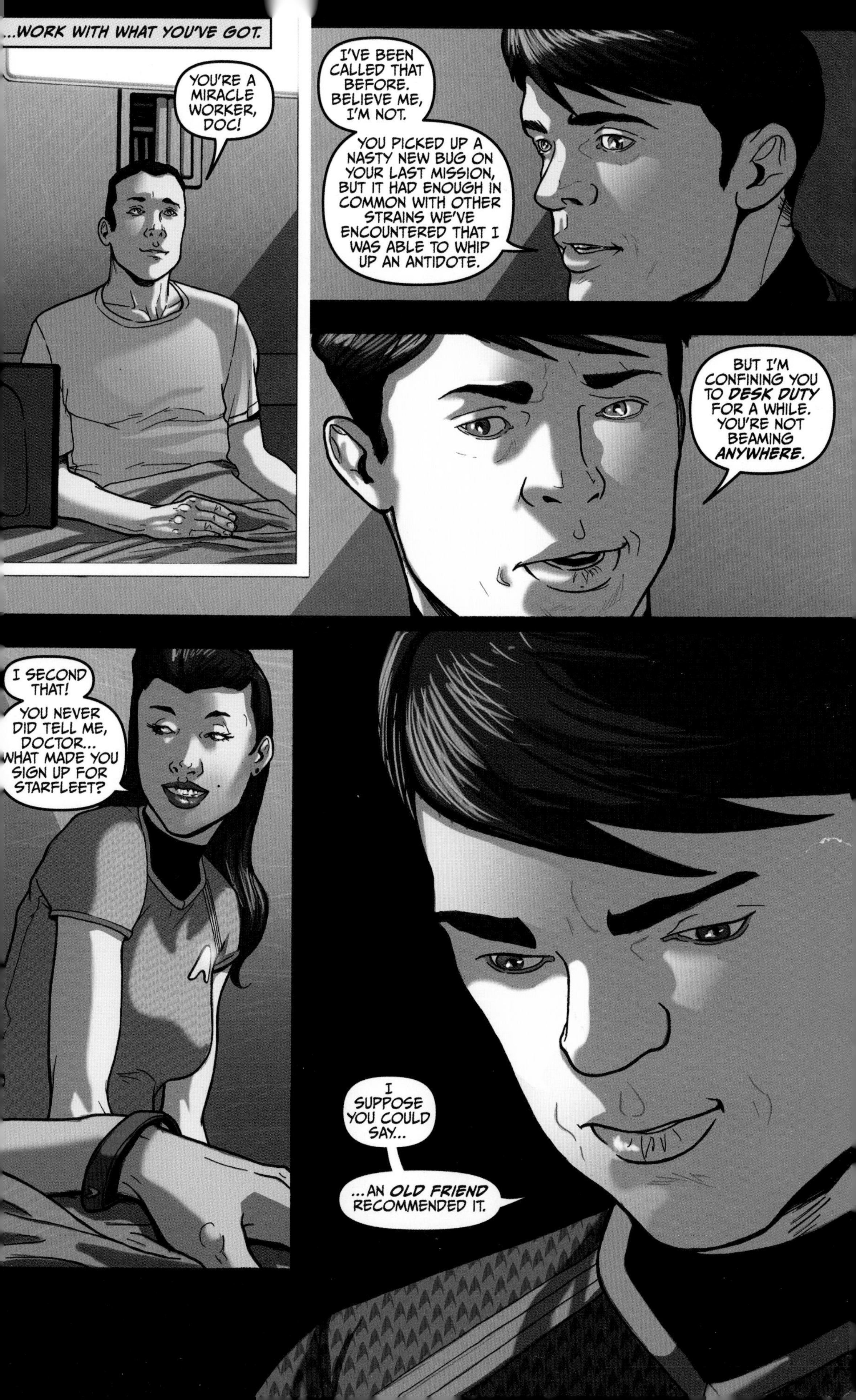
...WORK WITH WHAT YOU'VE GOT.
YOU'RE A MIRACLE WORKER, DOC!
I'VE BEEN CALLED THAT BEFORE. BELIEVE ME, I'M NOT.
YOU PICKED UP A NASTY NEW BUG ON YOUR LAST MISSION, BUT IT HAD ENOUGH IN COMMON WITH OTHER STRAINS WE'VE ENCOUNTERED THAT I WAS ABLE TO WHIP UP AN ANTIDOTE.
BUT I'M CONFINING YOU TO DESK DUTY FOR A WHILE. YOU'RE NOT BEAMING ANYWHERE.
I SECOND THAT!
YOU NEVER DID TELL ME, DOCTOR... WHAT MADE YOU SIGN UP FOR STARFLEET?
I SUPPOSE YOU COULD SAY...
...AN OLD FRIEND RECOMMENDED IT.

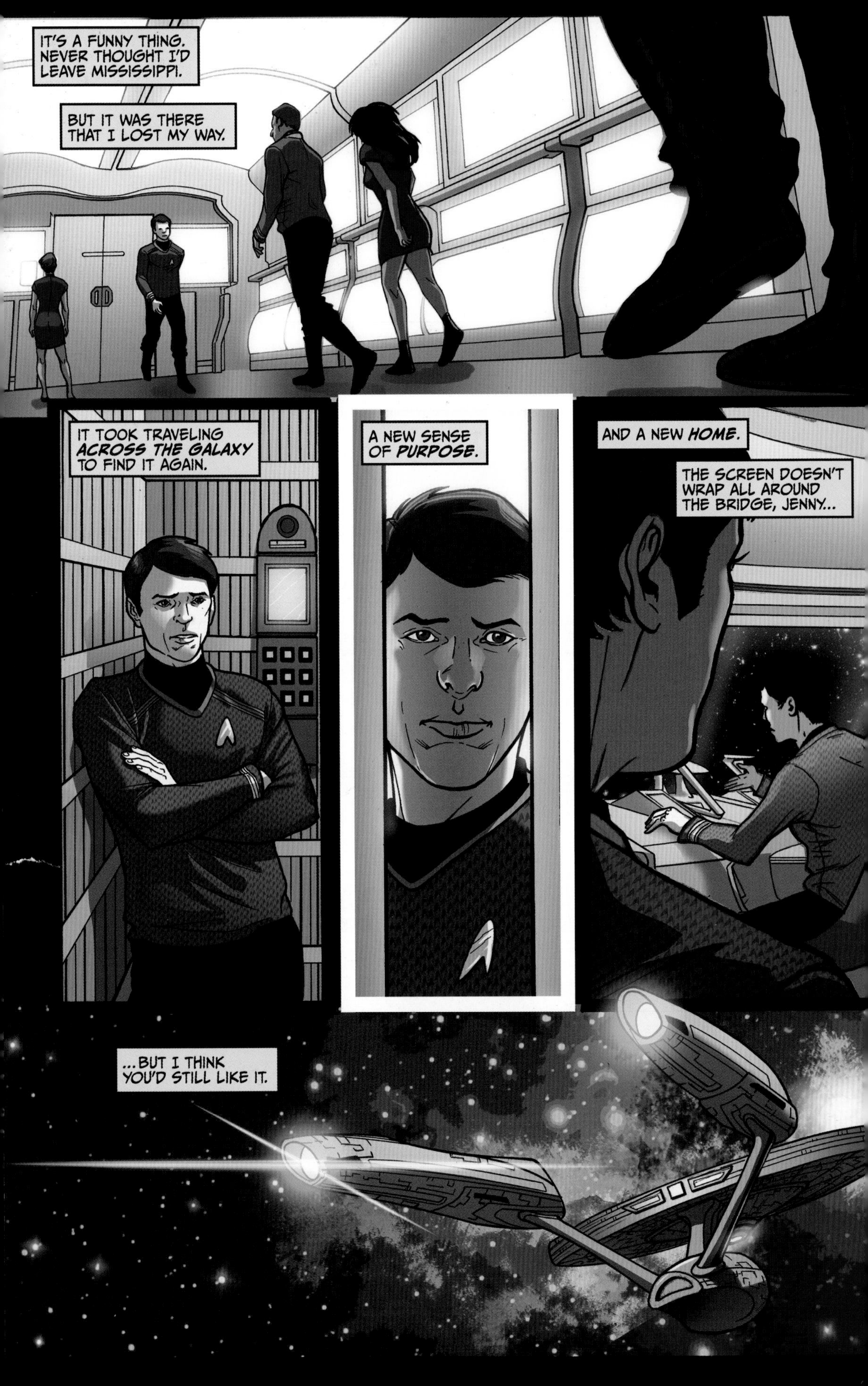
IT'S A FUNNY THING. NEVER THOUGHT I'D LEAVE MISSISSIPPI.
BUT IT WAS THERE THAT I LOST MY WAY.
IT TOOK TRAVELING *ACROSS THE GALAXY* TO FIND IT AGAIN.
A NEW SENSE OF *PURPOSE*.
AND A NEW *HOME*.
THE SCREEN DOESN'T WRAP ALL AROUND THE BRIDGE, JENNY...
...BUT I THINK YOU'D STILL LIKE IT.

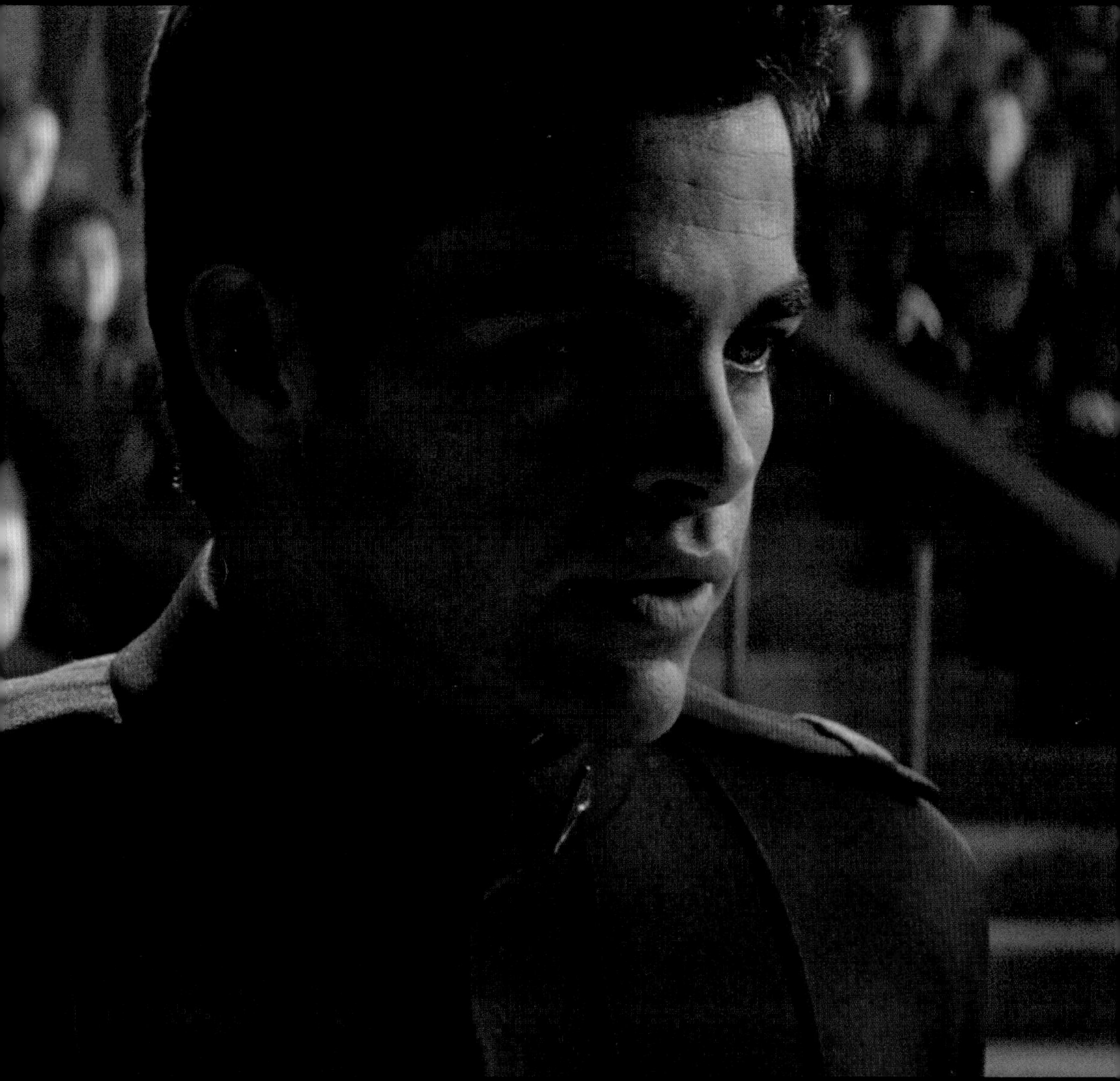

THE VOICE OF A FALLING STAR

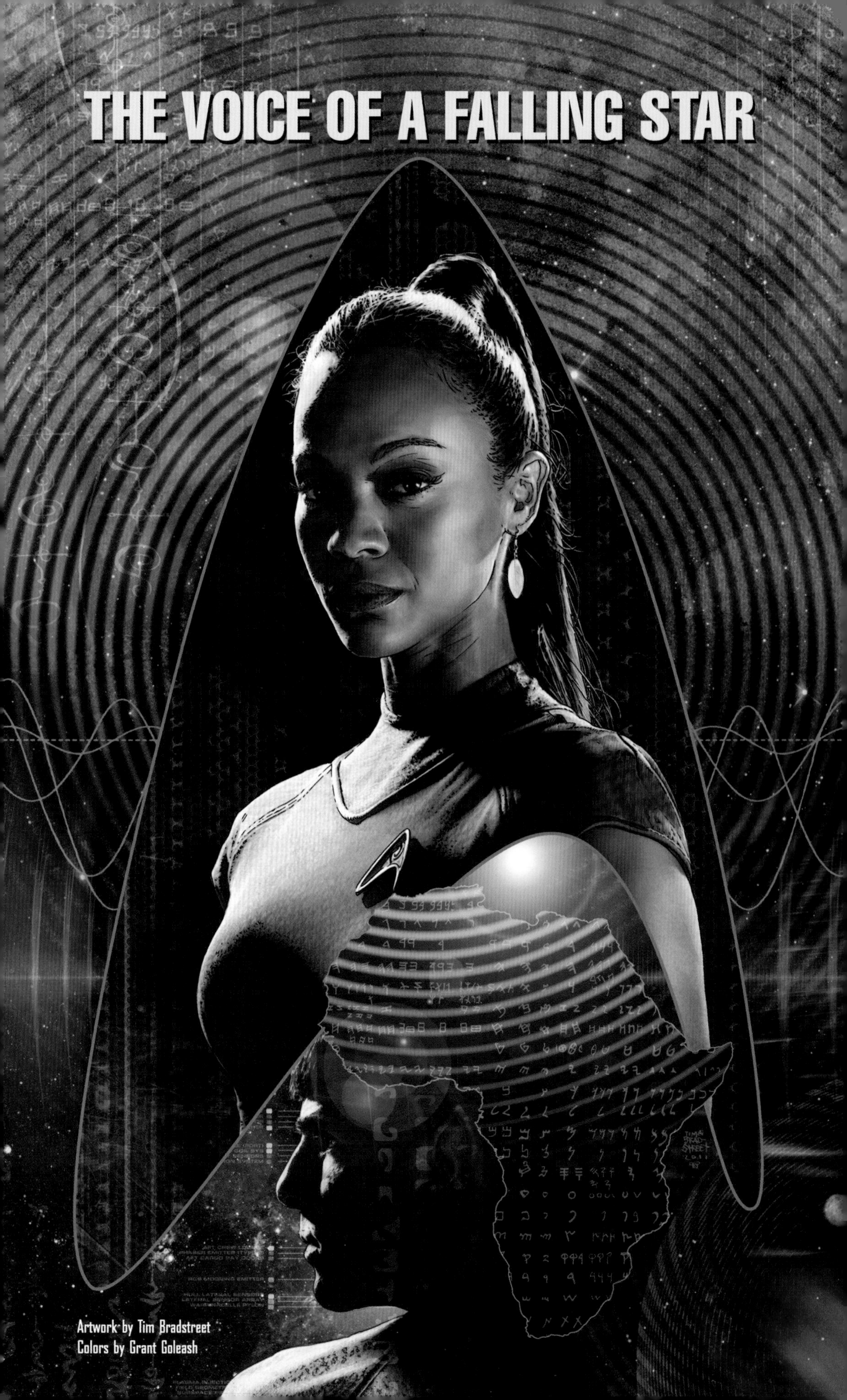

Artwork by Tim Bradstreet
Colors by Grant Goleash

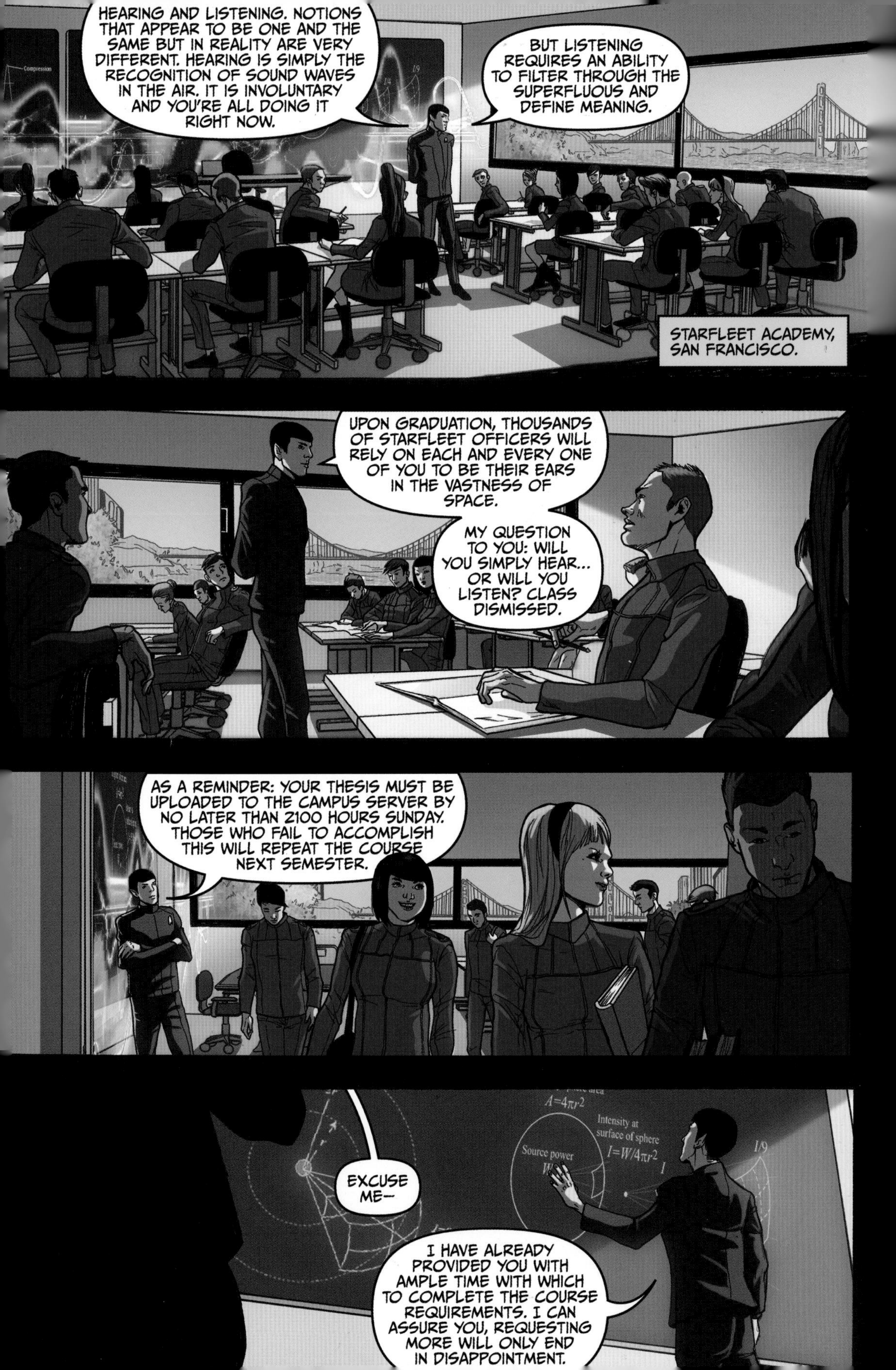
HEARING AND LISTENING. NOTIONS THAT APPEAR TO BE ONE AND THE SAME BUT IN REALITY ARE VERY DIFFERENT. HEARING IS SIMPLY THE RECOGNITION OF SOUND WAVES IN THE AIR. IT IS INVOLUNTARY AND YOU'RE ALL DOING IT RIGHT NOW.
BUT LISTENING REQUIRES AN ABILITY TO FILTER THROUGH THE SUPERFLUOUS AND DEFINE MEANING.
STARFLEET ACADEMY, SAN FRANCISCO.
UPON GRADUATION, THOUSANDS OF STARFLEET OFFICERS WILL RELY ON EACH AND EVERY ONE OF YOU TO BE THEIR EARS IN THE VASTNESS OF SPACE.
MY QUESTION TO YOU: WILL YOU SIMPLY HEAR... OR WILL YOU LISTEN? CLASS DISMISSED.
AS A REMINDER: YOUR THESIS MUST BE UPLOADED TO THE CAMPUS SERVER BY NO LATER THAN 2100 HOURS SUNDAY. THOSE WHO FAIL TO ACCOMPLISH THIS WILL REPEAT THE COURSE NEXT SEMESTER.
A=4πr²
Intensity at surface of sphere
I=W/4πr²
Source power
EXCUSE ME—
I HAVE ALREADY PROVIDED YOU WITH AMPLE TIME WITH WHICH TO COMPLETE THE COURSE REQUIREMENTS. I CAN ASSURE YOU, REQUESTING MORE WILL ONLY END IN DISAPPOINTMENT.

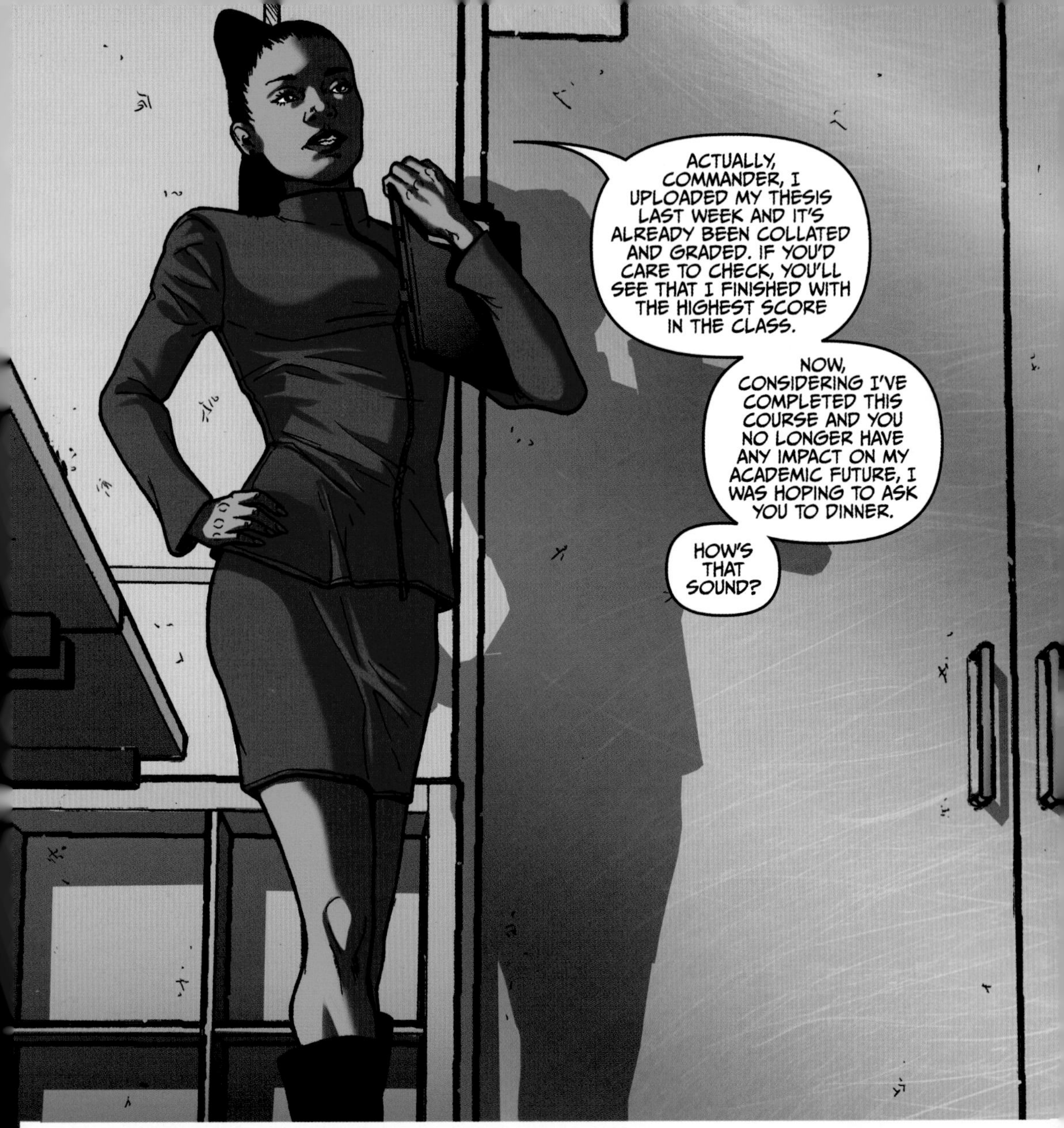
ACTUALLY, COMMANDER, I UPLOADED MY THESIS LAST WEEK AND IT'S ALREADY BEEN COLLATED AND GRADED. IF YOU'D CARE TO CHECK, YOU'LL SEE THAT I FINISHED WITH THE HIGHEST SCORE IN THE CLASS.
NOW, CONSIDERING I'VE COMPLETED THIS COURSE AND YOU NO LONGER HAVE ANY IMPACT ON MY ACADEMIC FUTURE, I WAS HOPING TO ASK YOU TO DINNER.
HOW'S THAT SOUND?

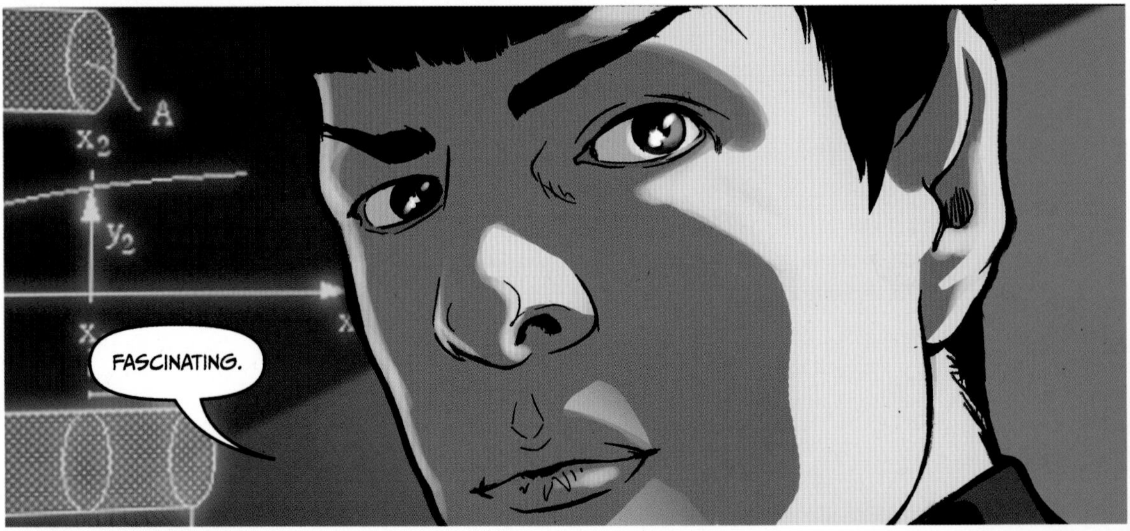
A
FASCINATING.

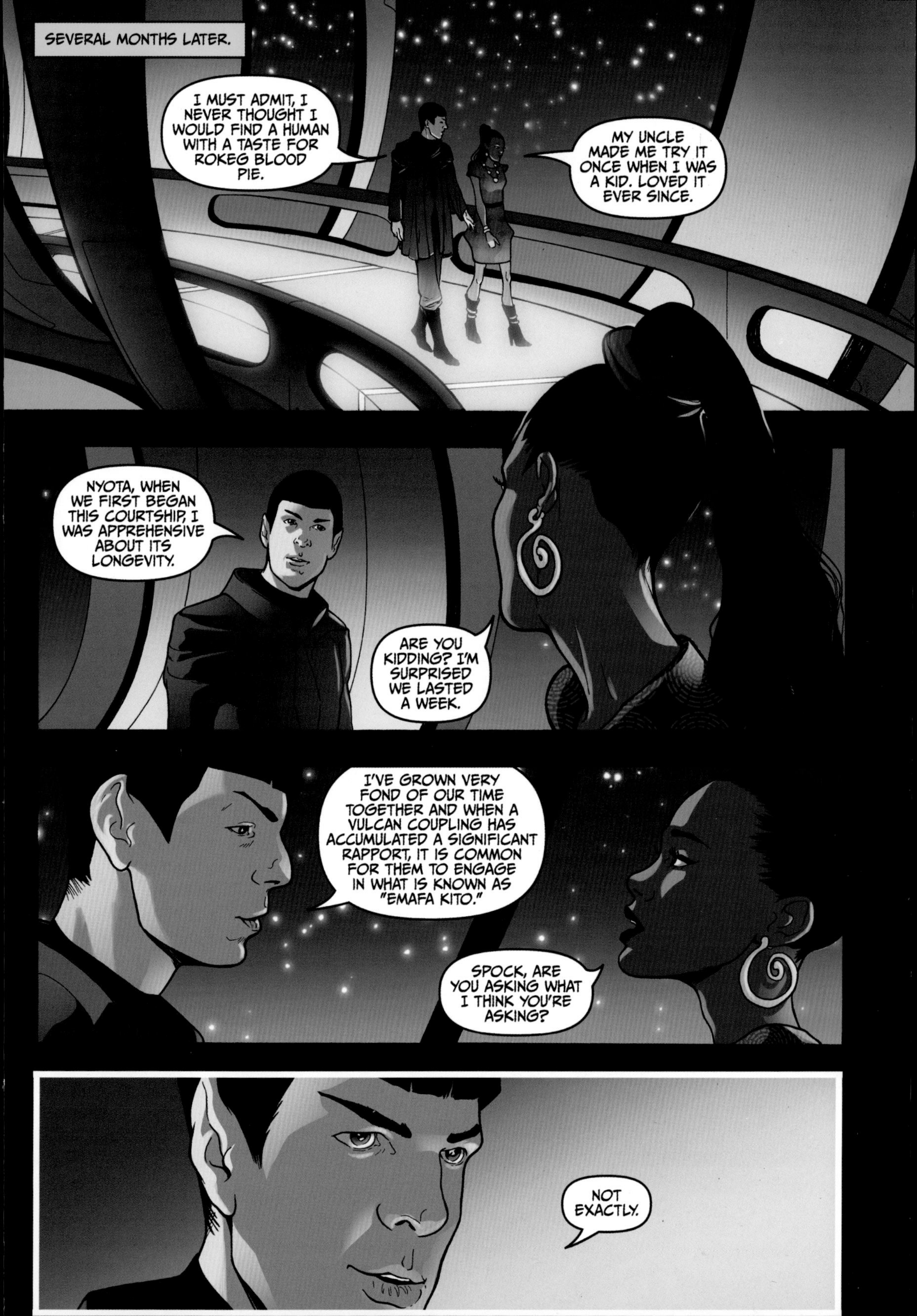
SEVERAL MONTHS LATER.
I MUST ADMIT, I NEVER THOUGHT I WOULD FIND A HUMAN WITH A TASTE FOR ROKEG BLOOD PIE.
MY UNCLE MADE ME TRY IT ONCE WHEN I WAS A KID. LOVED IT EVER SINCE.
NYOTA, WHEN WE FIRST BEGAN THIS COURTSHIP, I WAS APPREHENSIVE ABOUT ITS LONGEVITY.
ARE YOU KIDDING? I'M SURPRISED WE LASTED A WEEK.
I'VE GROWN VERY FOND OF OUR TIME TOGETHER AND WHEN A VULCAN COUPLING HAS ACCUMULATED A SIGNIFICANT RAPPORT, IT IS COMMON FOR THEM TO ENGAGE IN WHAT IS KNOWN AS "EMAFA KITO."
SPOCK, ARE YOU ASKING WHAT I THINK YOU'RE ASKING?
NOT EXACTLY.

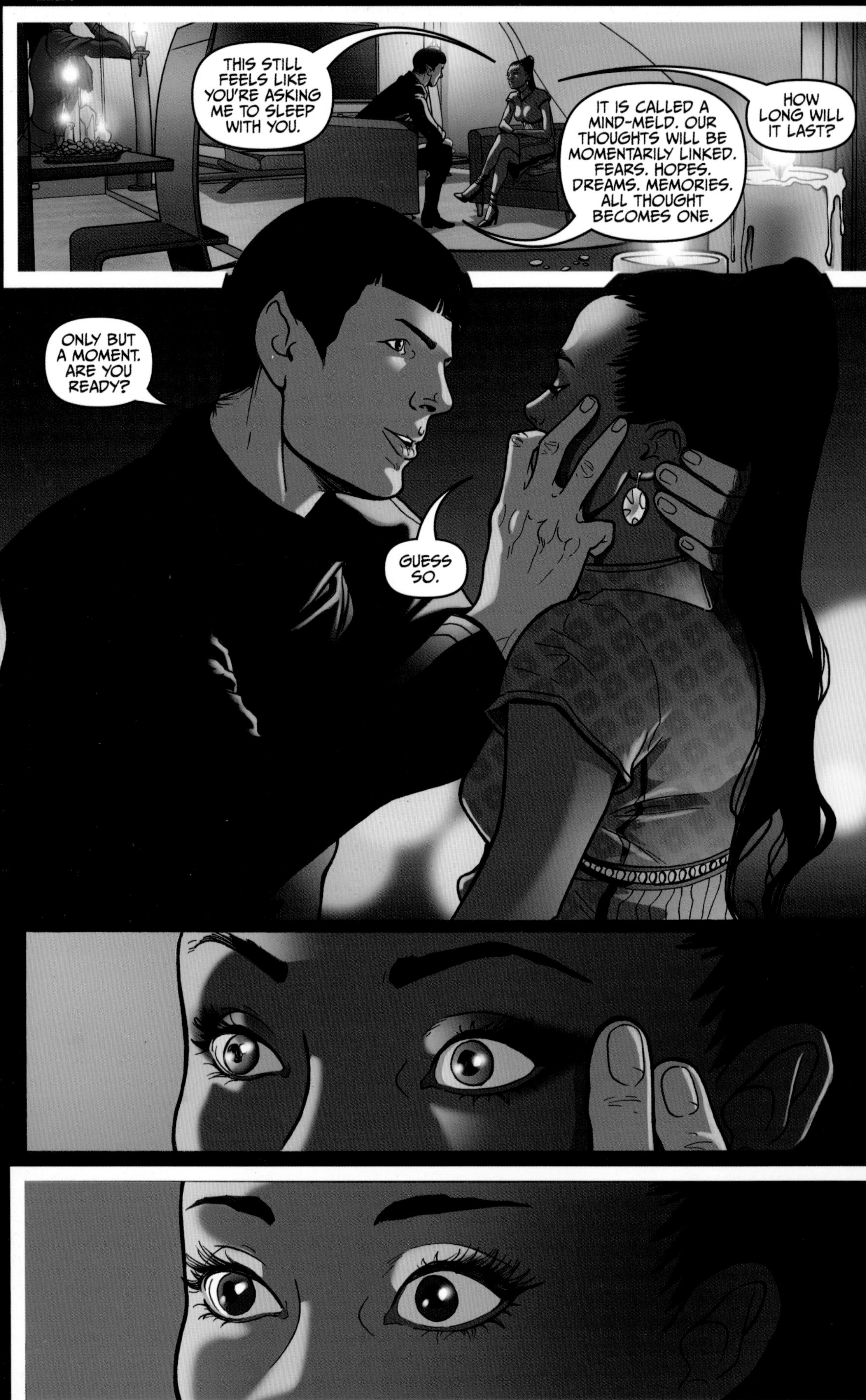
THIS STILL FEELS LIKE YOU'RE ASKING ME TO SLEEP WITH YOU.
IT IS CALLED A MIND-MELD. OUR THOUGHTS WILL BE MOMENTARILY LINKED. FEARS. HOPES. DREAMS. MEMORIES. ALL THOUGHT BECOMES ONE.
HOW LONG WILL IT LAST?
ONLY BUT A MOMENT. ARE YOU READY?
GUESS SO.

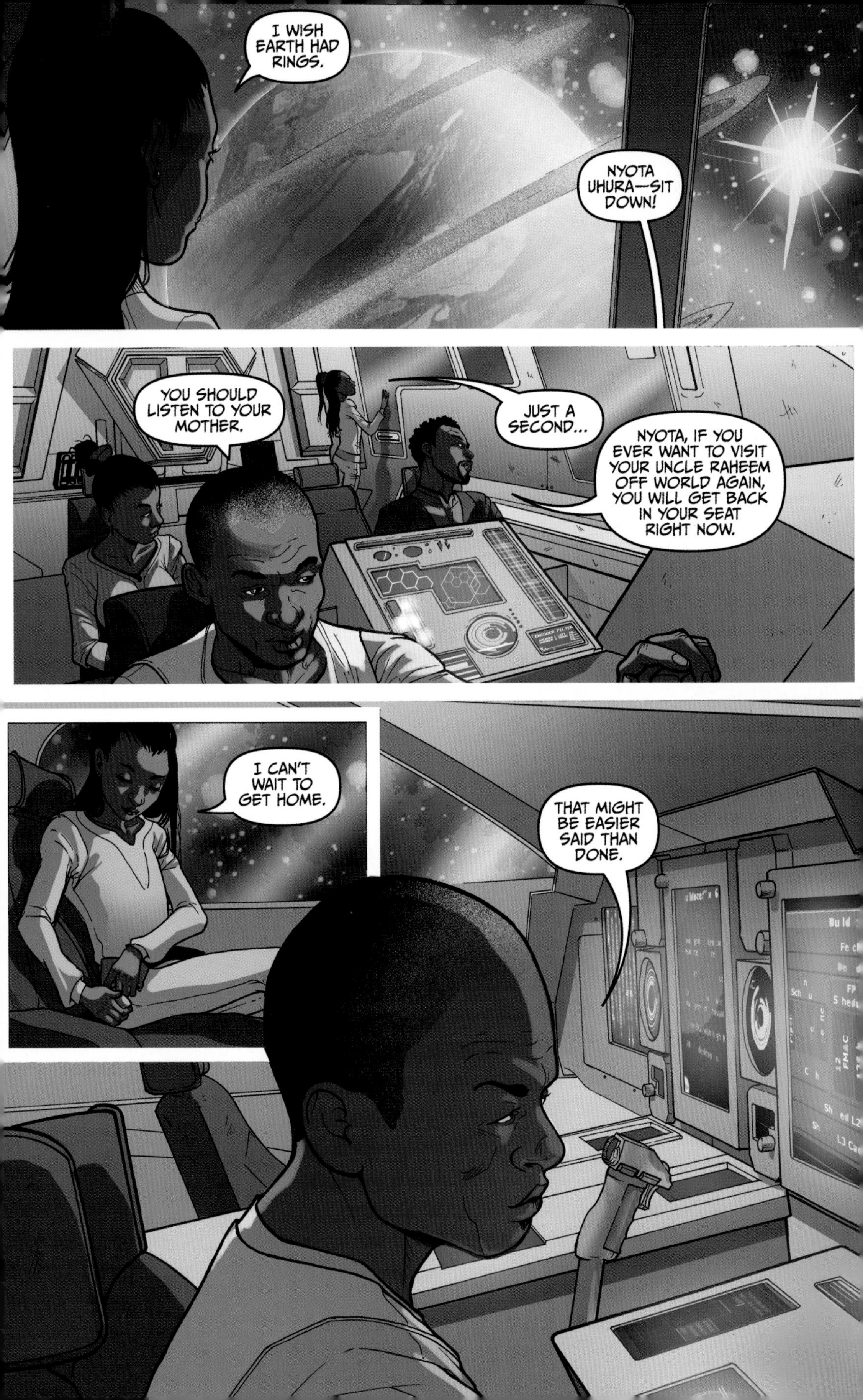
I WISH EARTH HAD RINGS.
NYOTA UHURA—SIT DOWN!
YOU SHOULD LISTEN TO YOUR MOTHER.
JUST A SECOND...
NYOTA, IF YOU EVER WANT TO VISIT YOUR UNCLE RAHEEM OFF WORLD AGAIN, YOU WILL GET BACK IN YOUR SEAT RIGHT NOW.
I CAN'T WAIT TO GET HOME.
THAT MIGHT BE EASIER SAID THAN DONE.

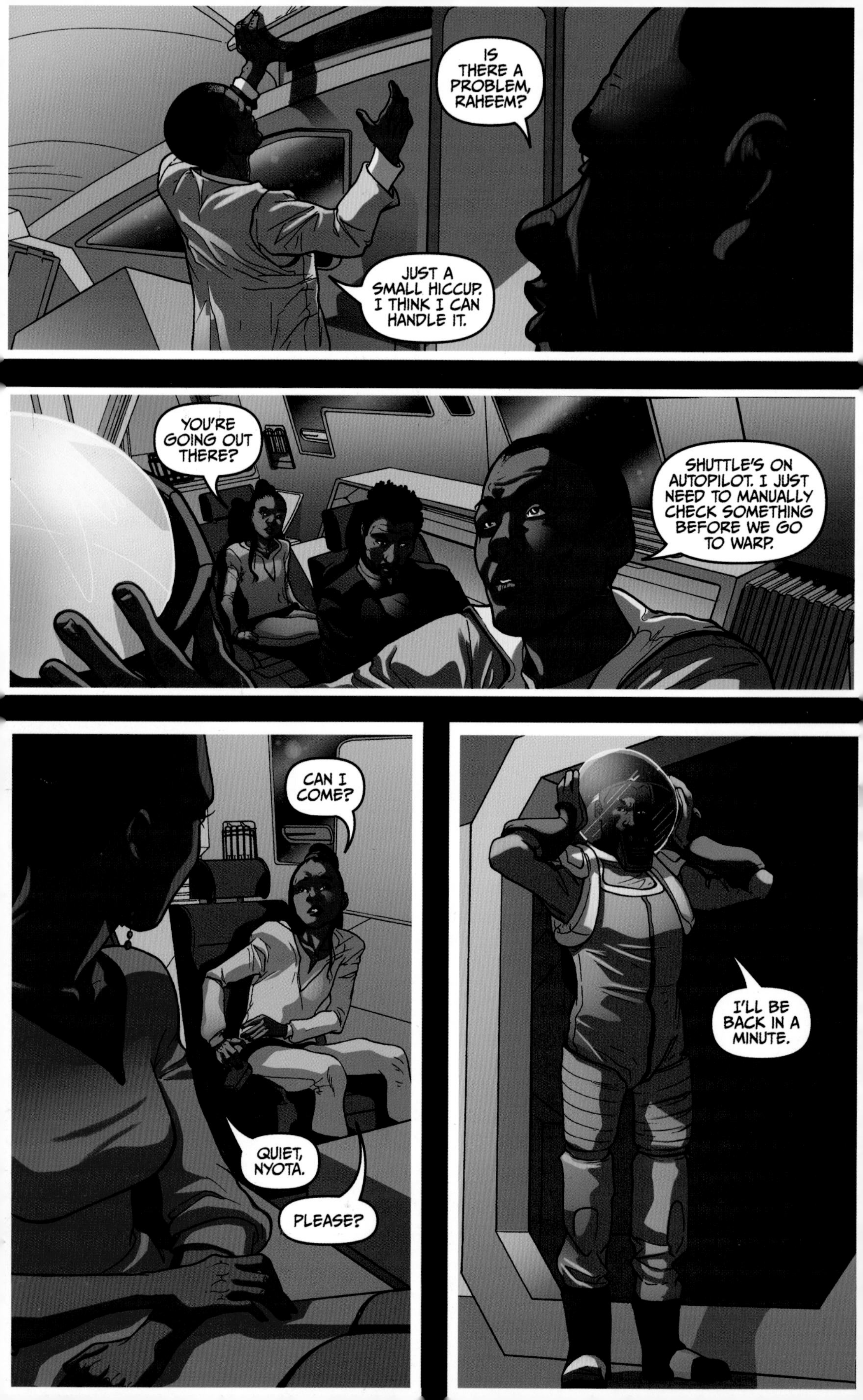
IS THERE A PROBLEM, RAHEEM?
JUST A SMALL HICCUP. I THINK I CAN HANDLE IT.
YOU'RE GOING OUT THERE?
SHUTTLE'S ON AUTOPILOT. I JUST NEED TO MANUALLY CHECK SOMETHING BEFORE WE GO TO WARP.
CAN I COME?
QUIET, NYOTA.
PLEASE?
I'LL BE BACK IN A MINUTE.

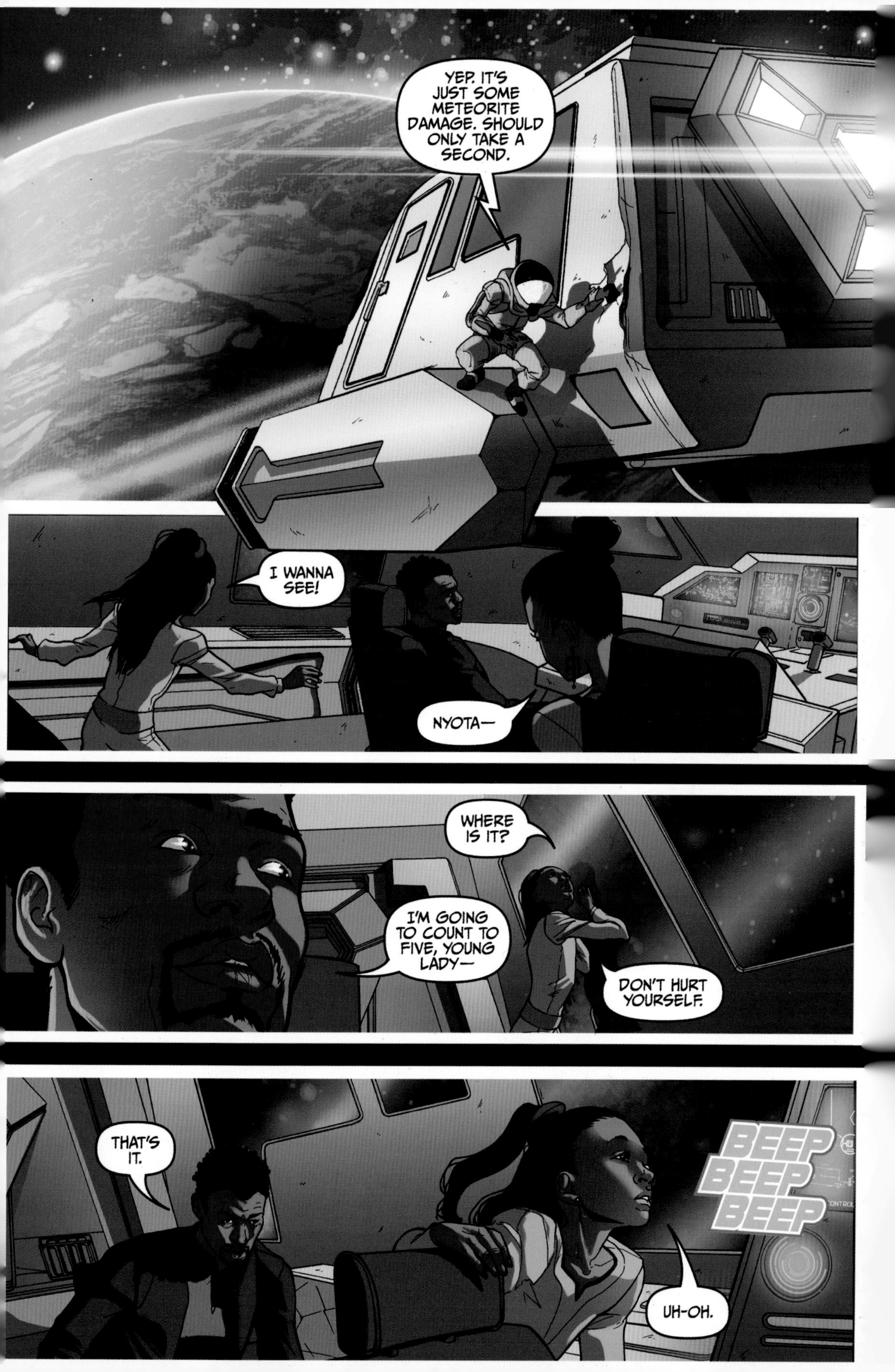
YEP. IT'S JUST SOME METEORITE DAMAGE. SHOULD ONLY TAKE A SECOND.
I WANNA SEE!
NYOTA—
WHERE IS IT?
I'M GOING TO COUNT TO FIVE, YOUNG LADY—
DON'T HURT YOURSELF.
THAT'S IT.
BEEP BEEP BEEP
UH-OH.

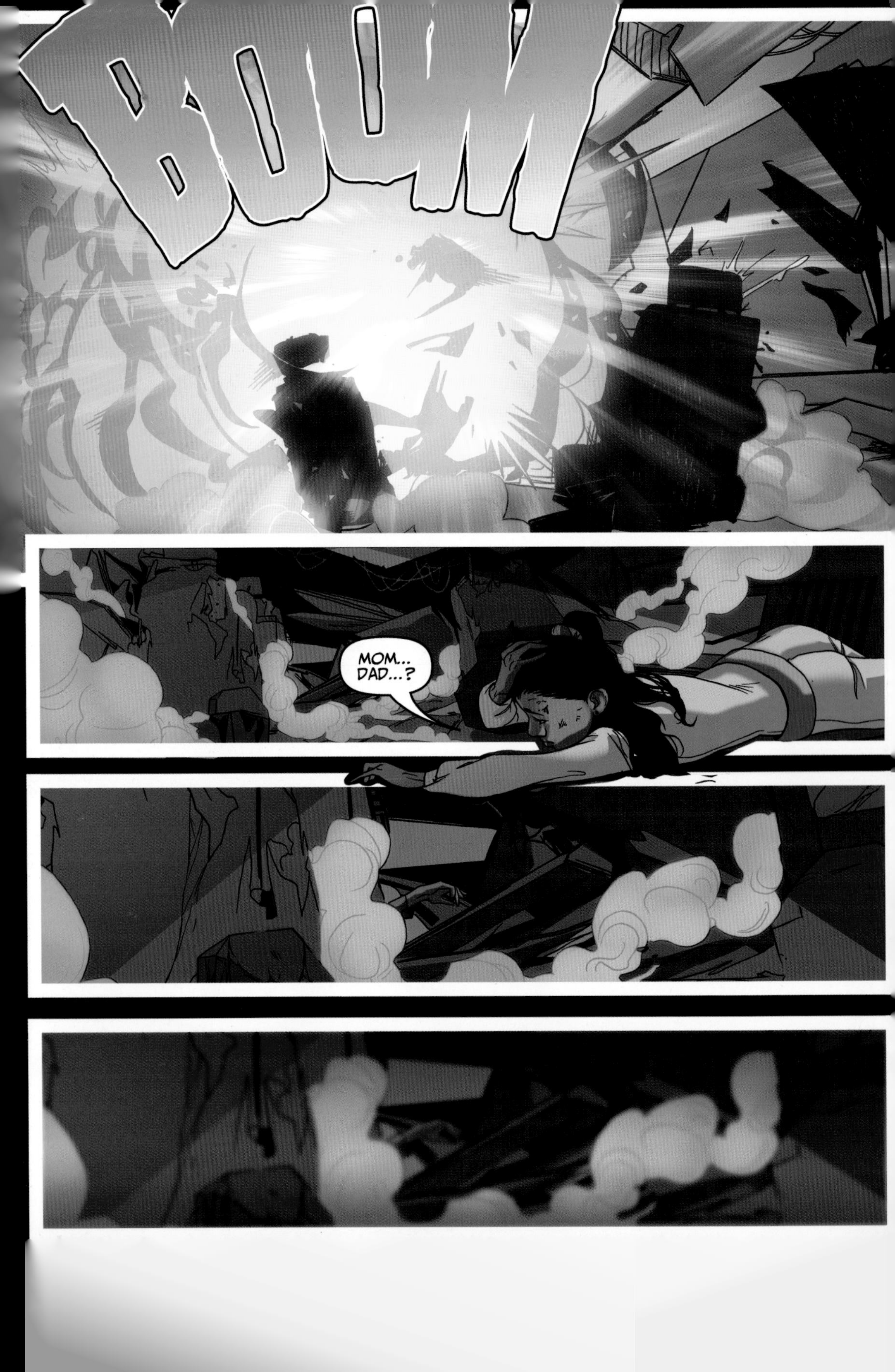
BOOM
MOM... DAD...?

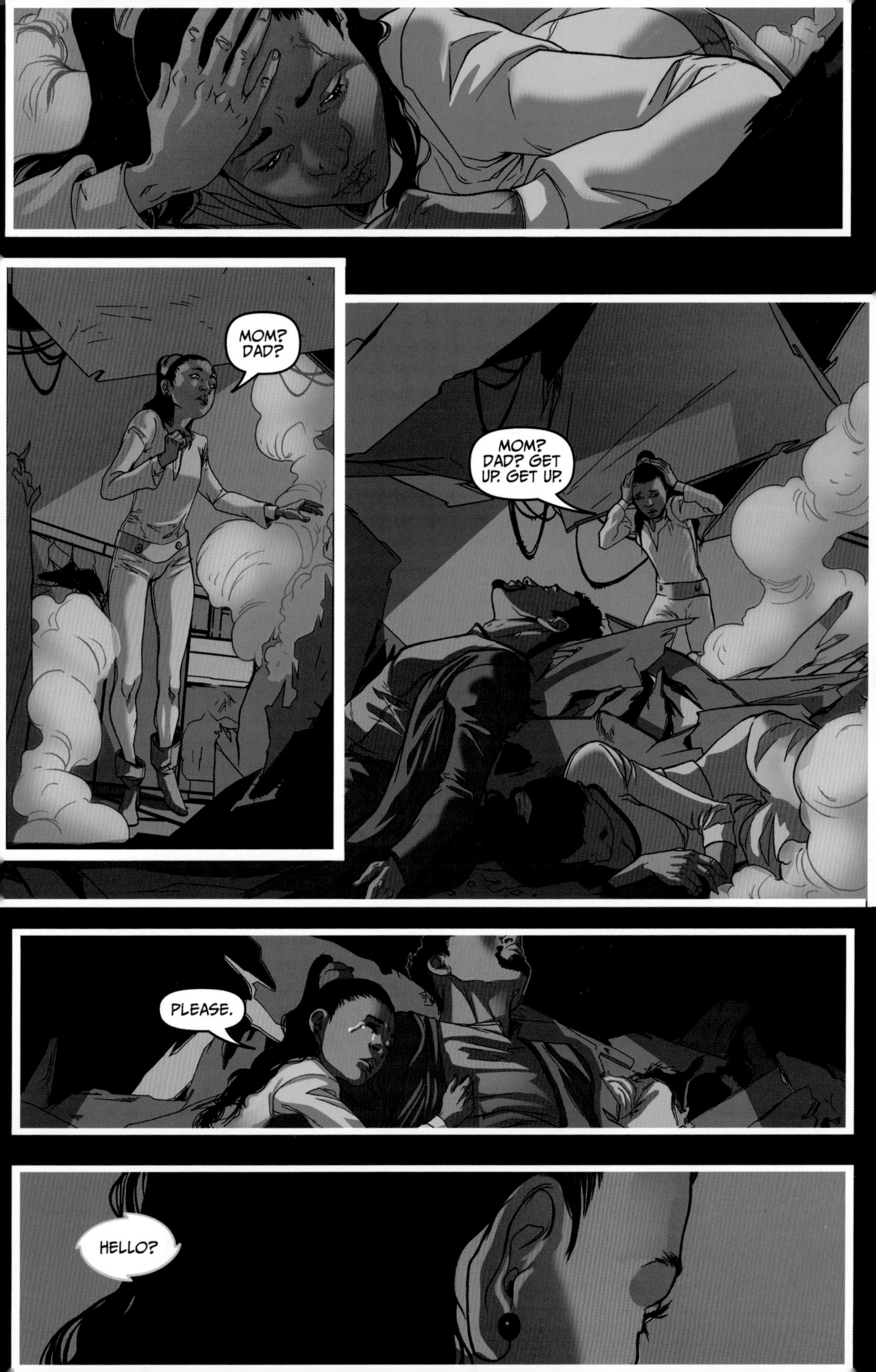
MOM? DAD?
MOM? DAD? GET UP. GET UP.
PLEASE.
HELLO?

WHO'S THERE? HELLO?

IS SOMEONE THERE?

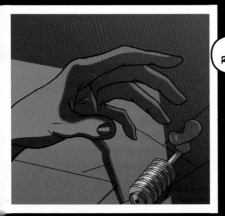

UNCLE RAHEEM?

NYOTA? OH, THANK GOD! ARE YOU ALL RIGHT?

I'M OKAY, I THINK. BUT MY PARENTS, THEY'RE NOT MOVING. THERE'S SMOKE EVERYWHERE. I'M SCARED... AND I DON'T KNOW WHAT TO DO.

WHERE ARE YOU?

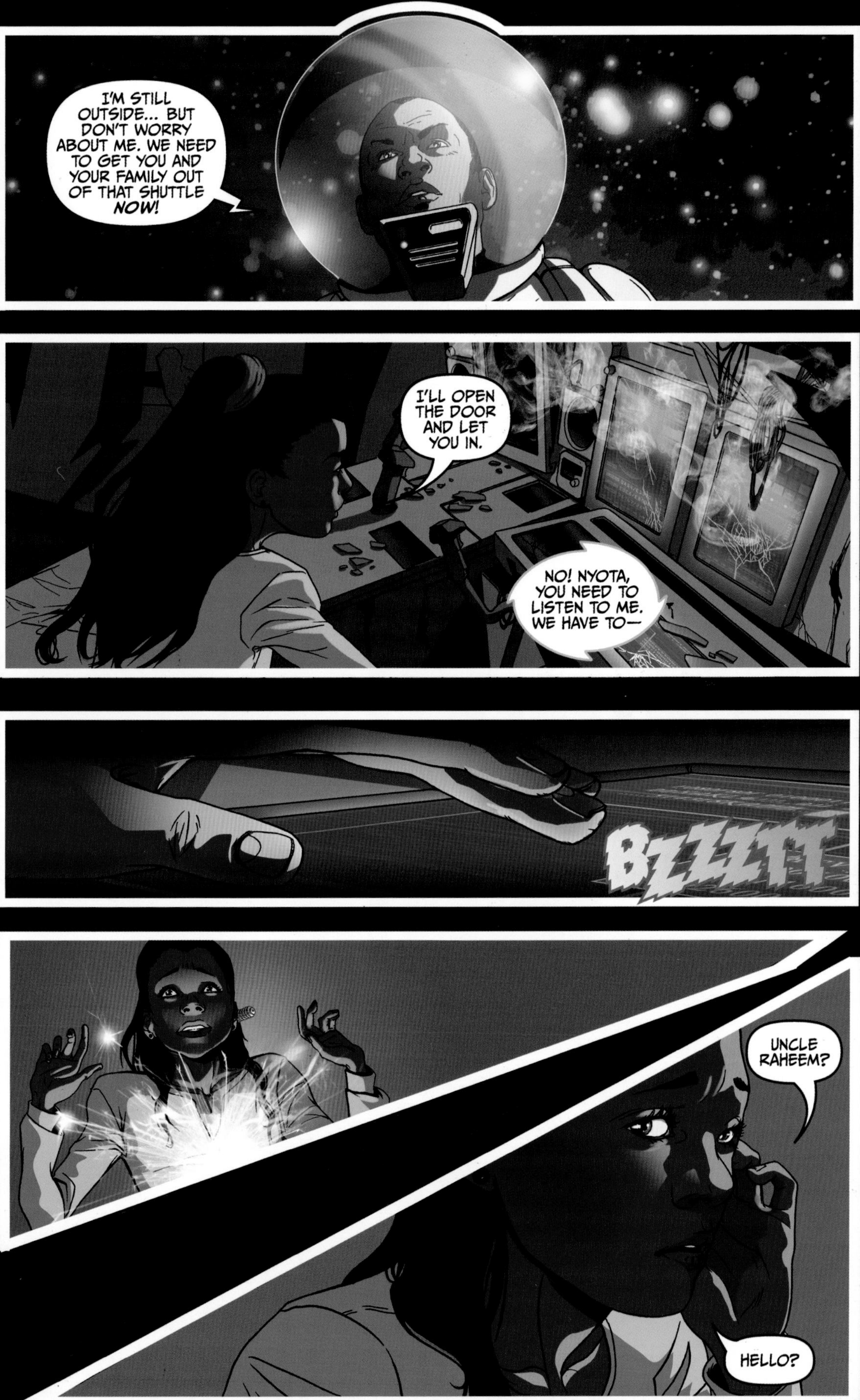
I'M STILL OUTSIDE... BUT DON'T WORRY ABOUT ME. WE NEED TO GET YOU AND YOUR FAMILY OUT OF THAT SHUTTLE *NOW!*
I'LL OPEN THE DOOR AND LET YOU IN.
NO! NYOTA, YOU NEED TO LISTEN TO ME. WE HAVE TO—
BZZZTT
UNCLE RAHEEM?
HELLO?

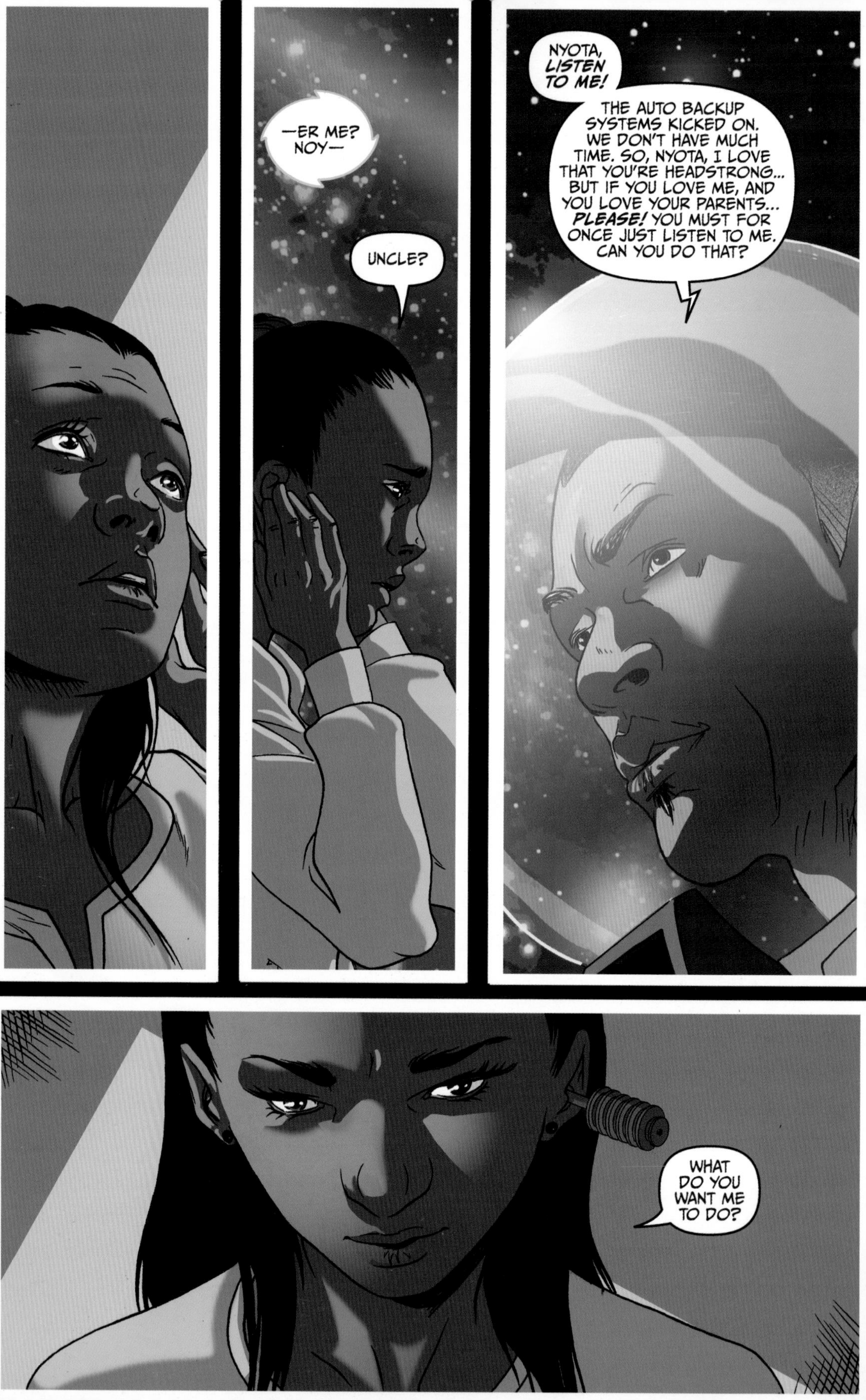
—ER ME? NOY—
UNCLE?
NYOTA, LISTEN TO ME!
THE AUTO BACKUP SYSTEMS KICKED ON. WE DON'T HAVE MUCH TIME. SO, NYOTA, I LOVE THAT YOU'RE HEADSTRONG... BUT IF YOU LOVE ME, AND YOU LOVE YOUR PARENTS... PLEASE! YOU MUST FOR ONCE JUST LISTEN TO ME. CAN YOU DO THAT?
WHAT DO YOU WANT ME TO DO?

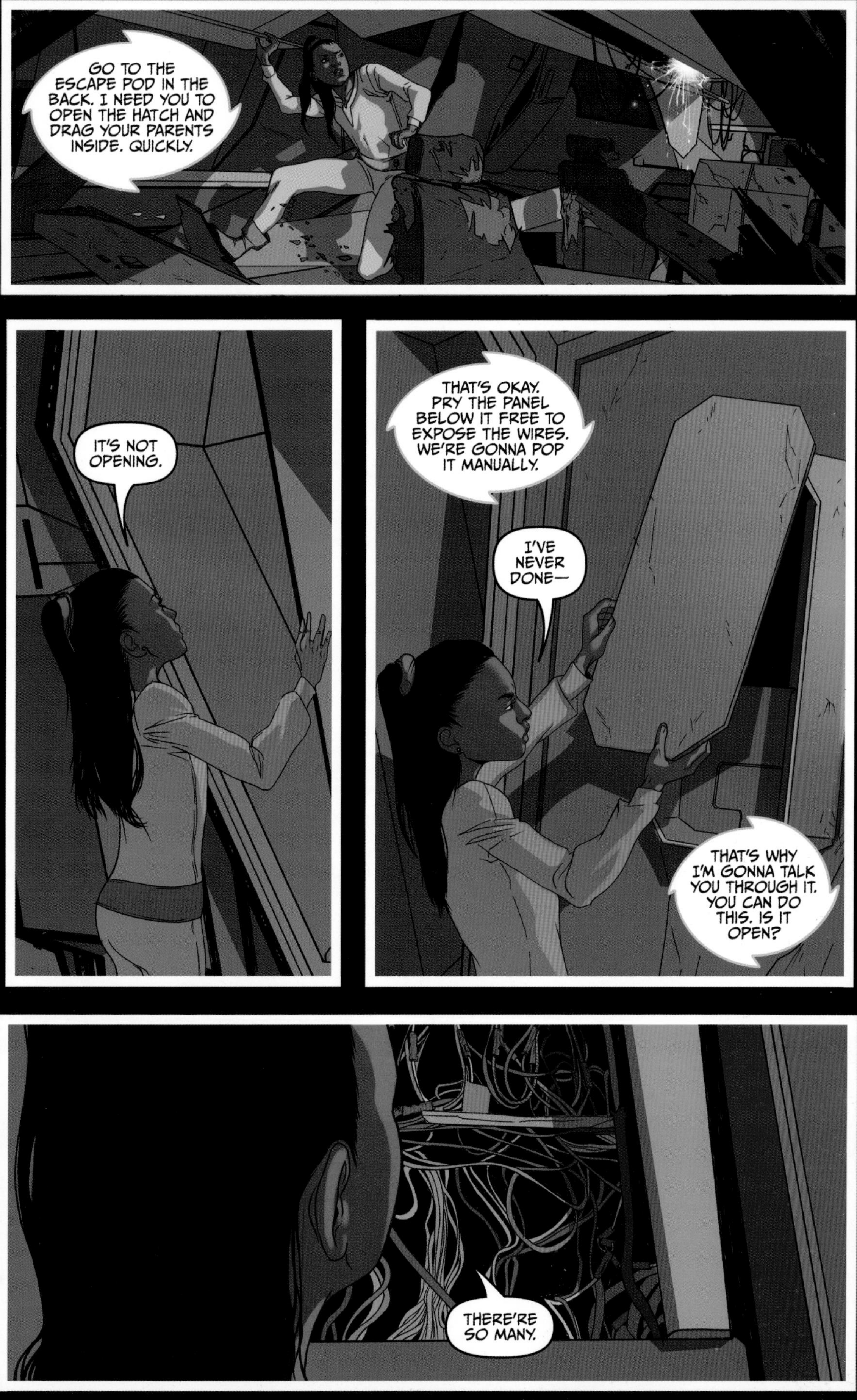
GO TO THE ESCAPE POD IN THE BACK. I NEED YOU TO OPEN THE HATCH AND DRAG YOUR PARENTS INSIDE. QUICKLY.
IT'S NOT OPENING.
THAT'S OKAY. PRY THE PANEL BELOW IT FREE TO EXPOSE THE WIRES. WE'RE GONNA POP IT MANUALLY.
I'VE NEVER DONE—
THAT'S WHY I'M GONNA TALK YOU THROUGH IT. YOU CAN DO THIS. IS IT OPEN?
THERE'RE SO MANY.

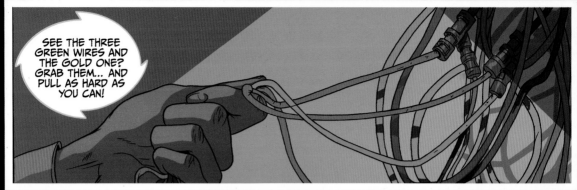

SEE THE THREE GREEN WIRES AND THE GOLD ONE? GRAB THEM... AND PULL AS HARD AS YOU CAN!

THAT SHOULD SHORT OUT POWER TO THE MAGNETIC LOCKS AND—

ZZZZZTT

IT OPENED!

GOOD GIRL. VERY GOOD. NOW COMES THE HARD PART...

...AND YOU NEED TO HURRY.

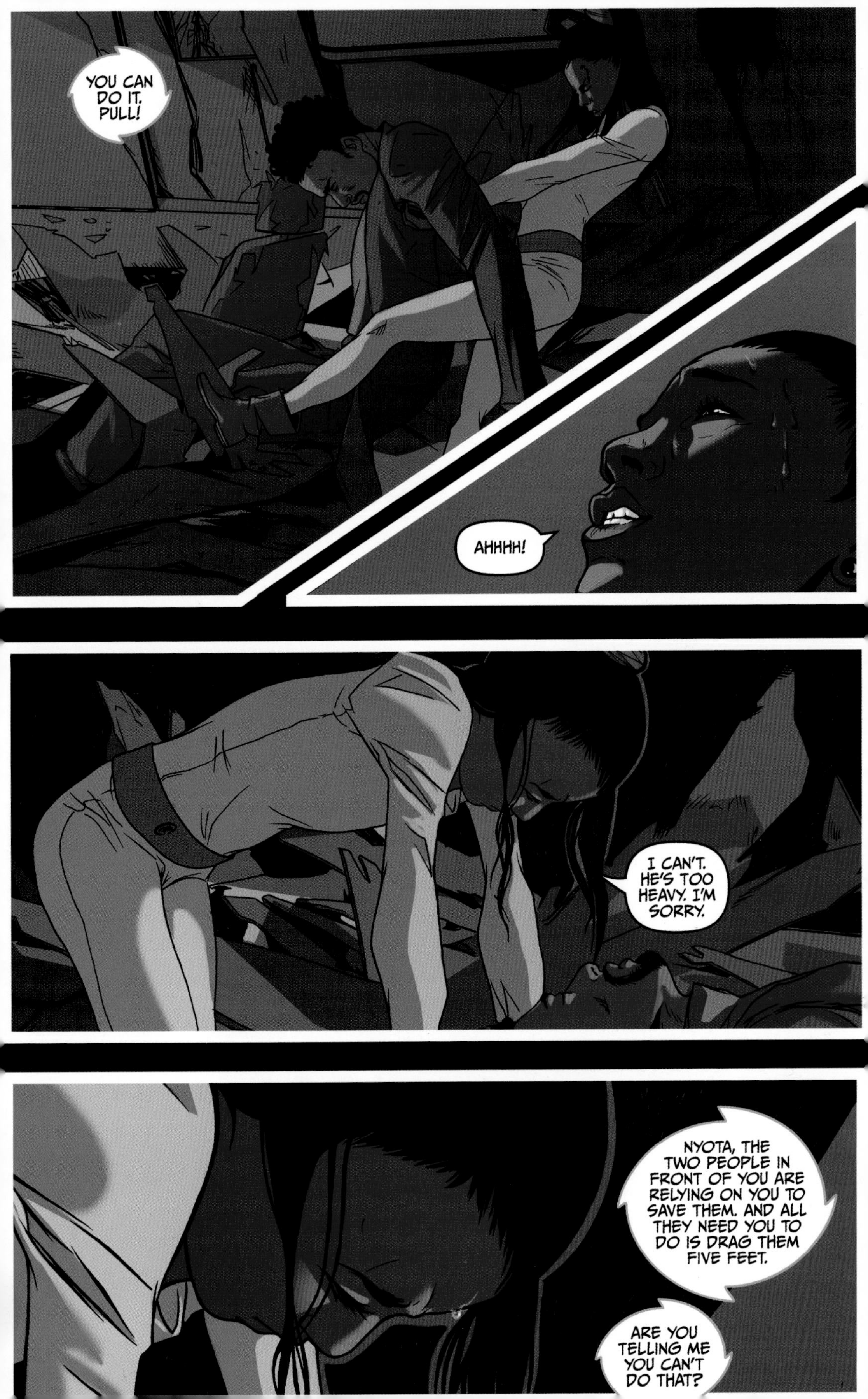
YOU CAN DO IT. PULL!
AHHHH!
I CAN'T. HE'S TOO HEAVY. I'M SORRY.
NYOTA, THE TWO PEOPLE IN FRONT OF YOU ARE RELYING ON YOU TO SAVE THEM. AND ALL THEY NEED YOU TO DO IS DRAG THEM FIVE FEET.
ARE YOU TELLING ME YOU CAN'T DO THAT?

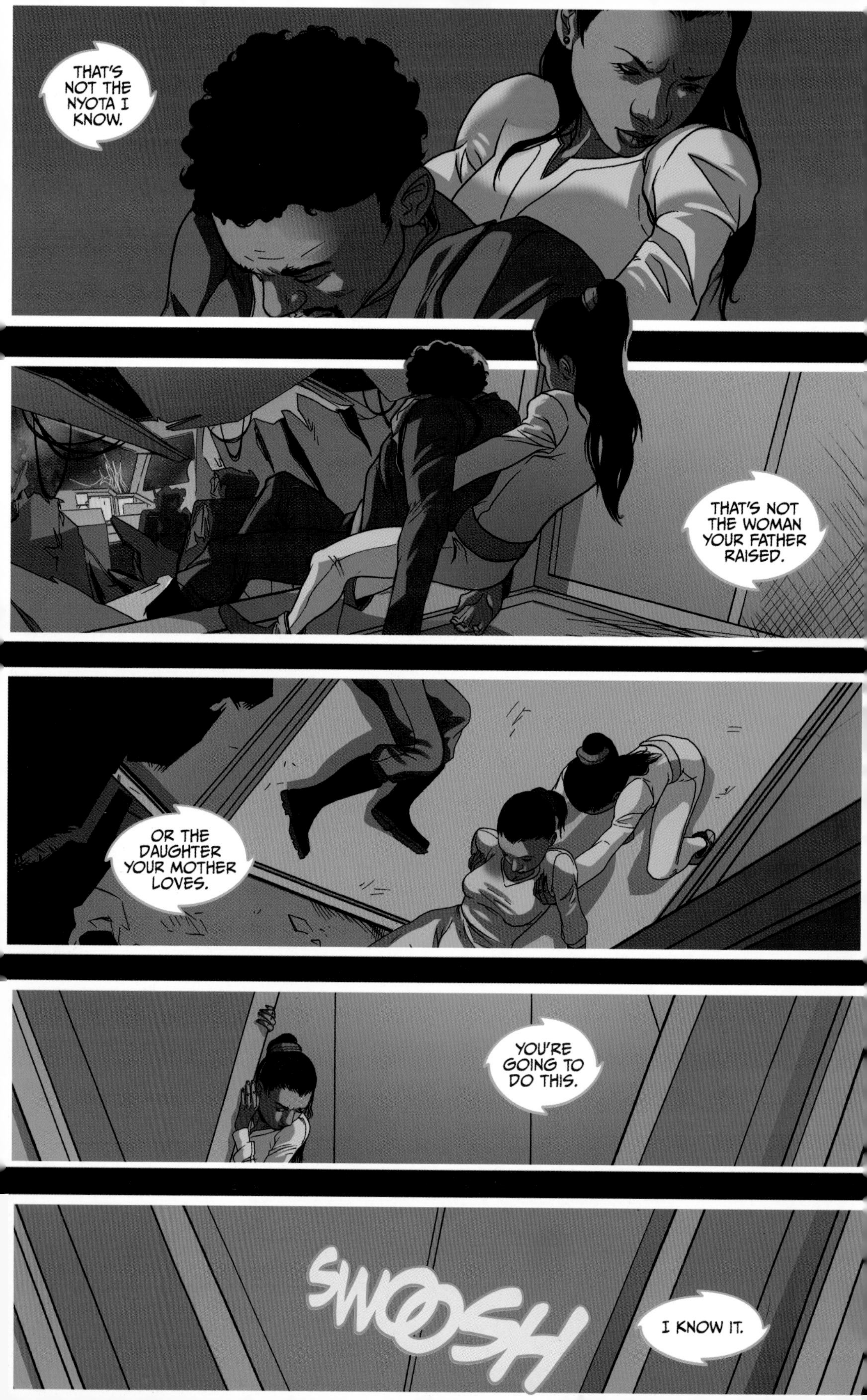
THAT'S NOT THE NYOTA I KNOW.
THAT'S NOT THE WOMAN YOUR FATHER RAISED.
OR THE DAUGHTER YOUR MOTHER LOVES.
YOU'RE GOING TO DO THIS.
SWOOSH
I KNOW IT.

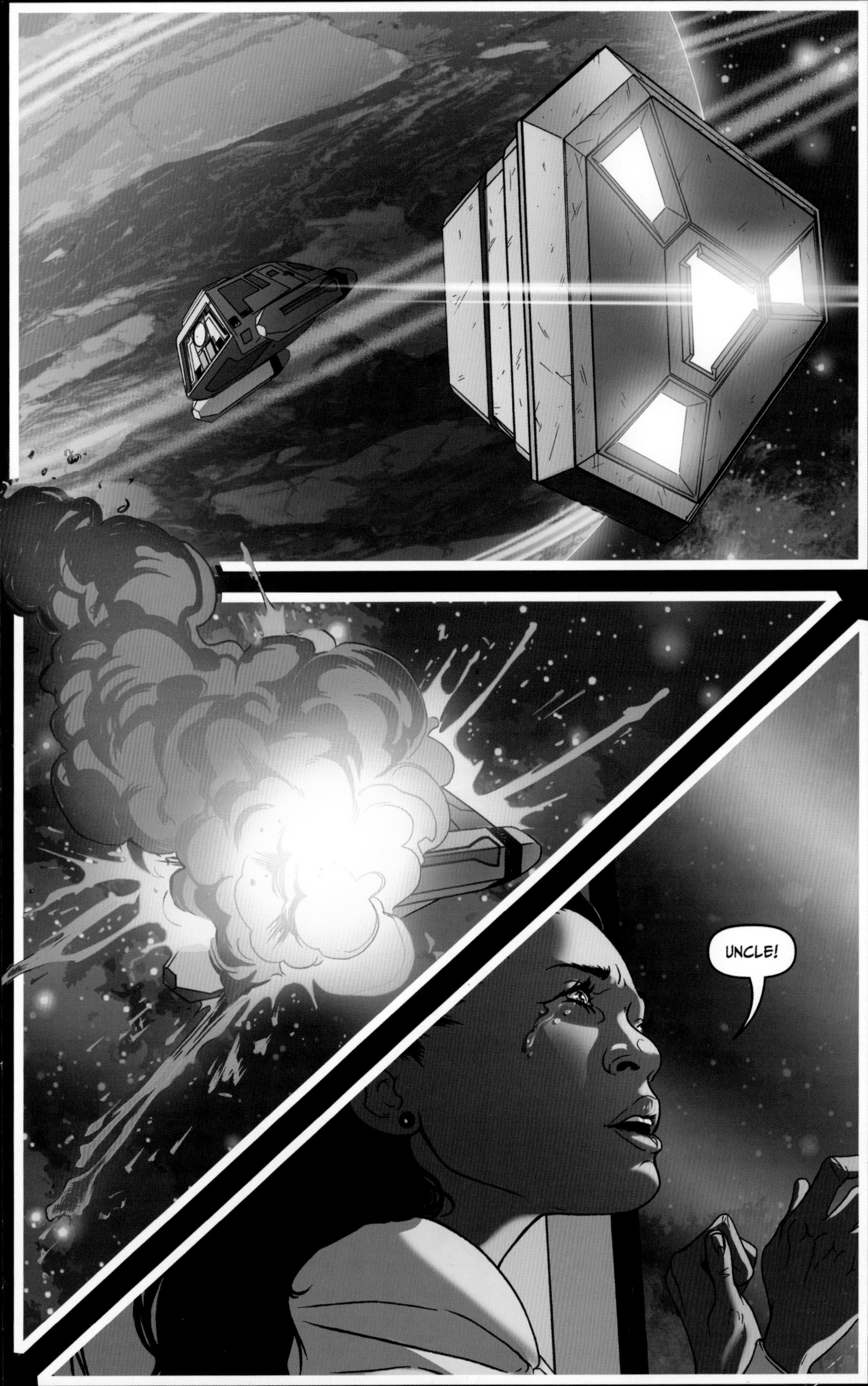
UNCLE!

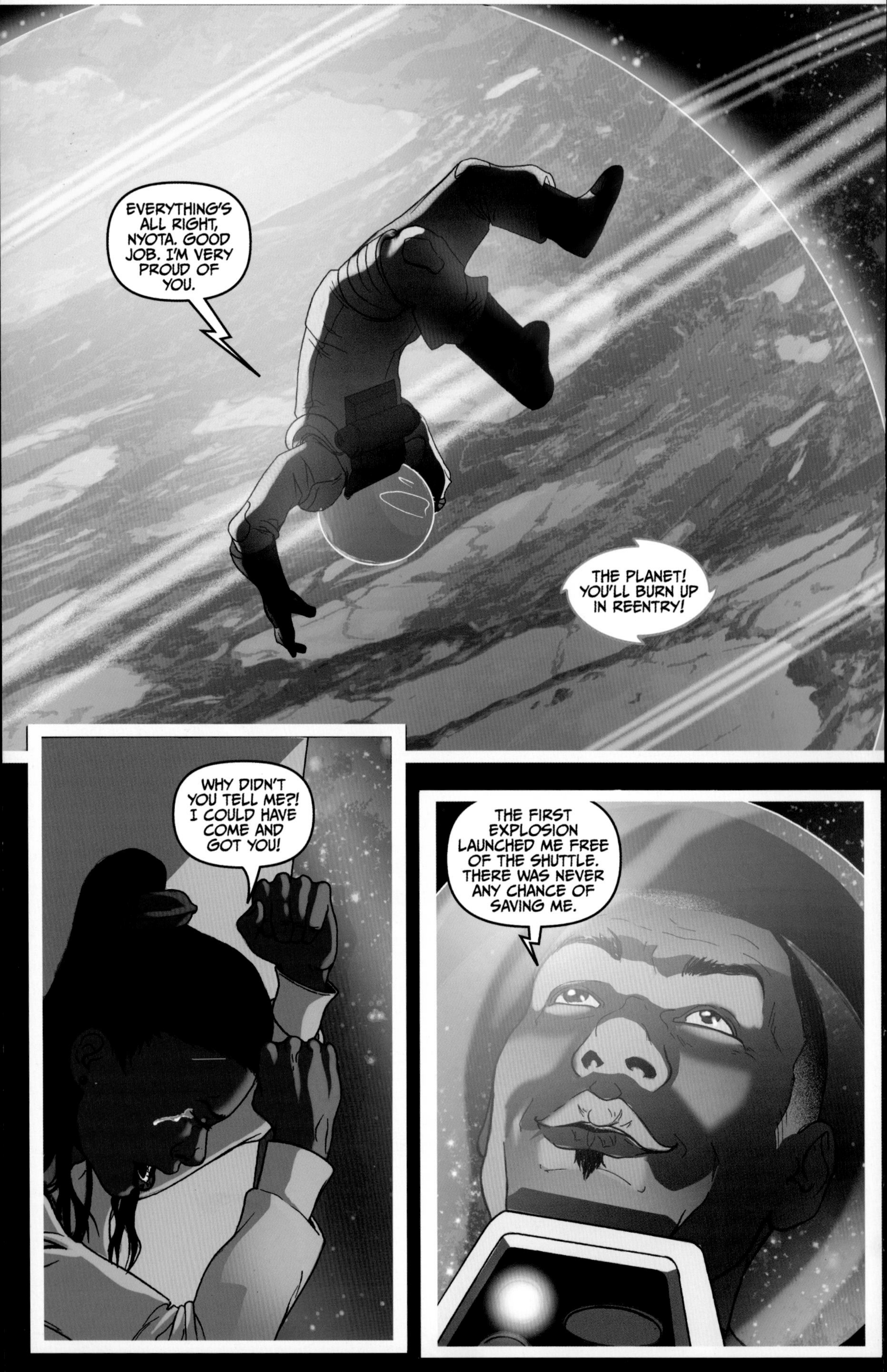
EVERYTHING'S ALL RIGHT, NYOTA. GOOD JOB. I'M VERY PROUD OF YOU.
THE PLANET! YOU'LL BURN UP IN REENTRY!
WHY DIDN'T YOU TELL ME?! I COULD HAVE COME AND GOT YOU!
THE FIRST EXPLOSION LAUNCHED ME FREE OF THE SHUTTLE. THERE WAS NEVER ANY CHANCE OF SAVING ME.

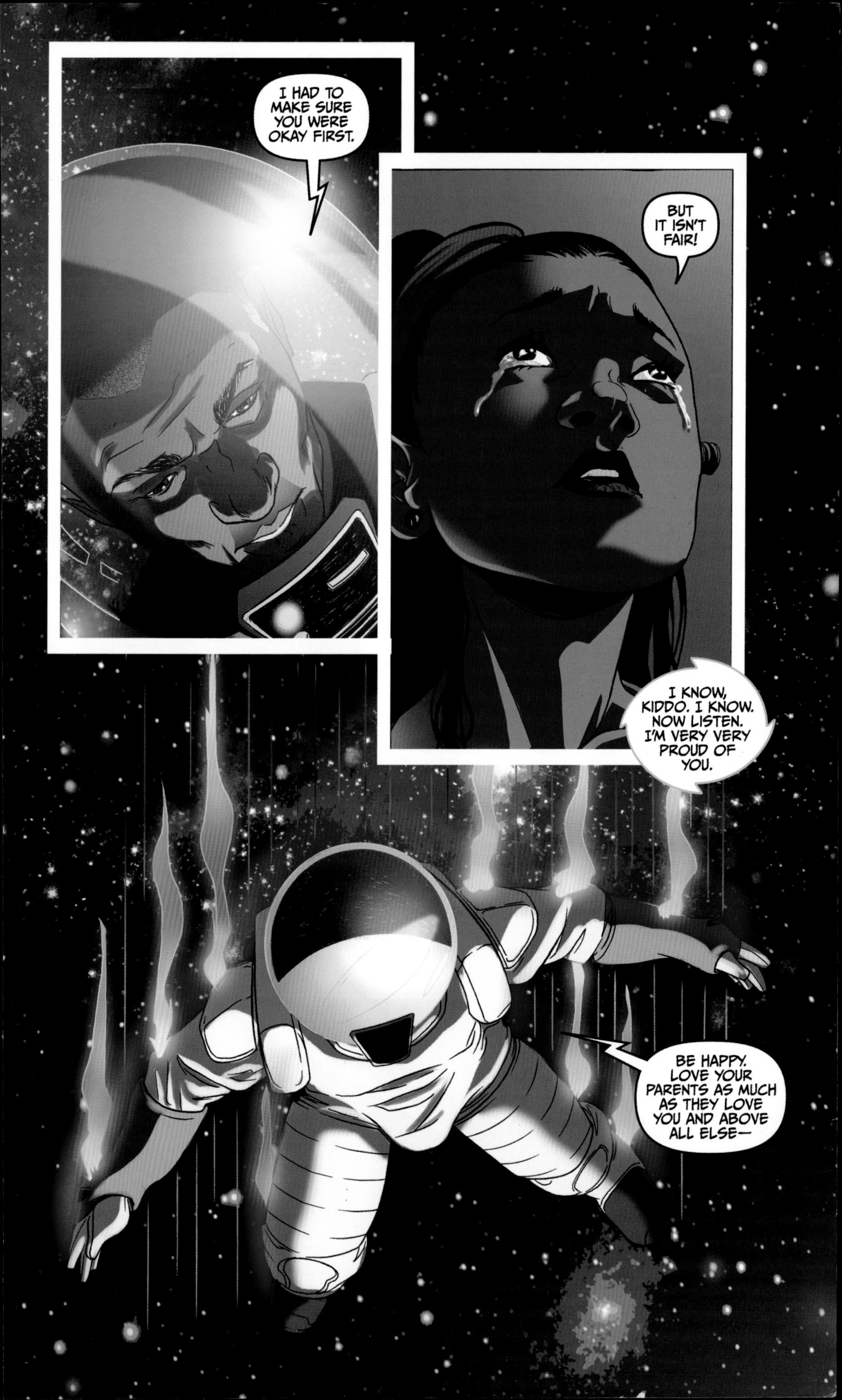
I HAD TO MAKE SURE YOU WERE OKAY FIRST.
BUT IT ISN'T FAIR!
I KNOW, KIDDO. I KNOW. NOW LISTEN. I'M VERY VERY PROUD OF YOU.
BE HAPPY. LOVE YOUR PARENTS AS MUCH AS THEY LOVE YOU AND ABOVE ALL ELSE—

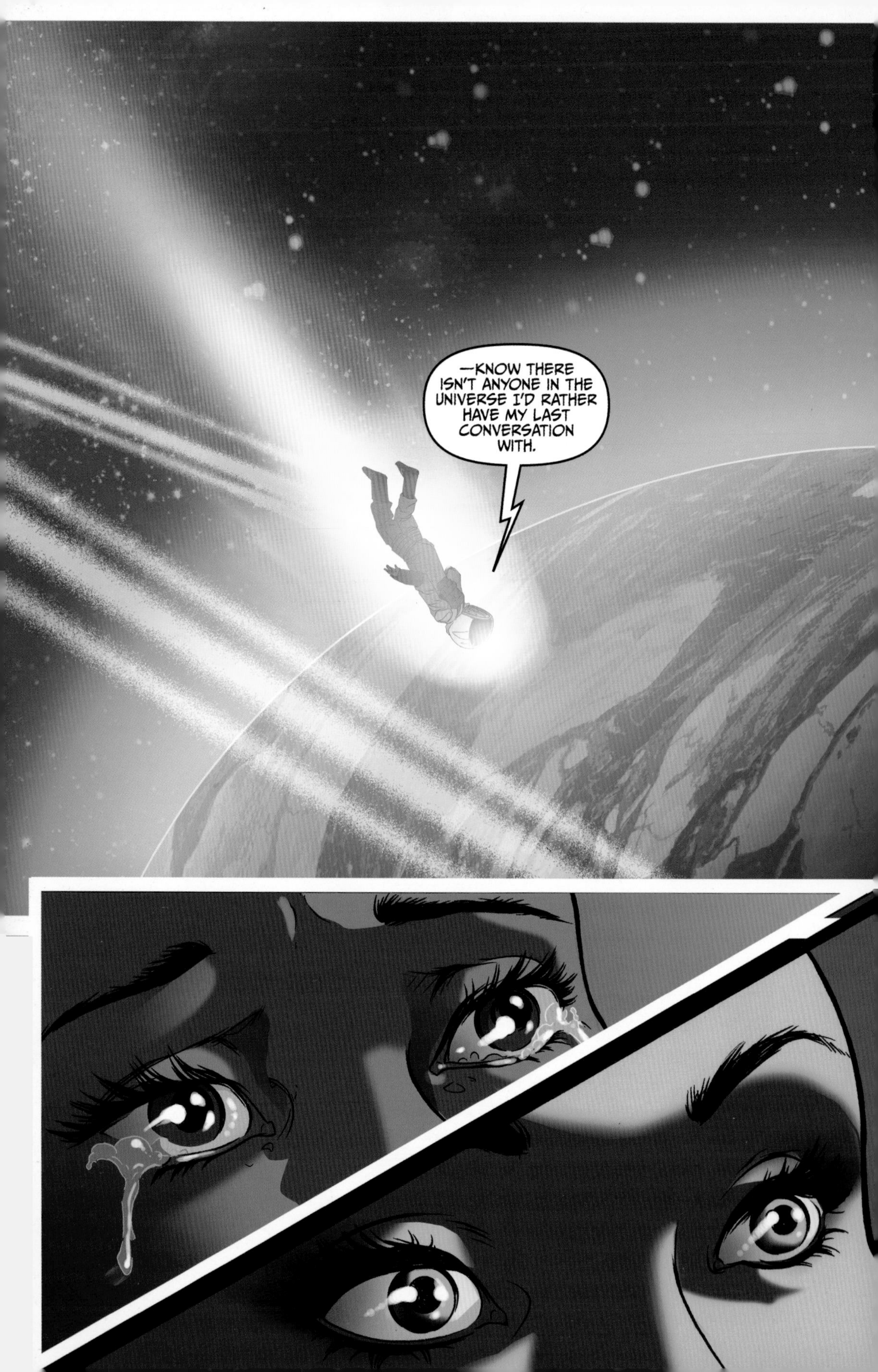
—KNOW THERE ISN'T ANYONE IN THE UNIVERSE I'D RATHER HAVE MY LAST CONVERSATION WITH.

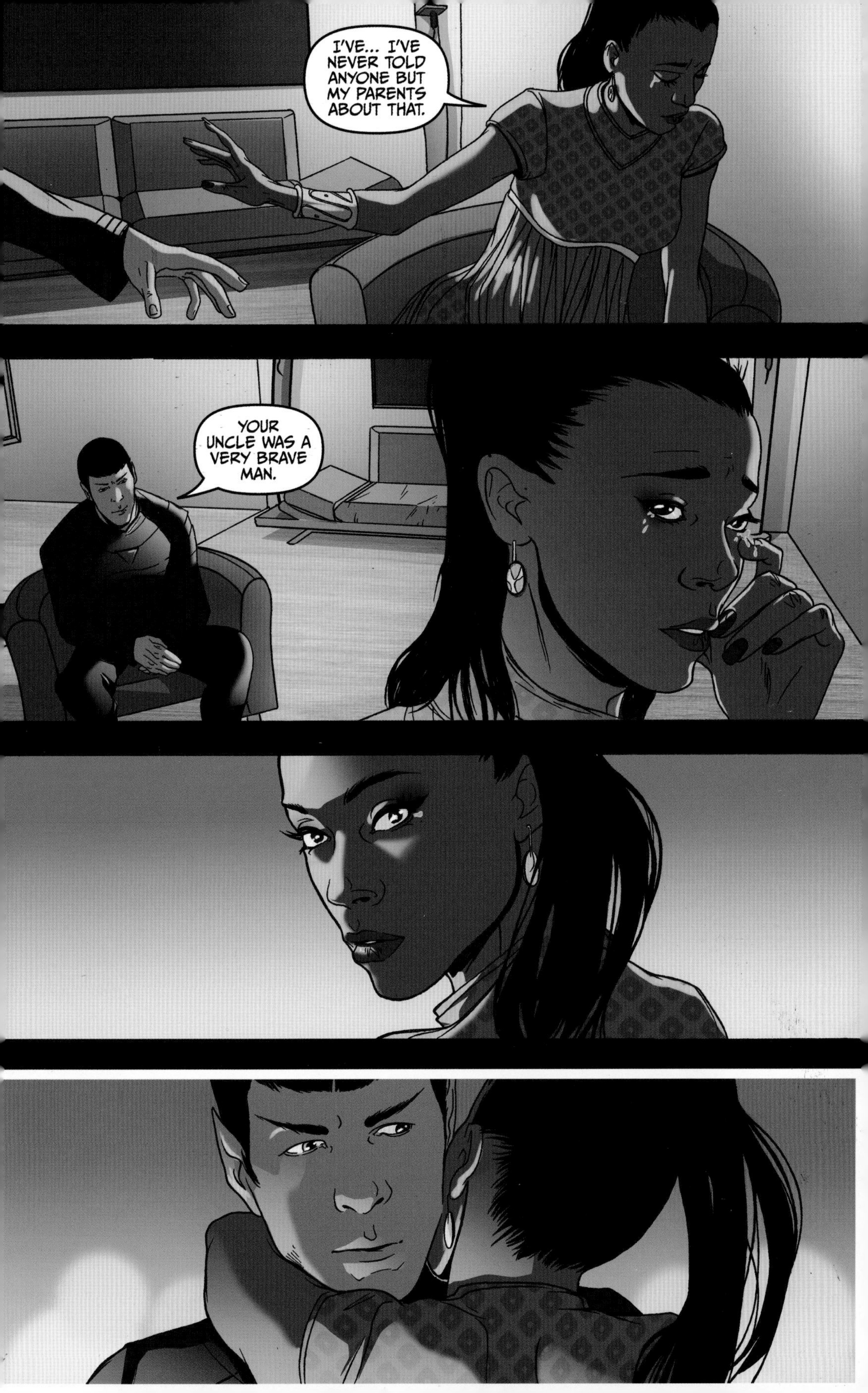
I'VE... I'VE NEVER TOLD ANYONE BUT MY PARENTS ABOUT THAT.
YOUR UNCLE WAS A VERY BRAVE MAN.

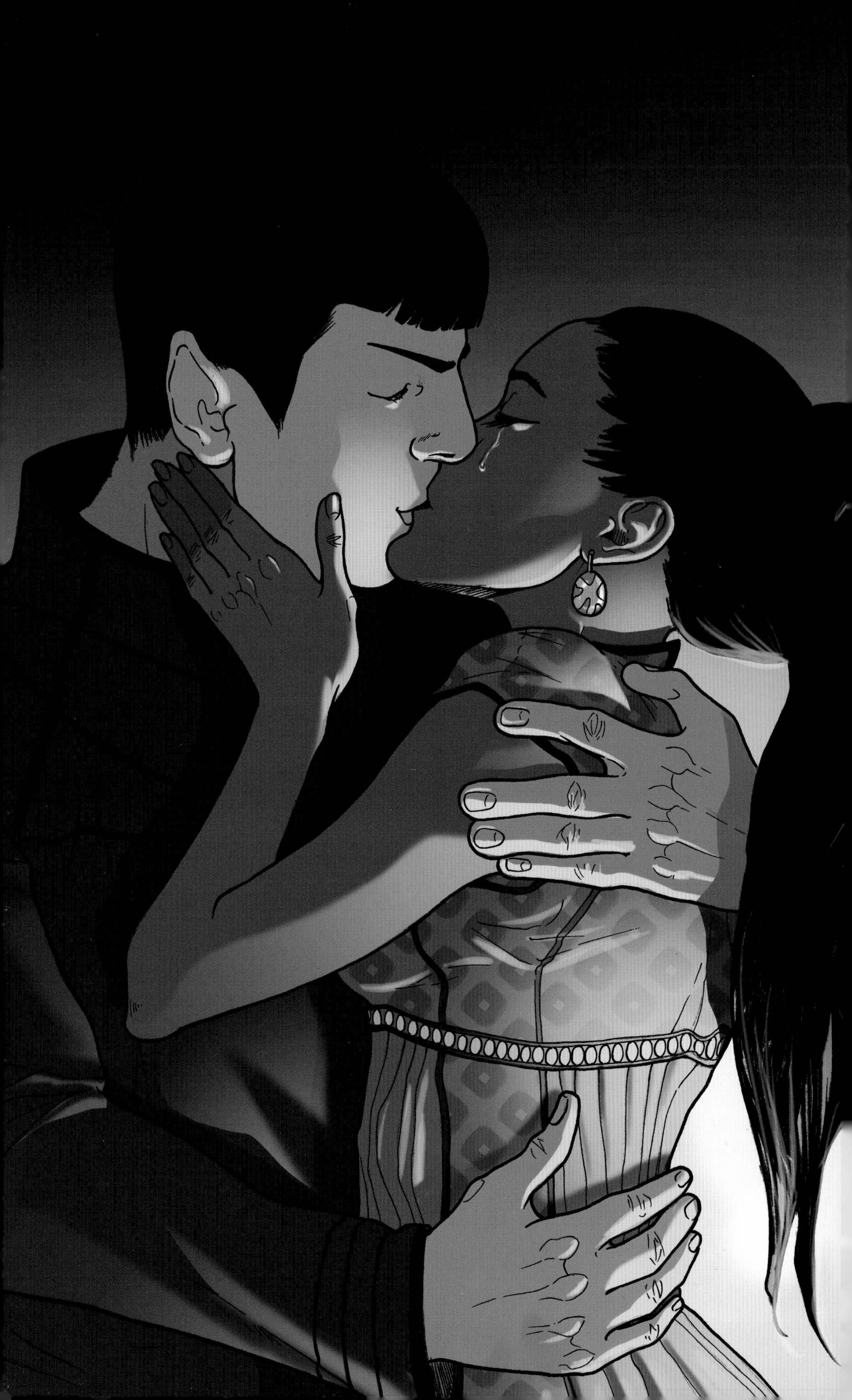

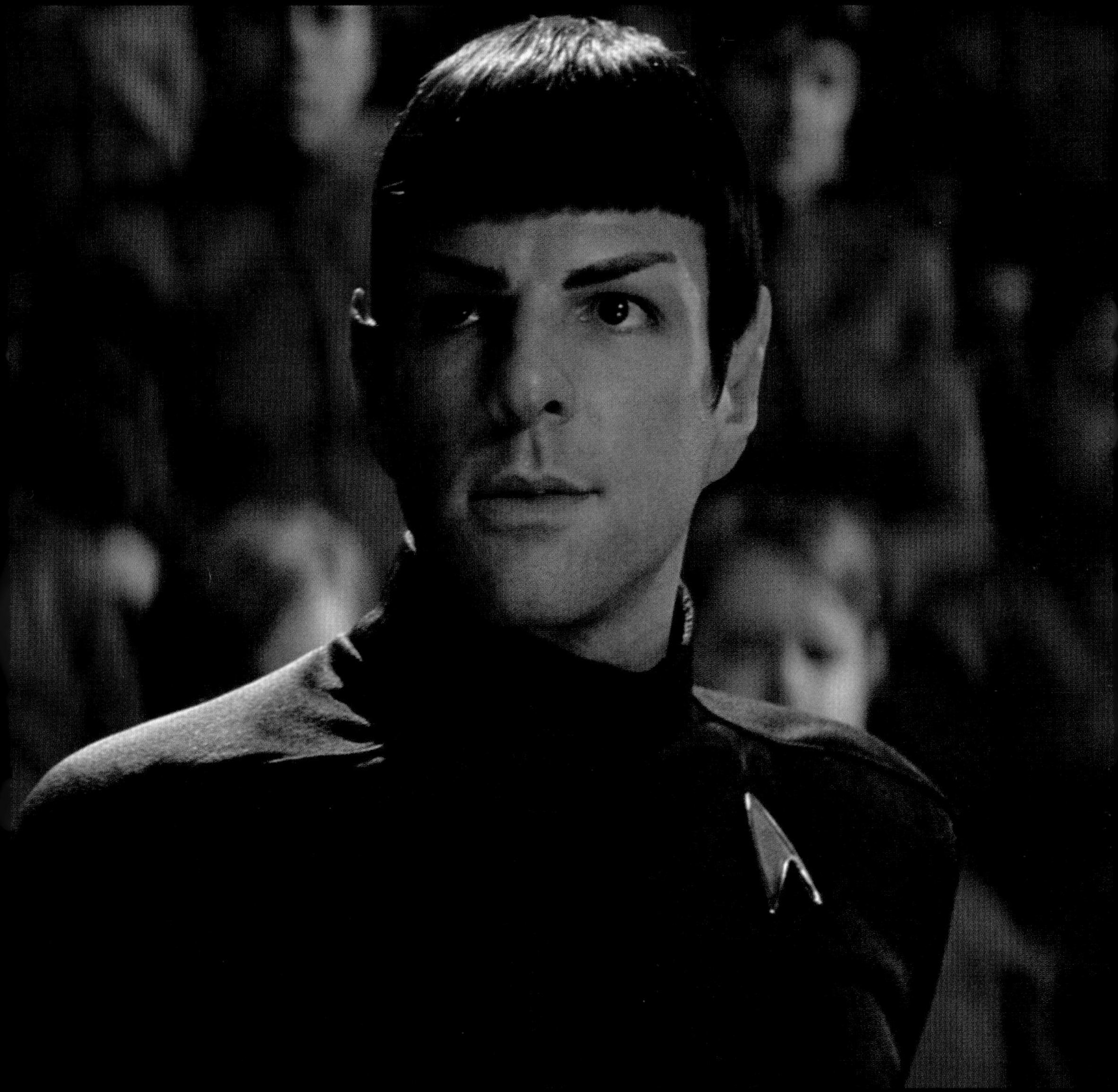

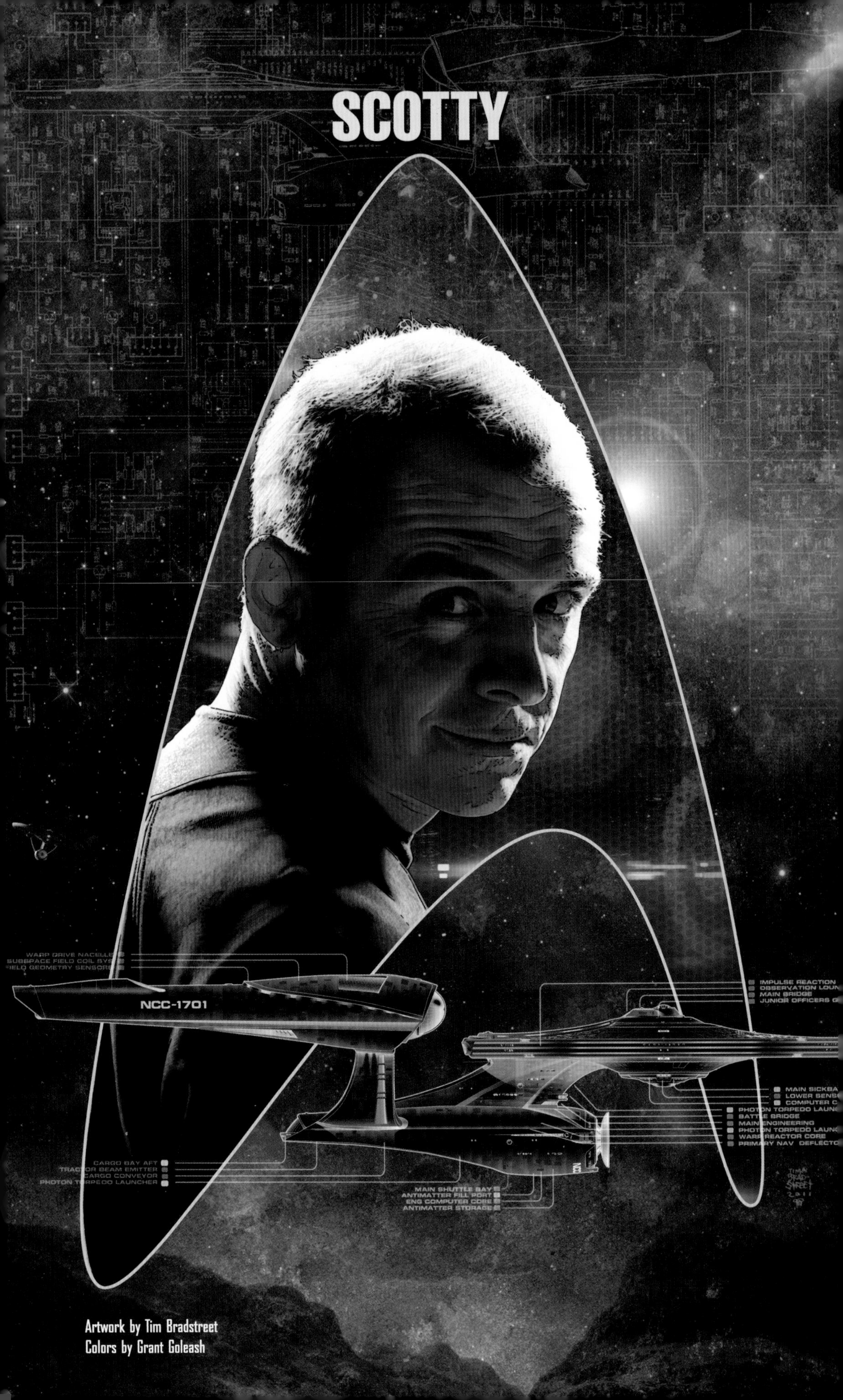
SCOTTY
WARP DRIVE NACELLE
NCC-1701
IMPULSE REACTION
MAIN BRIDGE
MAIN SICKBAY
BATTLE BRIDGE
MAIN ENGINEERING
WARP REACTOR CORE
CARGO BAY AFT
TRACTOR BEAM EMITTER
CARGO CONVEYOR
PHOTON TORPEDO LAUNCHER
MAIN SHUTTLE BAY
ANTIMATTER FILL PORT
ENG COMPUTER CORE
ANTIMATTER STORAGE

Artwork by Tim Bradstreet
Colors by Grant Goleash

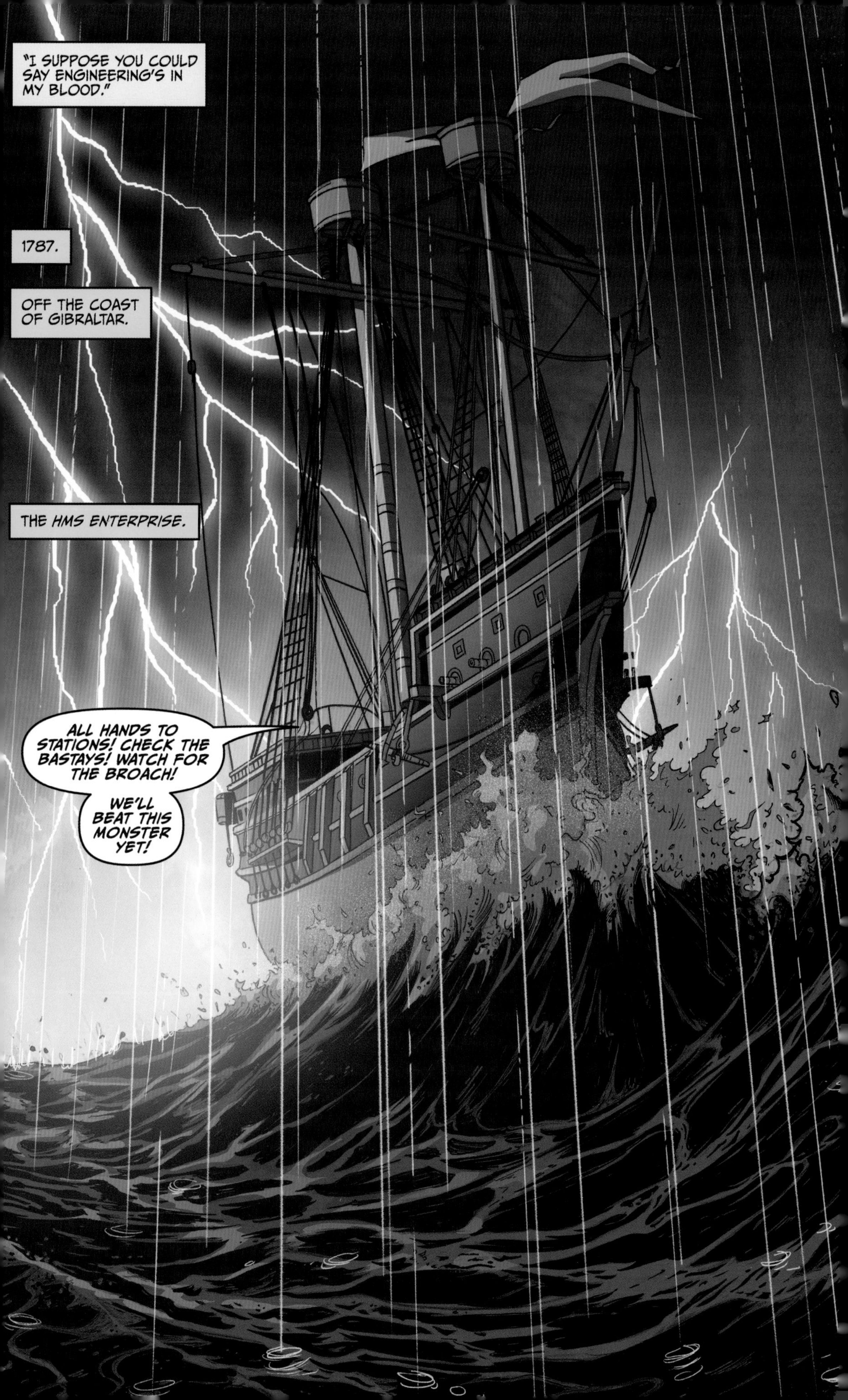
"I SUPPOSE YOU COULD SAY ENGINEERING'S IN MY BLOOD."
1787.
OFF THE COAST OF GIBRALTAR.
THE *HMS ENTERPRISE.*
ALL HANDS TO STATIONS! CHECK THE BASTAYS! WATCH FOR THE BROACH!
WE'LL BEAT THIS MONSTER YET!

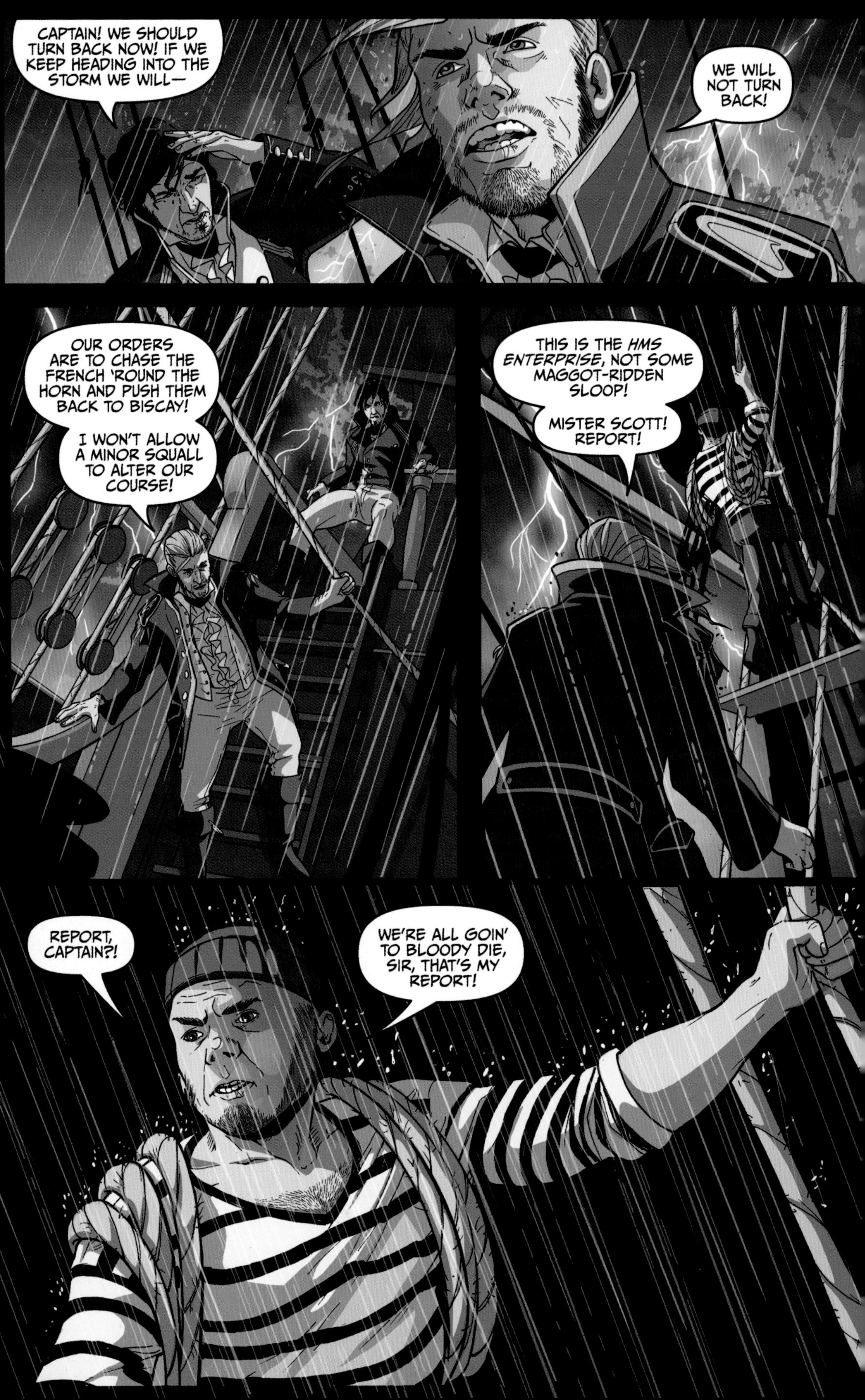
CAPTAIN! WE SHOULD TURN BACK NOW! IF WE KEEP HEADING INTO THE STORM WE WILL—
WE WILL NOT TURN BACK!
OUR ORDERS ARE TO CHASE THE FRENCH 'ROUND THE HORN AND PUSH THEM BACK TO BISCAY!
I WON'T ALLOW A MINOR SQUALL TO ALTER OUR COURSE!
THIS IS THE *HMS ENTERPRISE*, NOT SOME MAGGOT-RIDDEN SLOOP!
MISTER SCOTT! REPORT!
REPORT, CAPTAIN?!
WE'RE ALL GOIN' TO BLOODY DIE, SIR, THAT'S MY REPORT!

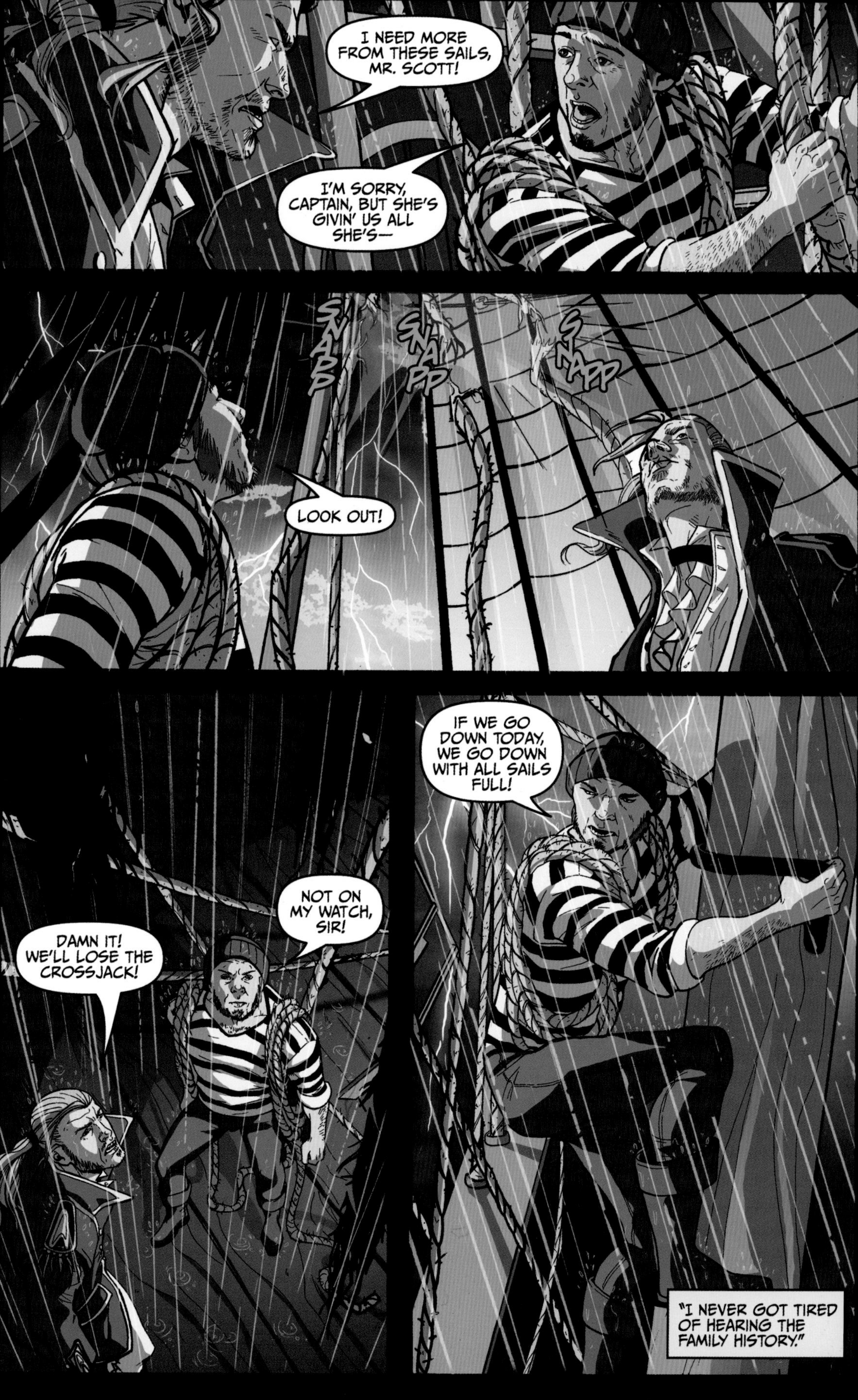
I NEED MORE FROM THESE SAILS, MR. SCOTT!
I'M SORRY, CAPTAIN, BUT SHE'S GIVIN' US ALL SHE'S—
SNAPP
SNAPP
SNAPP
LOOK OUT!
DAMN IT! WE'LL LOSE THE CROSSJACK!
NOT ON MY WATCH, SIR!
IF WE GO DOWN TODAY, WE GO DOWN WITH ALL SAILS FULL!
"I NEVER GOT TIRED OF HEARING THE FAMILY HISTORY."

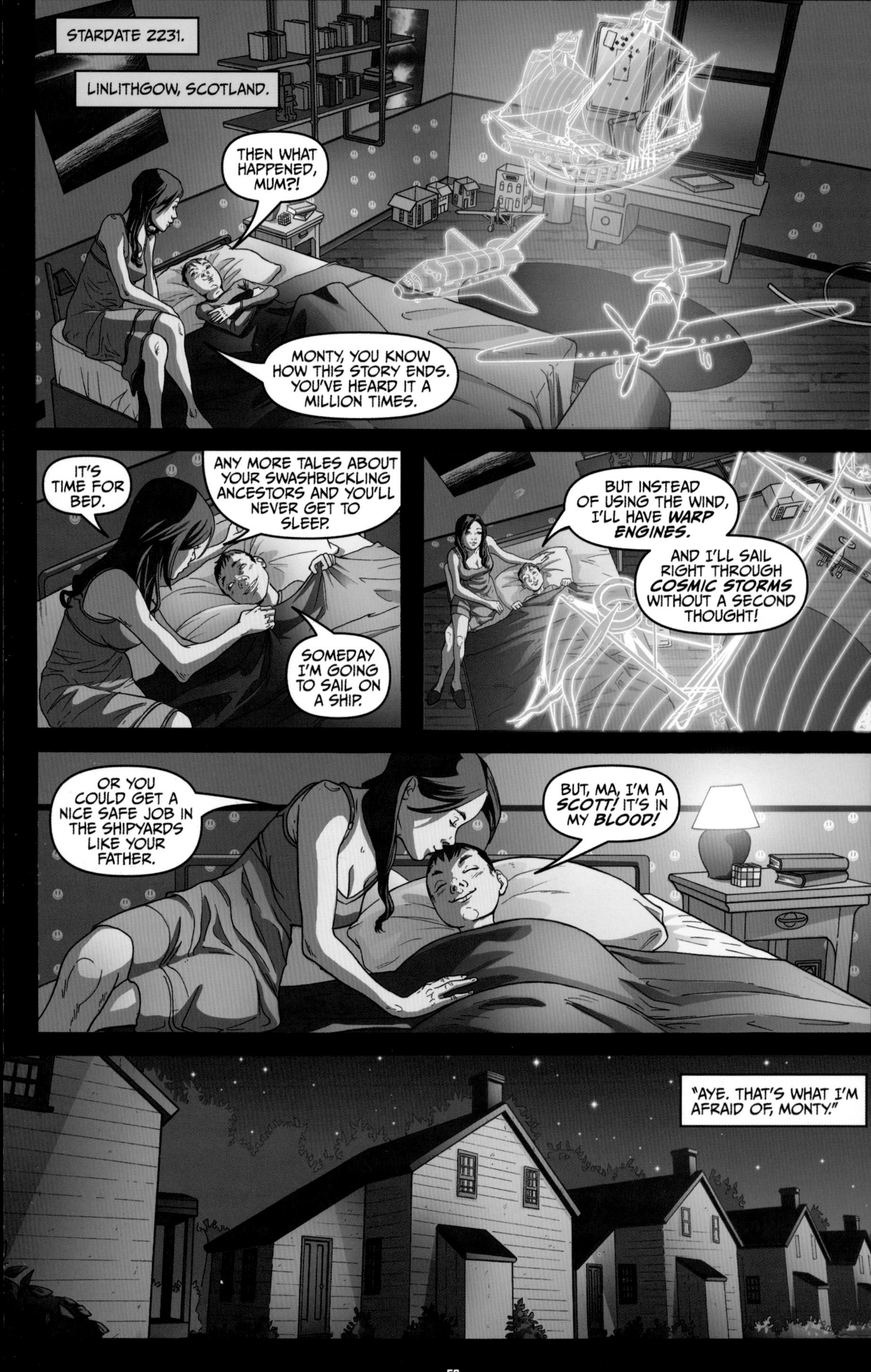
STARDATE 2231.
LINLITHGOW, SCOTLAND.
THEN WHAT HAPPENED, MUM?!
MONTY, YOU KNOW HOW THIS STORY ENDS. YOU'VE HEARD IT A MILLION TIMES.
IT'S TIME FOR BED.
ANY MORE TALES ABOUT YOUR SWASHBUCKLING ANCESTORS AND YOU'LL NEVER GET TO SLEEP.
SOMEDAY I'M GOING TO SAIL ON A SHIP.
BUT INSTEAD OF USING THE WIND, I'LL HAVE WARP ENGINES.
AND I'LL SAIL RIGHT THROUGH COSMIC STORMS WITHOUT A SECOND THOUGHT!
OR YOU COULD GET A NICE SAFE JOB IN THE SHIPYARDS LIKE YOUR FATHER.
BUT, MA, I'M A SCOTT! IT'S IN MY BLOOD!
"AYE. THAT'S WHAT I'M AFRAID OF, MONTY."

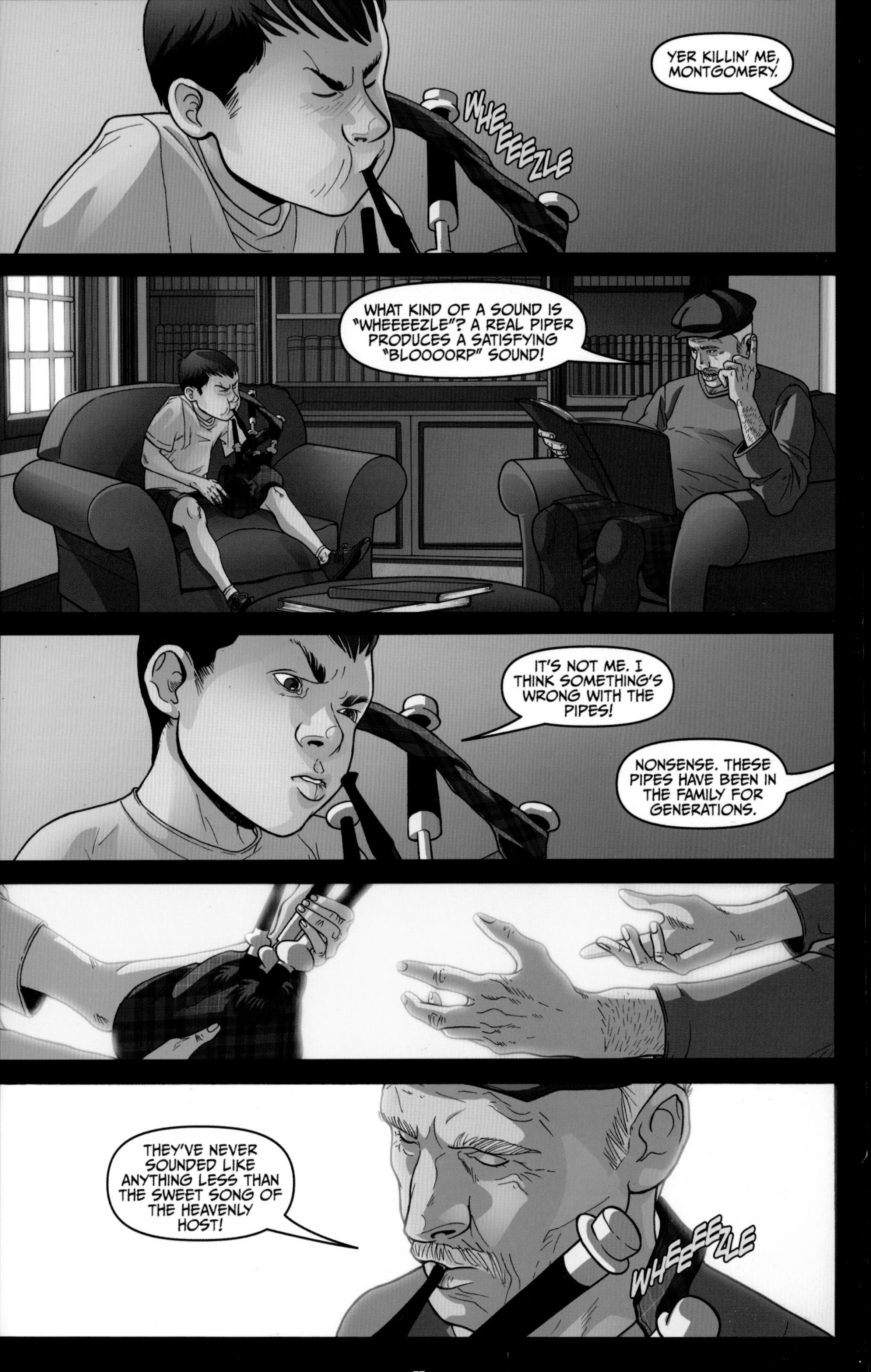
YER KILLIN' ME, MONTGOMERY.
WHEEEEZLE
WHAT KIND OF A SOUND IS "WHEEEEZLE"? A REAL PIPER PRODUCES A SATISFYING "BLOOOORP" SOUND!
IT'S NOT ME. I THINK SOMETHING'S WRONG WITH THE PIPES!
NONSENSE. THESE PIPES HAVE BEEN IN THE FAMILY FOR GENERATIONS.
THEY'VE NEVER SOUNDED LIKE ANYTHING LESS THAN THE SWEET SONG OF THE HEAVENLY HOST!
WHEEEEZLE

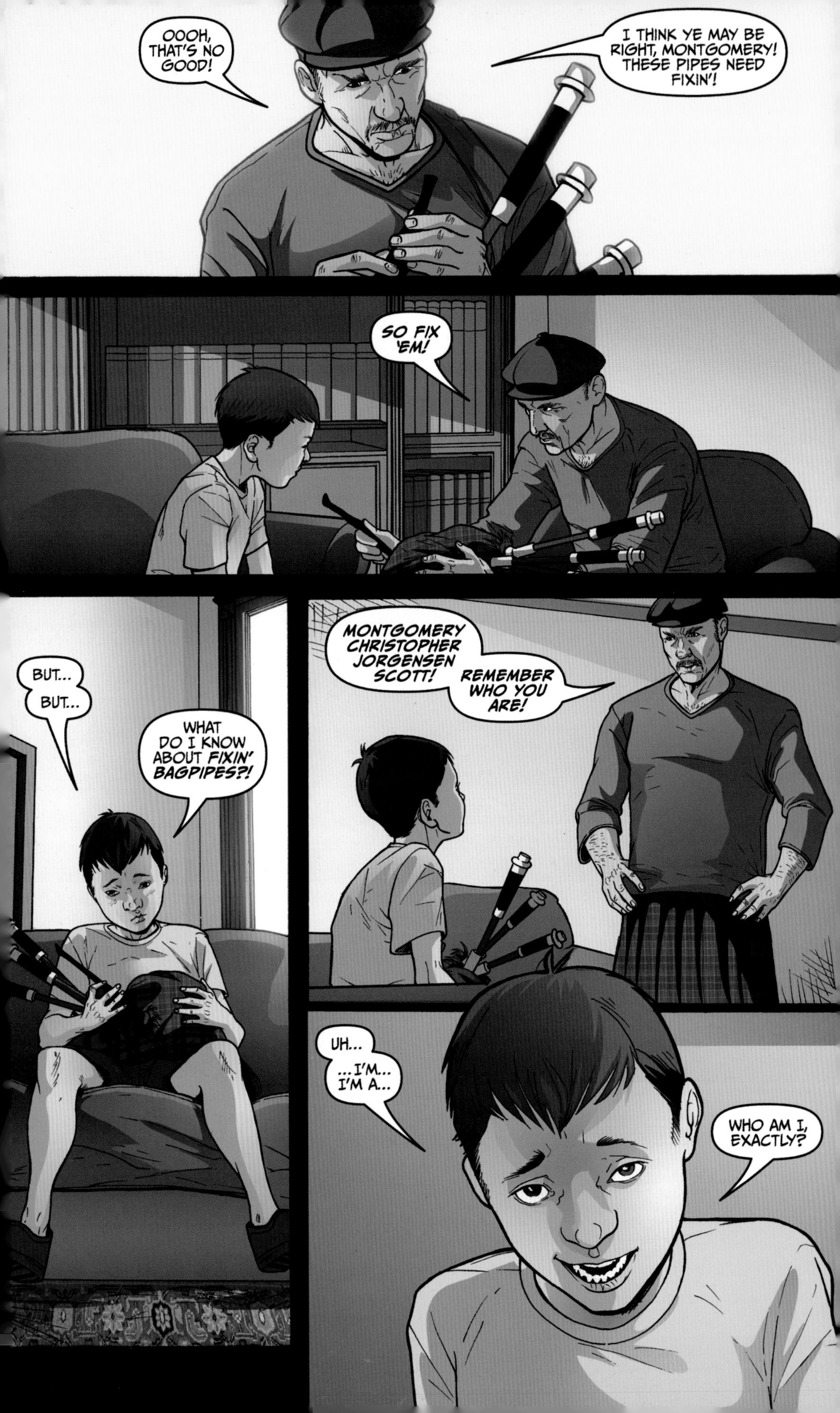
OOOH, THAT'S NO GOOD!
I THINK YE MAY BE RIGHT, MONTGOMERY! THESE PIPES NEED FIXIN'!
SO FIX 'EM!
BUT...
BUT...
WHAT DO I KNOW ABOUT FIXIN' BAGPIPES?!
MONTGOMERY CHRISTOPHER JORGENSEN SCOTT!
REMEMBER WHO YOU ARE!
UH...
...I'M... I'M A...
WHO AM I, EXACTLY?

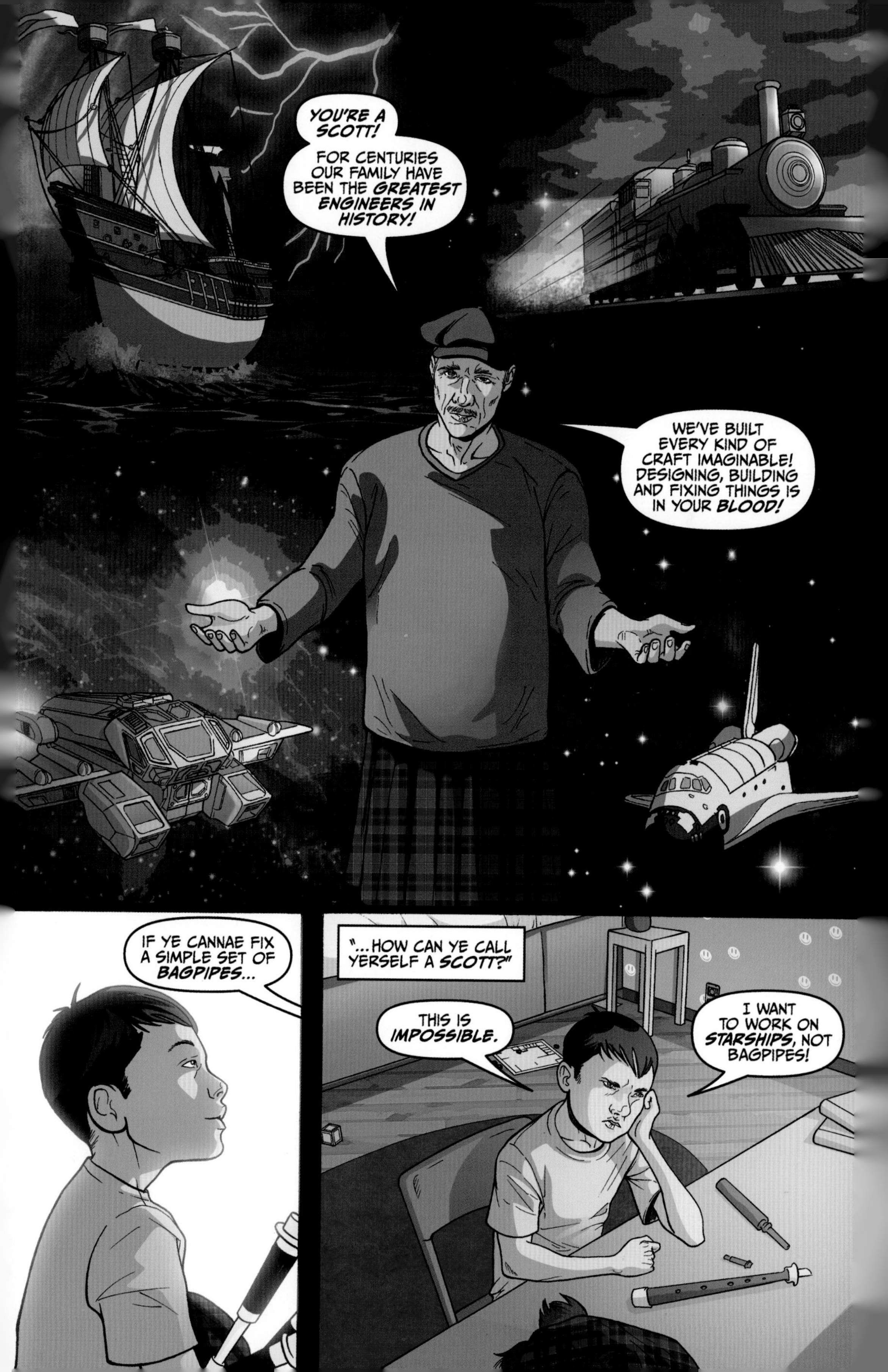
YOU'RE A SCOTT!
FOR CENTURIES OUR FAMILY HAVE BEEN THE GREATEST ENGINEERS IN HISTORY!
WE'VE BUILT EVERY KIND OF CRAFT IMAGINABLE! DESIGNING, BUILDING AND FIXING THINGS IS IN YOUR BLOOD!
IF YE CANNAE FIX A SIMPLE SET OF BAGPIPES...
"...HOW CAN YE CALL YERSELF A SCOTT?"
THIS IS IMPOSSIBLE.
I WANT TO WORK ON STARSHIPS, NOT BAGPIPES!

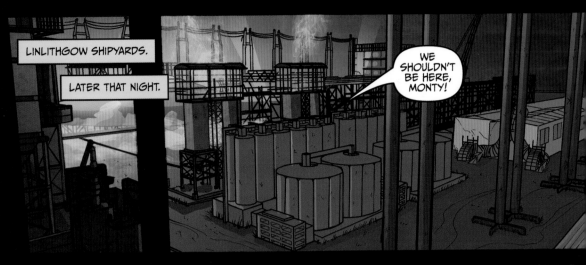

LINLITHGOW SHIPYARDS.

LATER THAT NIGHT.

WE SHOULDN'T BE HERE, MONTY!

MUM WILL KILL US FOR BEING OUT THIS LATE!

QUIT WORRYIN,' ROBBIE! I STUFFED PILLOWS IN OUR BEDSHEETS. SHE'LL PEEK IN AND THINK WE'RE ASLEEP!

WHAT ARE WE EVEN DOIN' HERE, MONTY?

WE'RE EXPLORIN'! WE'VE GOT THIS INCREDIBLE PLACE RIGHT IN OUR BACKYARD, FULL OF THINGS JUST WAITING TO BE—

—DISCOVERED!

OH...

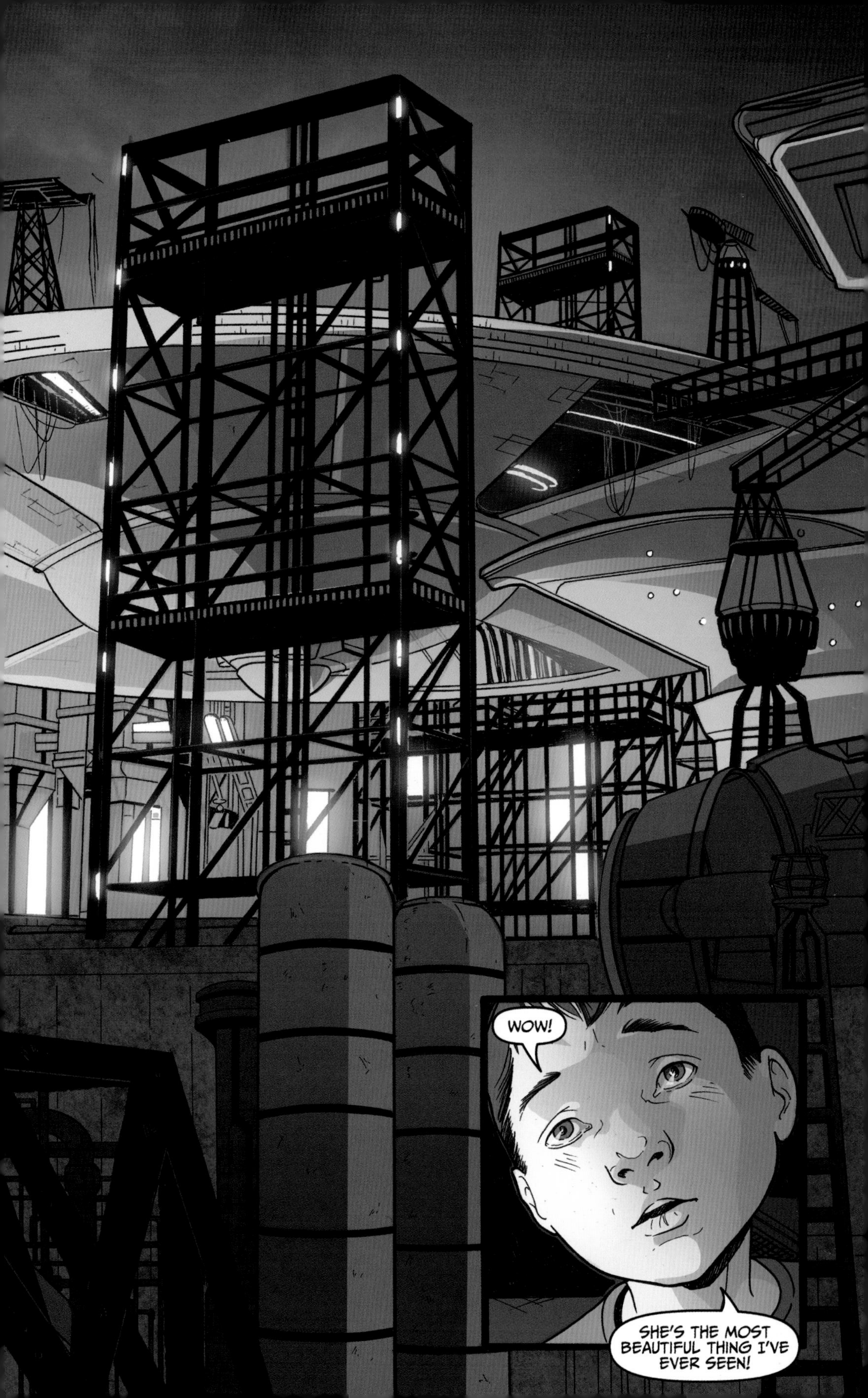
WOW!
SHE'S THE MOST BEAUTIFUL THING I'VE EVER SEEN!

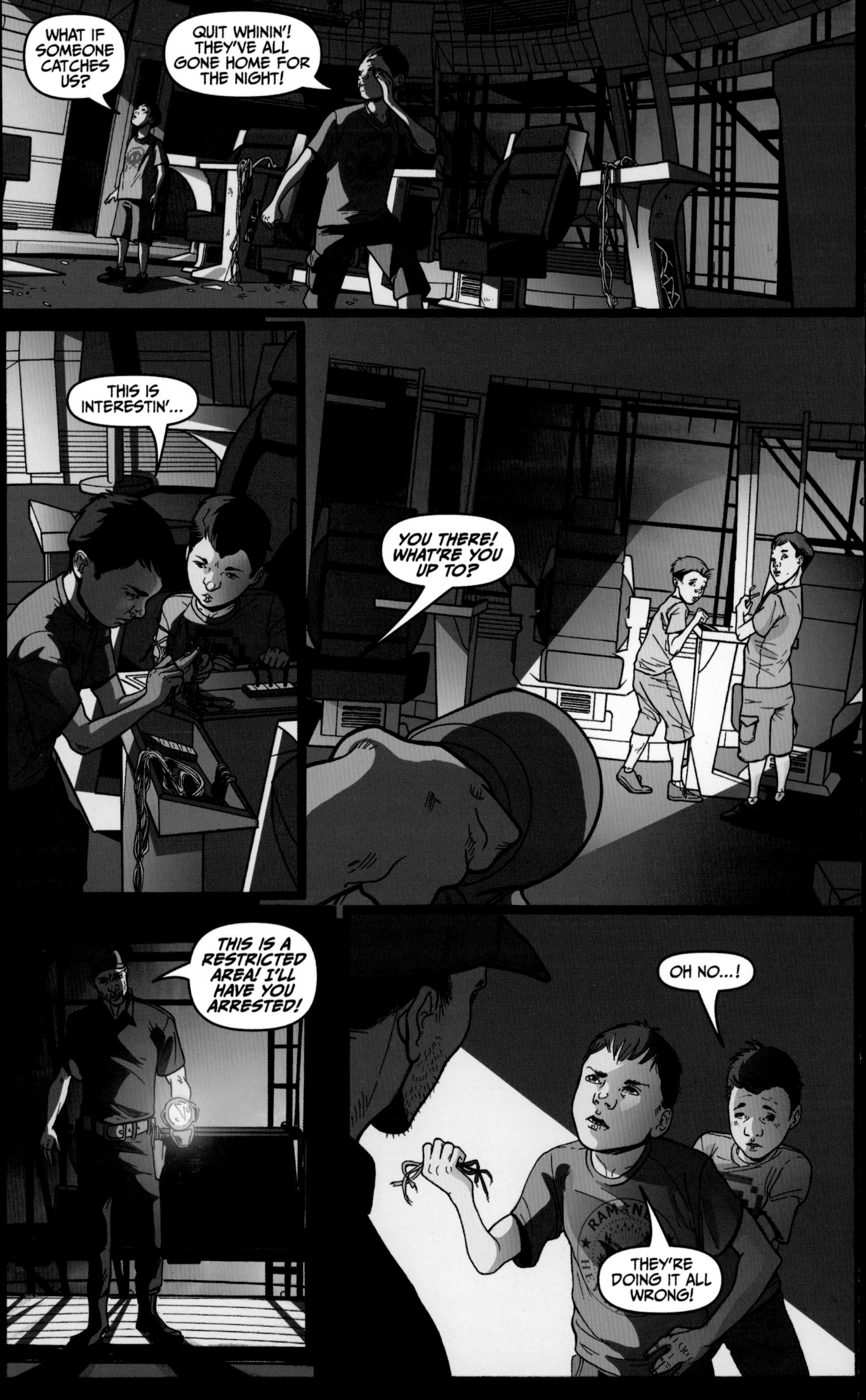
WHAT IF SOMEONE CATCHES US?
QUIT WHININ'! THEY'VE ALL GONE HOME FOR THE NIGHT!
THIS IS INTERESTIN'...
YOU THERE! WHAT'RE YOU UP TO?
THIS IS A RESTRICTED AREA! I'LL HAVE YOU ARRESTED!
OH NO...!
THEY'RE DOING IT ALL WRONG!

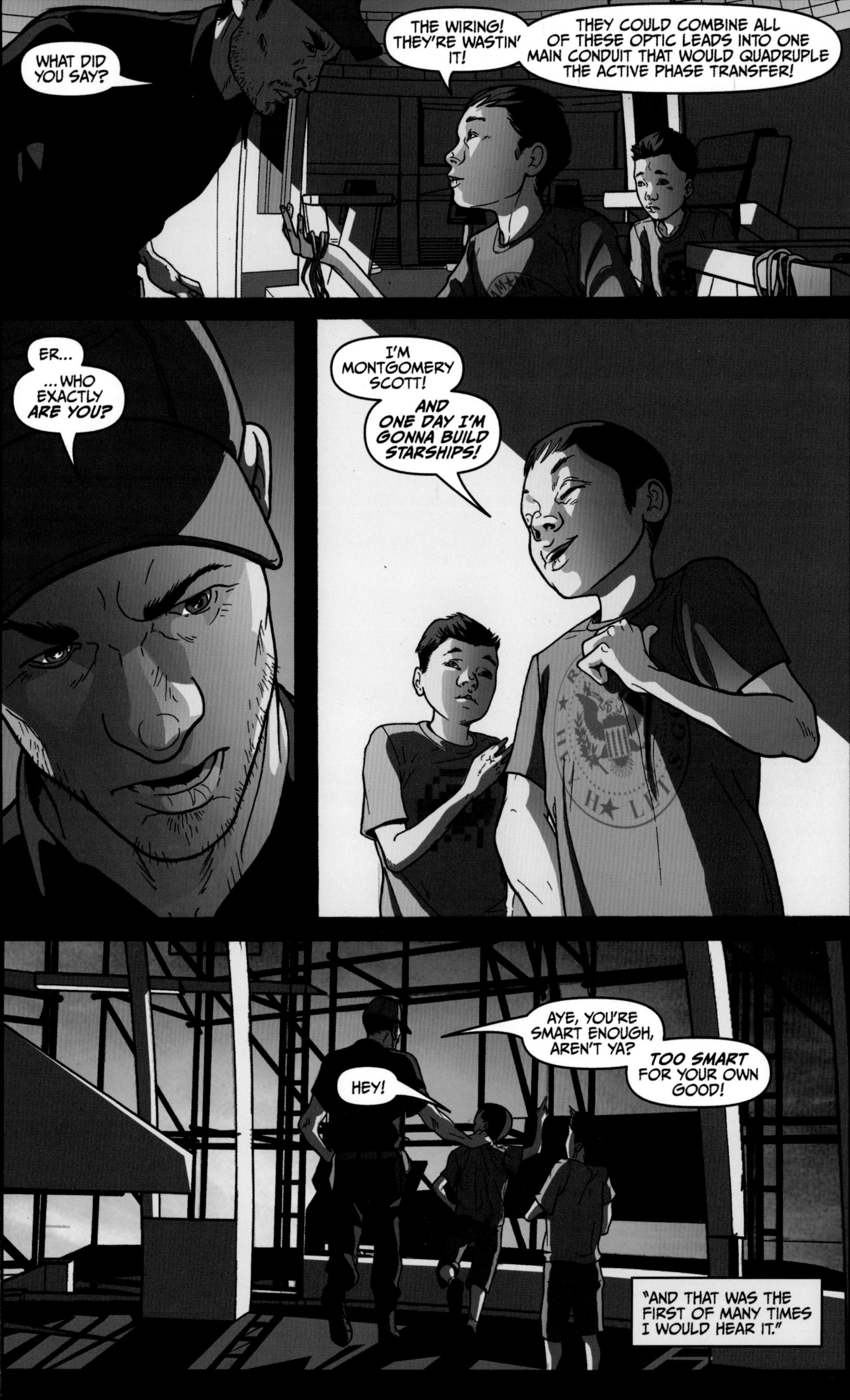

WHAT DID YOU SAY?
THE WIRING! THEY'RE WASTIN' IT!
THEY COULD COMBINE ALL OF THESE OPTIC LEADS INTO ONE MAIN CONDUIT THAT WOULD QUADRUPLE THE ACTIVE PHASE TRANSFER!
ER...
...WHO EXACTLY *ARE YOU?*
I'M MONTGOMERY SCOTT!
AND ONE DAY I'M GONNA BUILD STARSHIPS!
AYE, YOU'RE SMART ENOUGH, AREN'T YA?
TOO SMART FOR YOUR OWN GOOD!
HEY!
"AND THAT WAS THE FIRST OF MANY TIMES I WOULD HEAR IT."

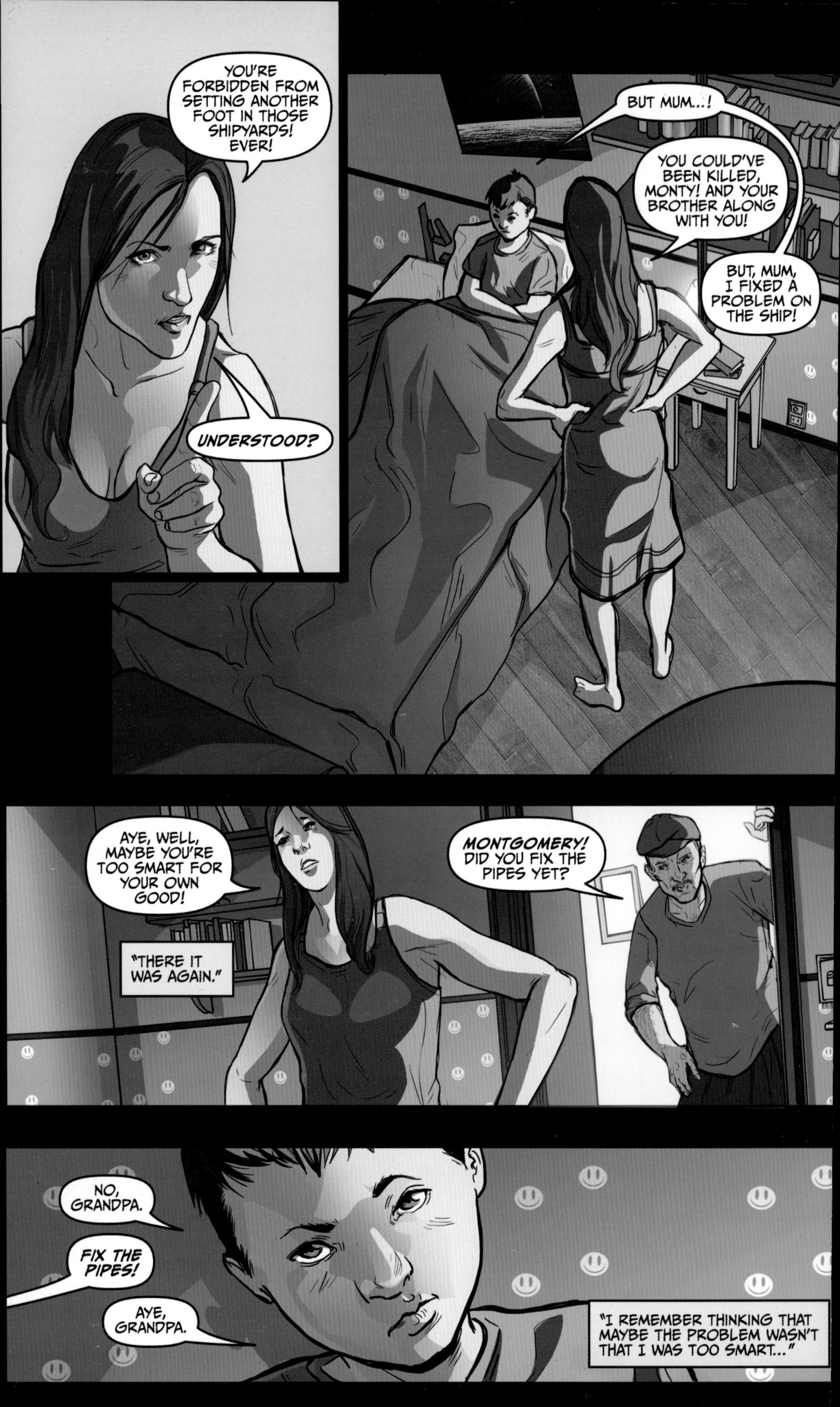
YOU'RE FORBIDDEN FROM SETTING ANOTHER FOOT IN THOSE SHIPYARDS! EVER!
UNDERSTOOD?
BUT MUM...!
YOU COULD'VE BEEN KILLED, MONTY! AND YOUR BROTHER ALONG WITH YOU!
BUT, MUM, I FIXED A PROBLEM ON THE SHIP!
AYE, WELL, MAYBE YOU'RE TOO SMART FOR YOUR OWN GOOD!
"THERE IT WAS AGAIN."
MONTGOMERY! DID YOU FIX THE PIPES YET?
NO, GRANDPA.
FIX THE PIPES!
AYE, GRANDPA.
"I REMEMBER THINKING THAT MAYBE THE PROBLEM WASN'T THAT I WAS TOO SMART..."

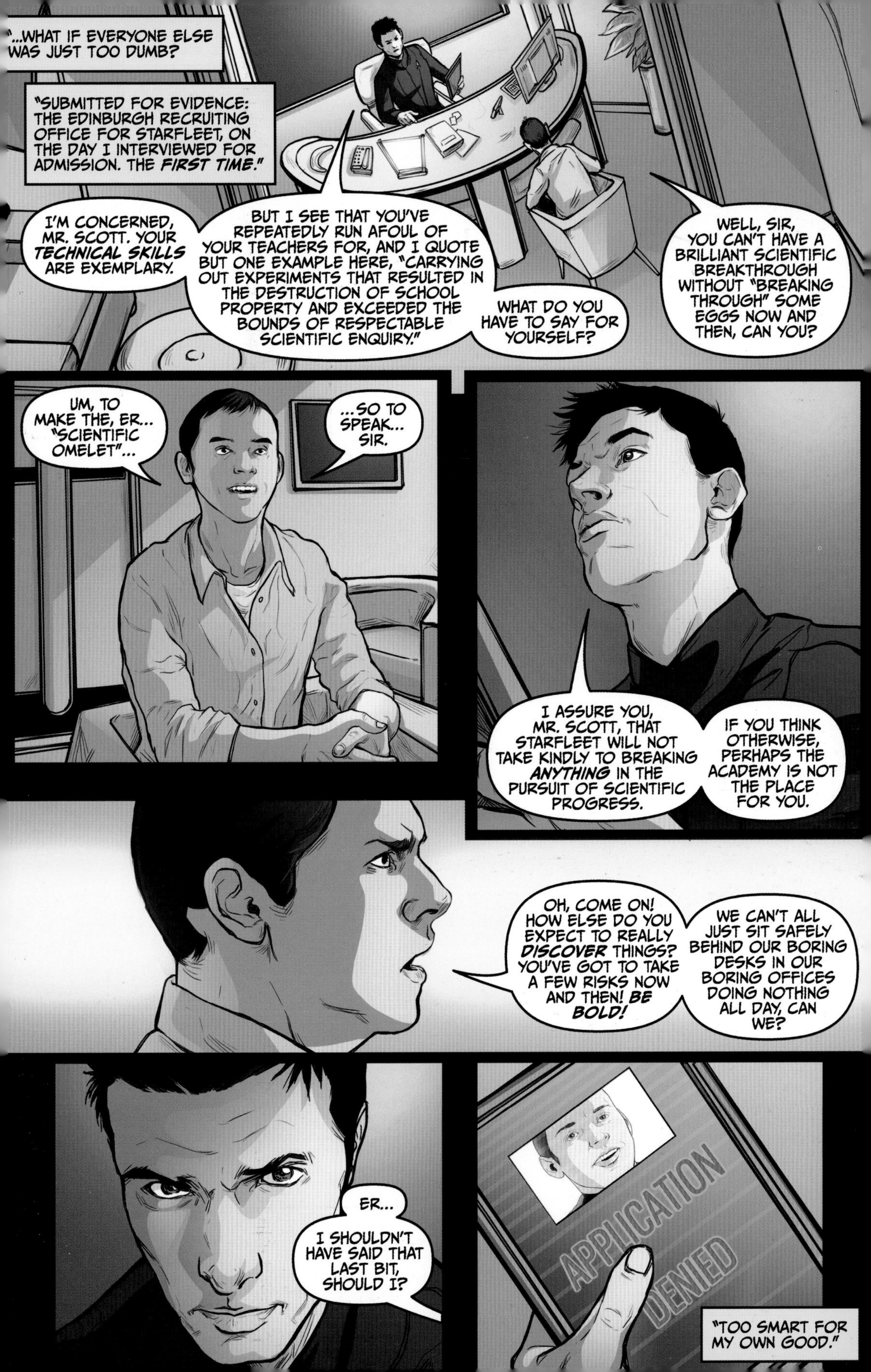
"...WHAT IF EVERYONE ELSE WAS JUST TOO DUMB?
"SUBMITTED FOR EVIDENCE: THE EDINBURGH RECRUITING OFFICE FOR STARFLEET, ON THE DAY I INTERVIEWED FOR ADMISSION. THE *FIRST TIME*."
I'M CONCERNED, MR. SCOTT. YOUR ***TECHNICAL SKILLS*** ARE EXEMPLARY.
BUT I SEE THAT YOU'VE REPEATEDLY RUN AFOUL OF YOUR TEACHERS FOR, AND I QUOTE BUT ONE EXAMPLE HERE, "CARRYING OUT EXPERIMENTS THAT RESULTED IN THE DESTRUCTION OF SCHOOL PROPERTY AND EXCEEDED THE BOUNDS OF RESPECTABLE SCIENTIFIC ENQUIRY."
WHAT DO YOU HAVE TO SAY FOR YOURSELF?
WELL, SIR, YOU CAN'T HAVE A BRILLIANT SCIENTIFIC BREAKTHROUGH WITHOUT "BREAKING THROUGH" SOME EGGS NOW AND THEN, CAN YOU?
UM, TO MAKE THE, ER... "SCIENTIFIC OMELET"...
...SO TO SPEAK... SIR.
I ASSURE YOU, MR. SCOTT, THAT STARFLEET WILL NOT TAKE KINDLY TO BREAKING ***ANYTHING*** IN THE PURSUIT OF SCIENTIFIC PROGRESS.
IF YOU THINK OTHERWISE, PERHAPS THE ACADEMY IS NOT THE PLACE FOR YOU.
OH, COME ON! HOW ELSE DO YOU EXPECT TO REALLY ***DISCOVER*** THINGS? YOU'VE GOT TO TAKE A FEW RISKS NOW AND THEN! ***BE BOLD!***
WE CAN'T ALL JUST SIT SAFELY BEHIND OUR BORING DESKS IN OUR BORING OFFICES DOING NOTHING ALL DAY, CAN WE?
ER...
I SHOULDN'T HAVE SAID THAT LAST BIT, SHOULD I?
APPLICATION DENIED
"TOO SMART FOR MY OWN GOOD."

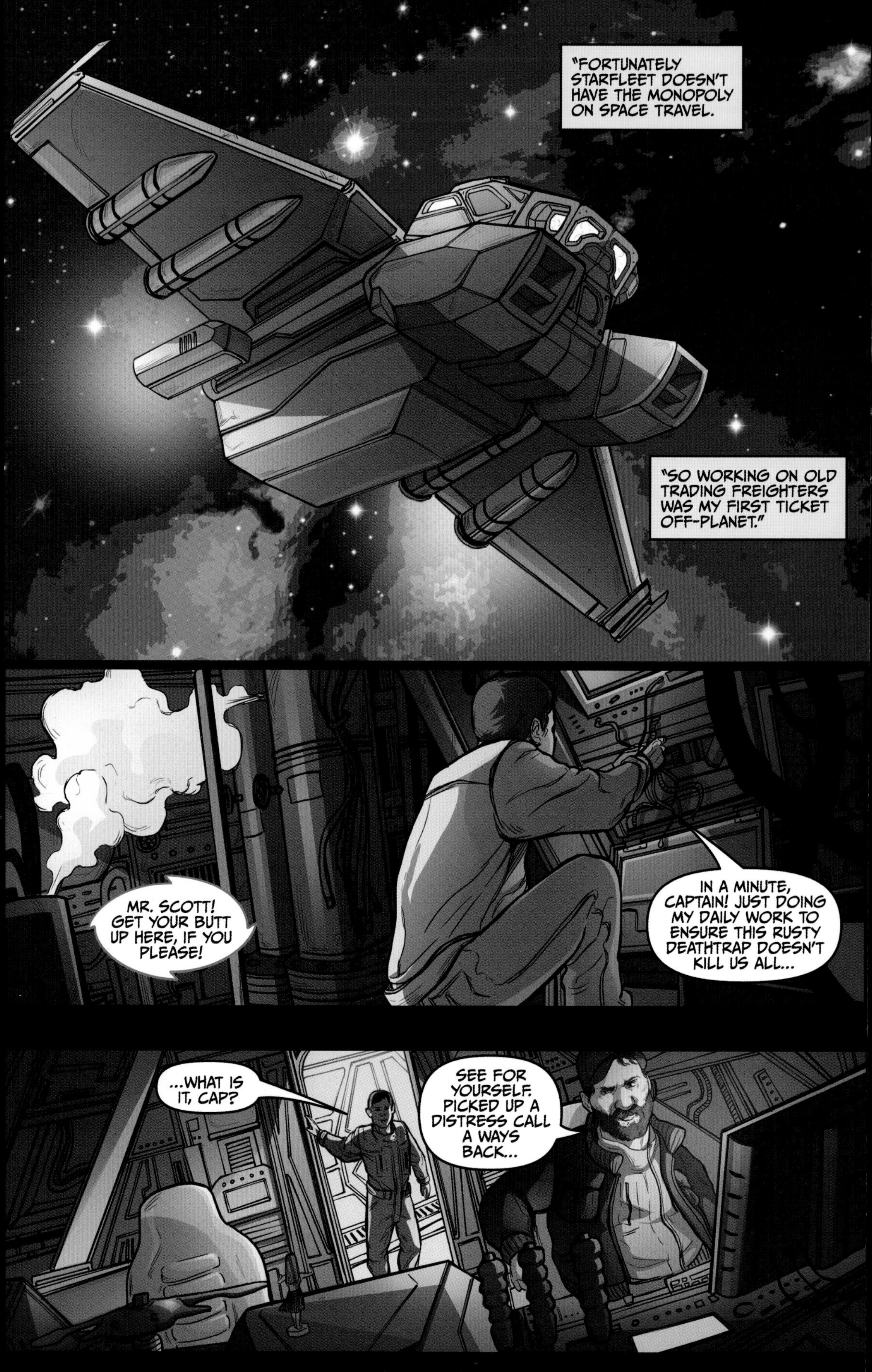
"FORTUNATELY STARFLEET DOESN'T HAVE THE MONOPOLY ON SPACE TRAVEL.
"SO WORKING ON OLD TRADING FREIGHTERS WAS MY FIRST TICKET OFF-PLANET."
MR. SCOTT! GET YOUR BUTT UP HERE, IF YOU PLEASE!
IN A MINUTE, CAPTAIN! JUST DOING MY DAILY WORK TO ENSURE THIS RUSTY DEATHTRAP DOESN'T KILL US ALL...
...WHAT IS IT, CAP?
SEE FOR YOURSELF. PICKED UP A DISTRESS CALL A WAYS BACK...

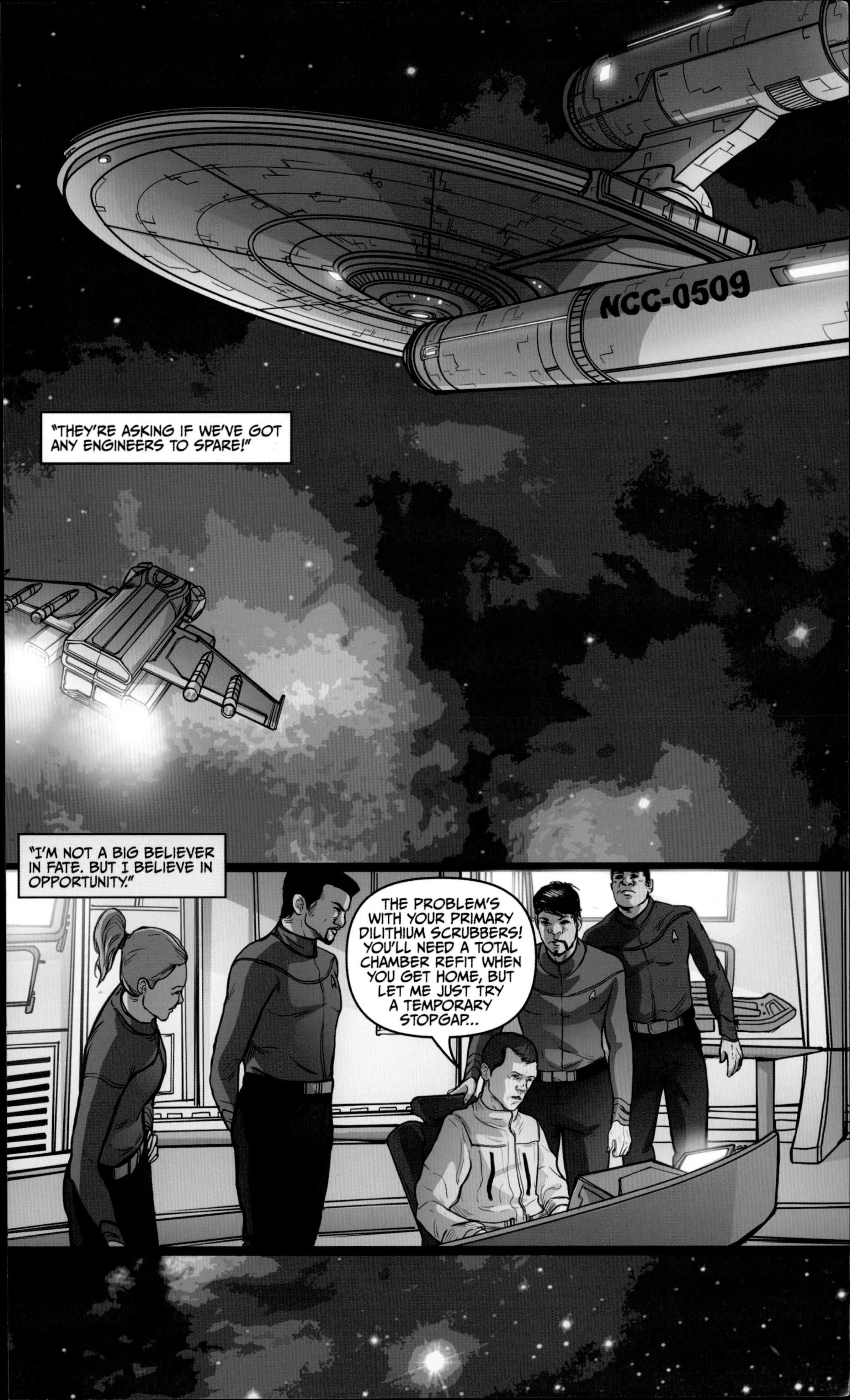
NCC-0509
"THEY'RE ASKING IF WE'VE GOT ANY ENGINEERS TO SPARE!"
"I'M NOT A BIG BELIEVER IN FATE. BUT I BELIEVE IN OPPORTUNITY."
THE PROBLEM'S WITH YOUR PRIMARY DILITHIUM SCRUBBERS! YOU'LL NEED A TOTAL CHAMBER REFIT WHEN YOU GET HOME, BUT LET ME JUST TRY A TEMPORARY STOPGAP...

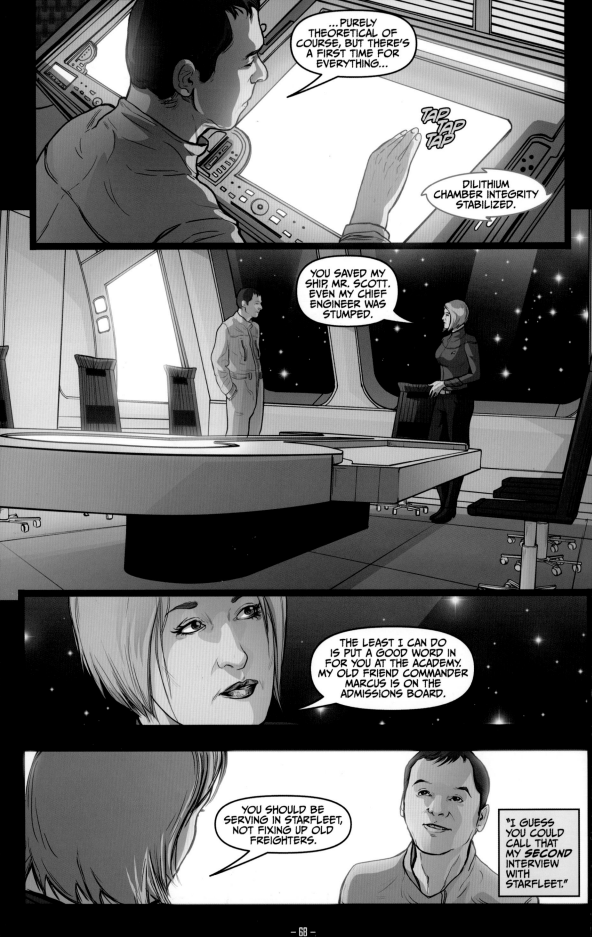

...PURELY THEORETICAL OF COURSE, BUT THERE'S A FIRST TIME FOR EVERYTHING...

TAP TAP TAP

DILITHIUM CHAMBER INTEGRITY STABILIZED.

YOU SAVED MY SHIP, MR. SCOTT. EVEN MY CHIEF ENGINEER WAS STUMPED.

THE LEAST I CAN DO IS PUT A GOOD WORD IN FOR YOU AT THE ACADEMY. MY OLD FRIEND COMMANDER MARCUS IS ON THE ADMISSIONS BOARD.

YOU SHOULD BE SERVING IN STARFLEET, NOT FIXING UP OLD FREIGHTERS.

"I GUESS YOU COULD CALL THAT MY *SECOND* INTERVIEW WITH STARFLEET."

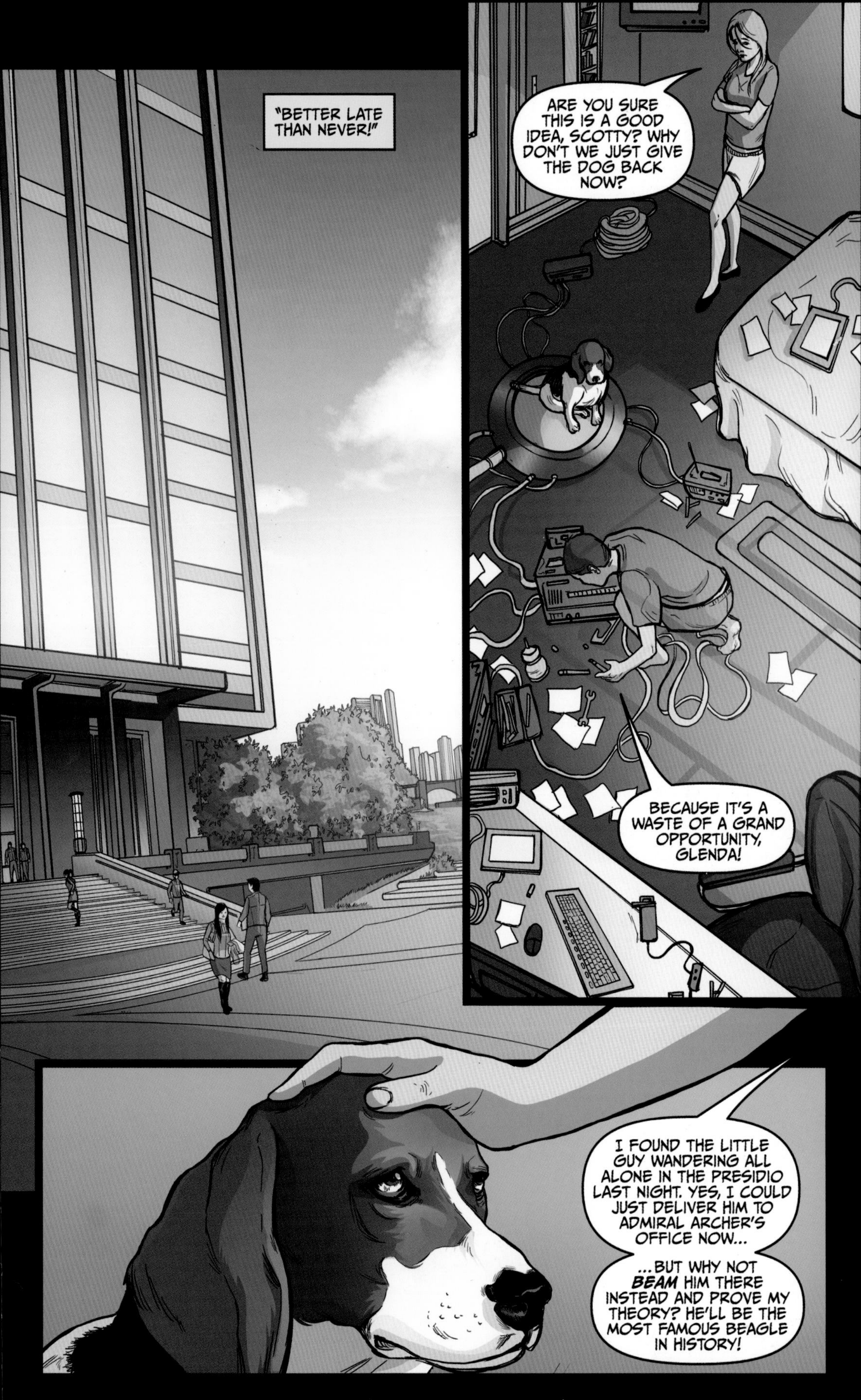
"BETTER LATE THAN NEVER!"
ARE YOU SURE THIS IS A GOOD IDEA, SCOTTY? WHY DON'T WE JUST GIVE THE DOG BACK NOW?
BECAUSE IT'S A WASTE OF A GRAND OPPORTUNITY, GLENDA!
I FOUND THE LITTLE GUY WANDERING ALL ALONE IN THE PRESIDIO LAST NIGHT. YES, I COULD JUST DELIVER HIM TO ADMIRAL ARCHER'S OFFICE NOW...
...BUT WHY NOT BEAM HIM THERE INSTEAD AND PROVE MY THEORY? HE'LL BE THE MOST FAMOUS BEAGLE IN HISTORY!

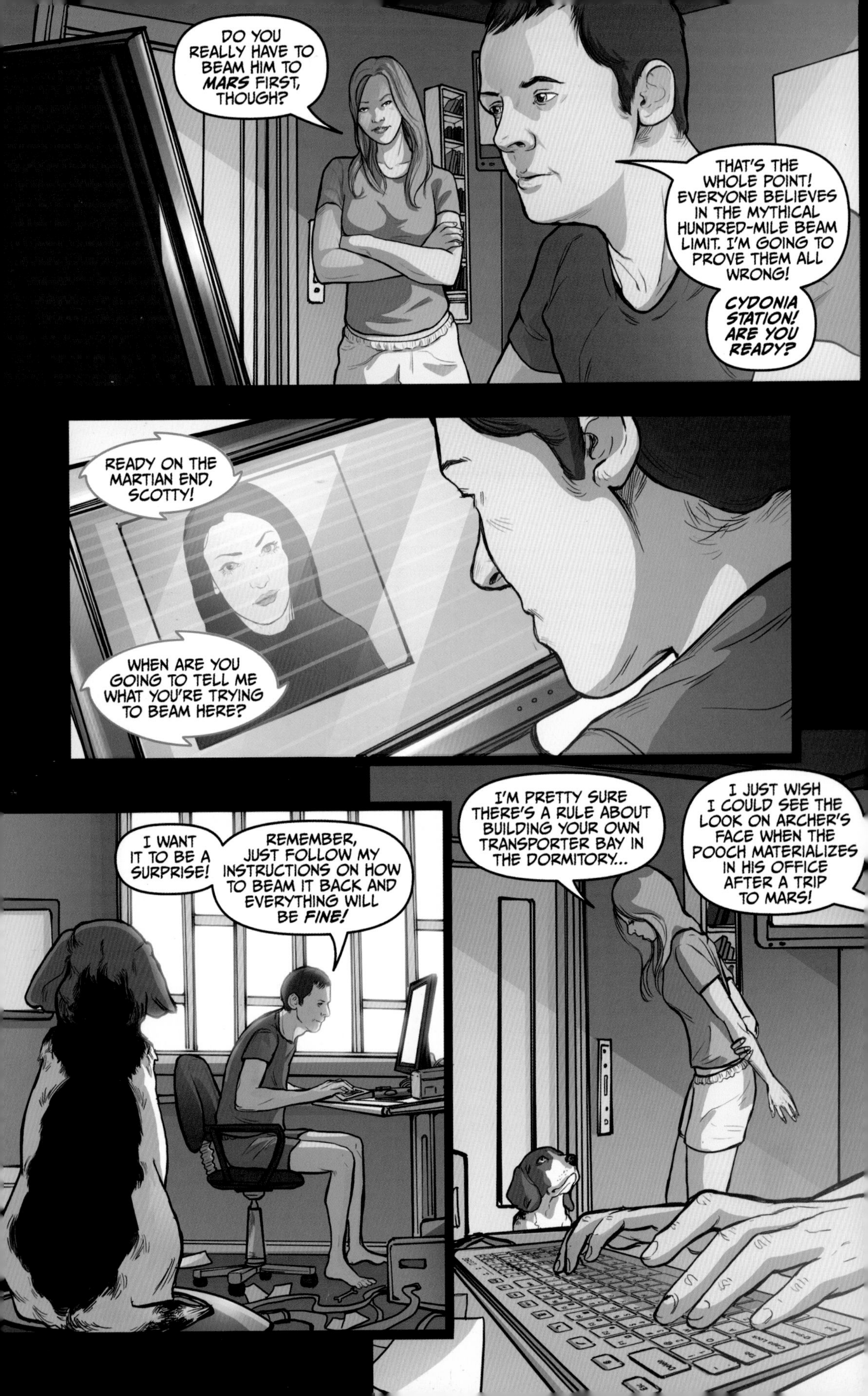
DO YOU REALLY HAVE TO BEAM HIM TO *MARS* FIRST, THOUGH?
THAT'S THE WHOLE POINT! EVERYONE BELIEVES IN THE MYTHICAL HUNDRED-MILE BEAM LIMIT. I'M GOING TO PROVE THEM ALL WRONG!
CYDONIA STATION! ARE YOU READY?
READY ON THE MARTIAN END, SCOTTY!
WHEN ARE YOU GOING TO TELL ME WHAT YOU'RE TRYING TO BEAM HERE?
I WANT IT TO BE A SURPRISE!
REMEMBER, JUST FOLLOW MY INSTRUCTIONS ON HOW TO BEAM IT BACK AND EVERYTHING WILL BE *FINE!*
I'M PRETTY SURE THERE'S A RULE ABOUT BUILDING YOUR OWN TRANSPORTER BAY IN THE DORMITORY...
I JUST WISH I COULD SEE THE LOOK ON ARCHER'S FACE WHEN THE POOCH MATERIALIZES IN HIS OFFICE AFTER A TRIP TO MARS!

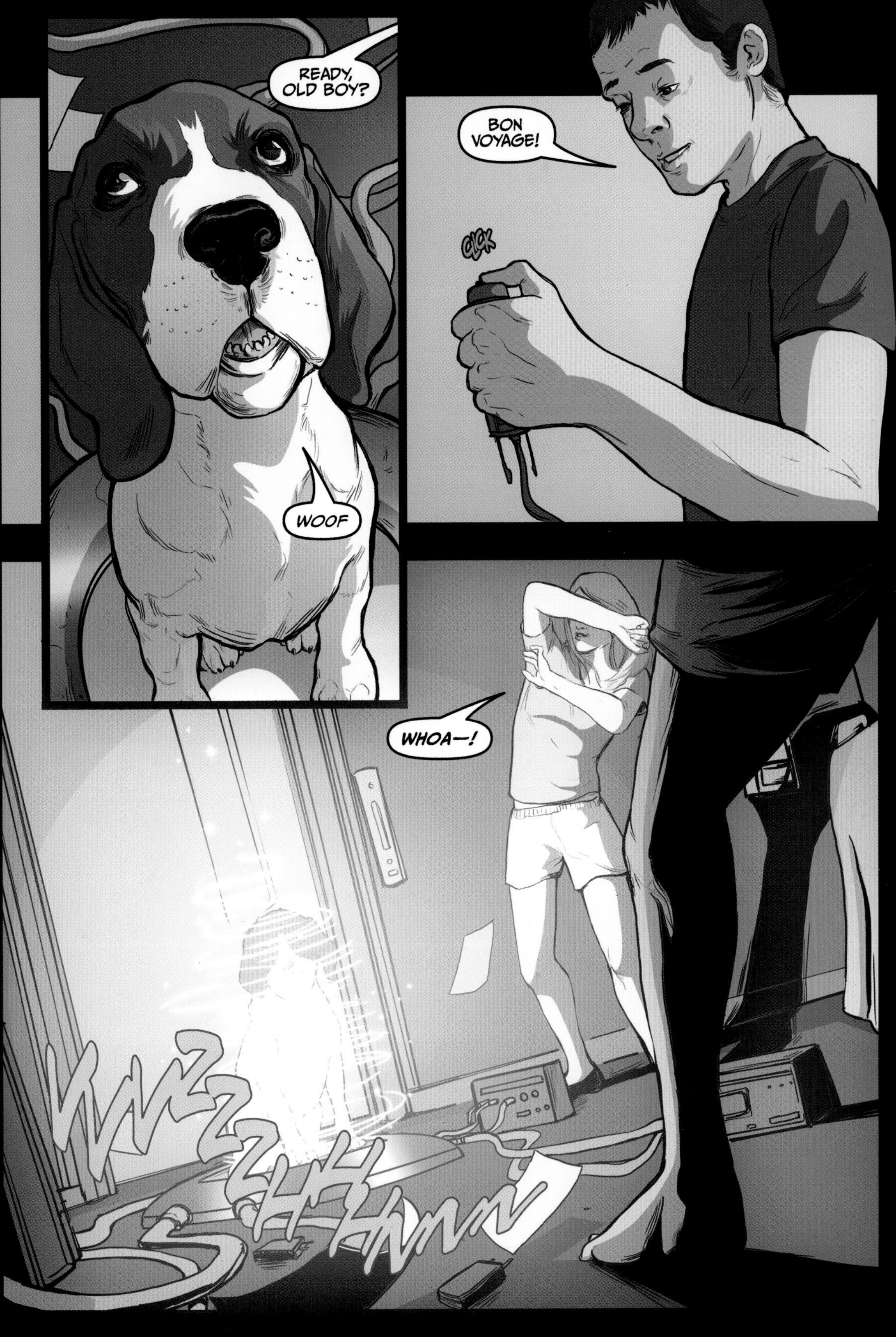
READY, OLD BOY?
BON VOYAGE!
CLICK
WOOF
WHOA—!
VVVZZZZHHHNNN

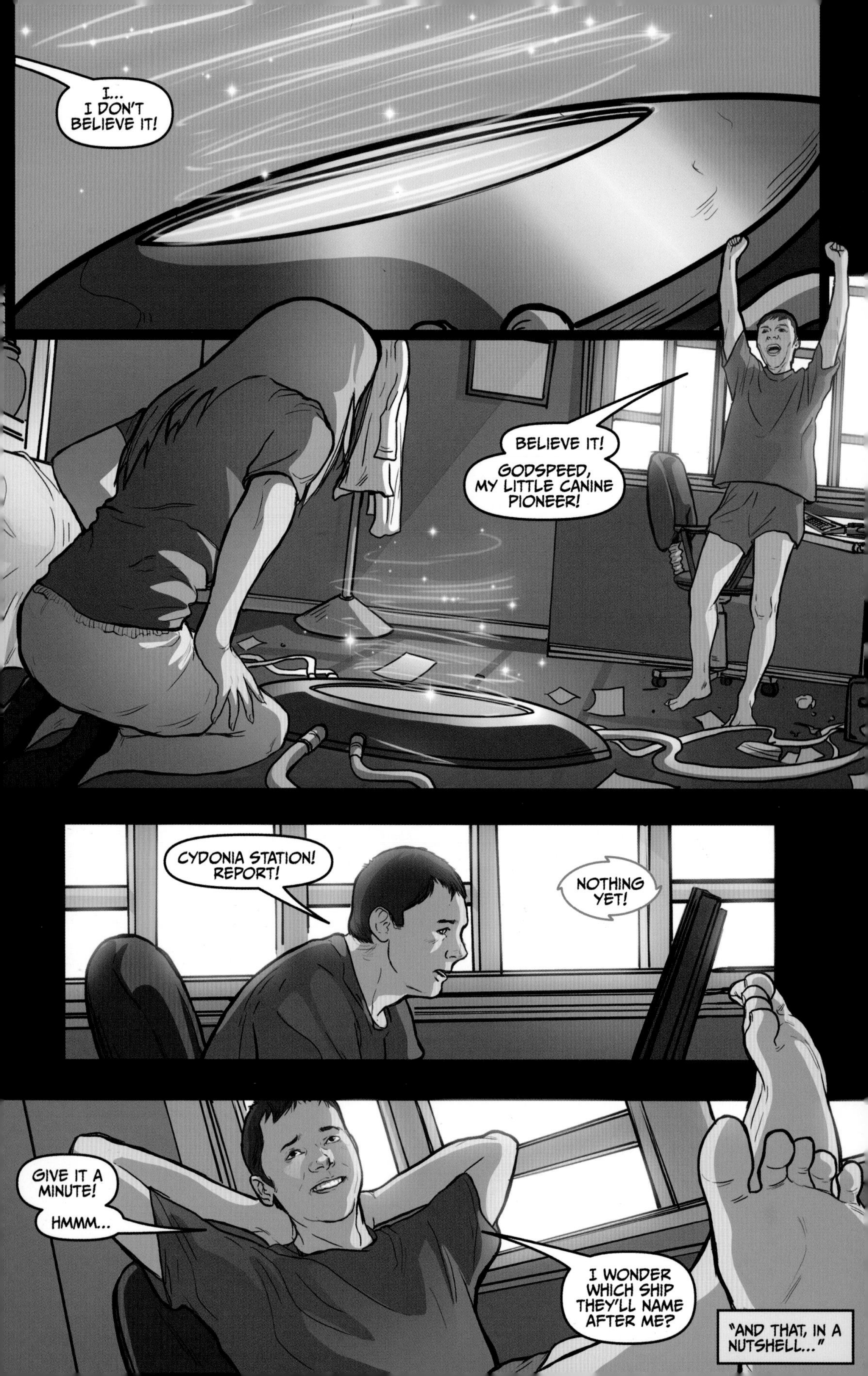
I... I DON'T BELIEVE IT!
BELIEVE IT! GODSPEED, MY LITTLE CANINE PIONEER!
CYDONIA STATION! REPORT!
NOTHING YET!
GIVE IT A MINUTE!
HMMM...
I WONDER WHICH SHIP THEY'LL NAME AFTER ME?
"AND THAT, IN A NUTSHELL..."

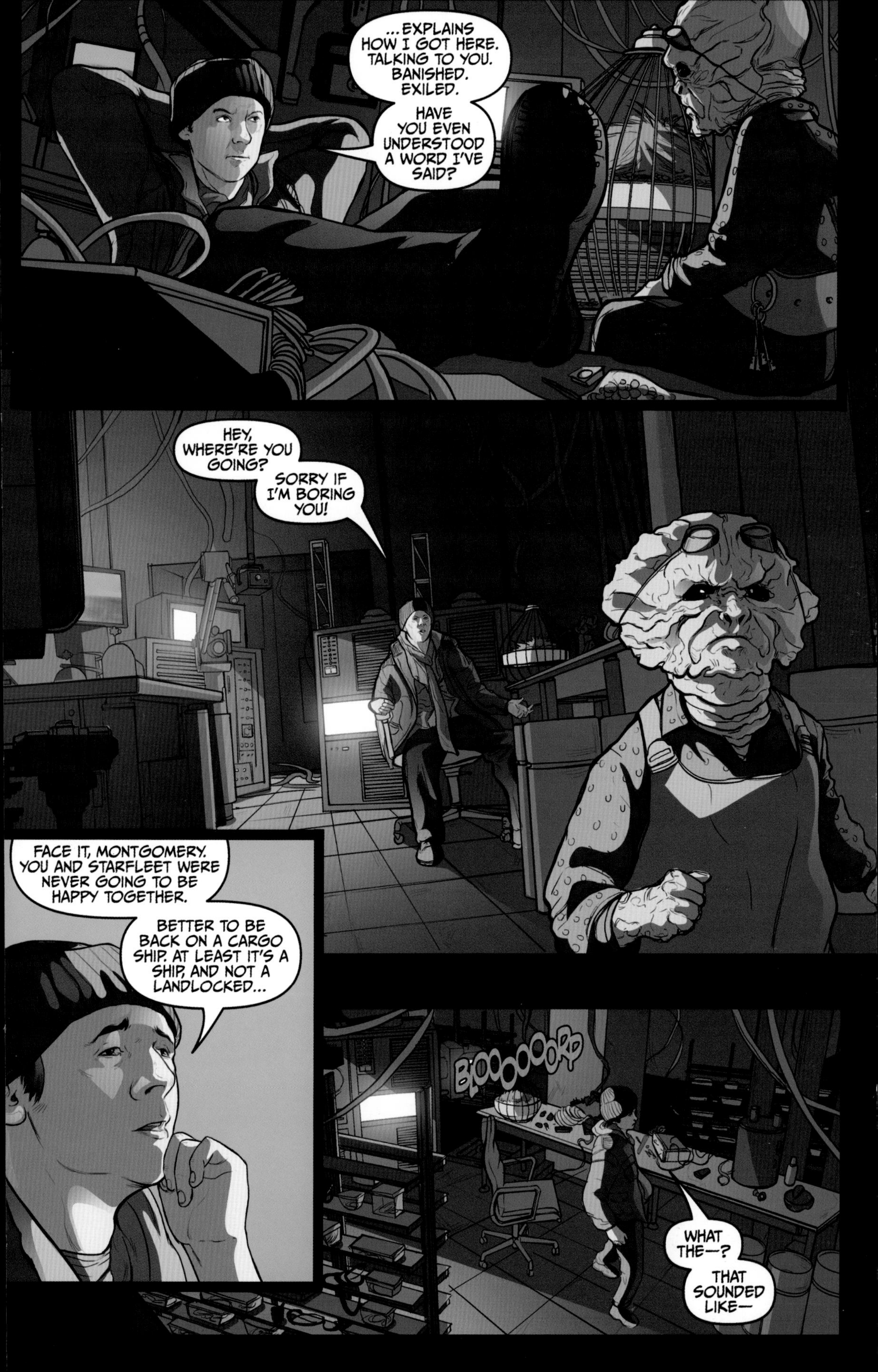
...EXPLAINS HOW I GOT HERE. TALKING TO YOU. BANISHED. EXILED.
HAVE YOU EVEN UNDERSTOOD A WORD I'VE SAID?
HEY, WHERE'RE YOU GOING?
SORRY IF I'M BORING YOU!
FACE IT, MONTGOMERY. YOU AND STARFLEET WERE NEVER GOING TO BE HAPPY TOGETHER.
BETTER TO BE BACK ON A CARGO SHIP. AT LEAST IT'S A SHIP, AND NOT A LANDLOCKED...
BLOOOOOORP
WHAT THE—?
THAT SOUNDED LIKE—

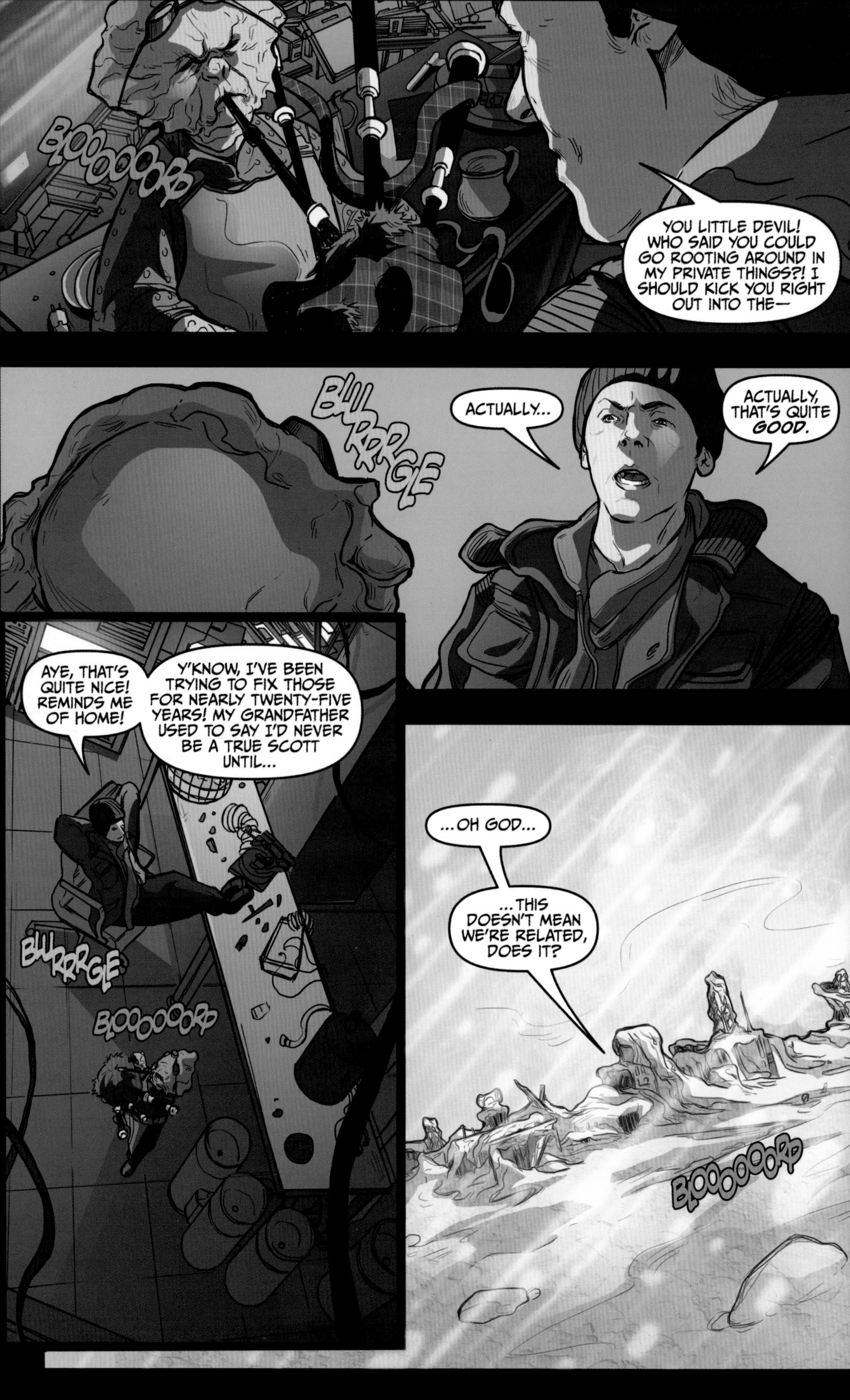
BLOOOOOORP
YOU LITTLE DEVIL! WHO SAID YOU COULD GO ROOTING AROUND IN MY PRIVATE THINGS?! I SHOULD KICK YOU RIGHT OUT INTO THE—
BLURRRGLE
ACTUALLY...
ACTUALLY, THAT'S QUITE GOOD.
AYE, THAT'S QUITE NICE! REMINDS ME OF HOME!
Y'KNOW, I'VE BEEN TRYING TO FIX THOSE FOR NEARLY TWENTY-FIVE YEARS! MY GRANDFATHER USED TO SAY I'D NEVER BE A TRUE SCOTT UNTIL...
BLURRRGLE
BLOOOOOORP
...OH GOD...
...THIS DOESN'T MEAN WE'RE RELATED, DOES IT?
BLOOOOOORP

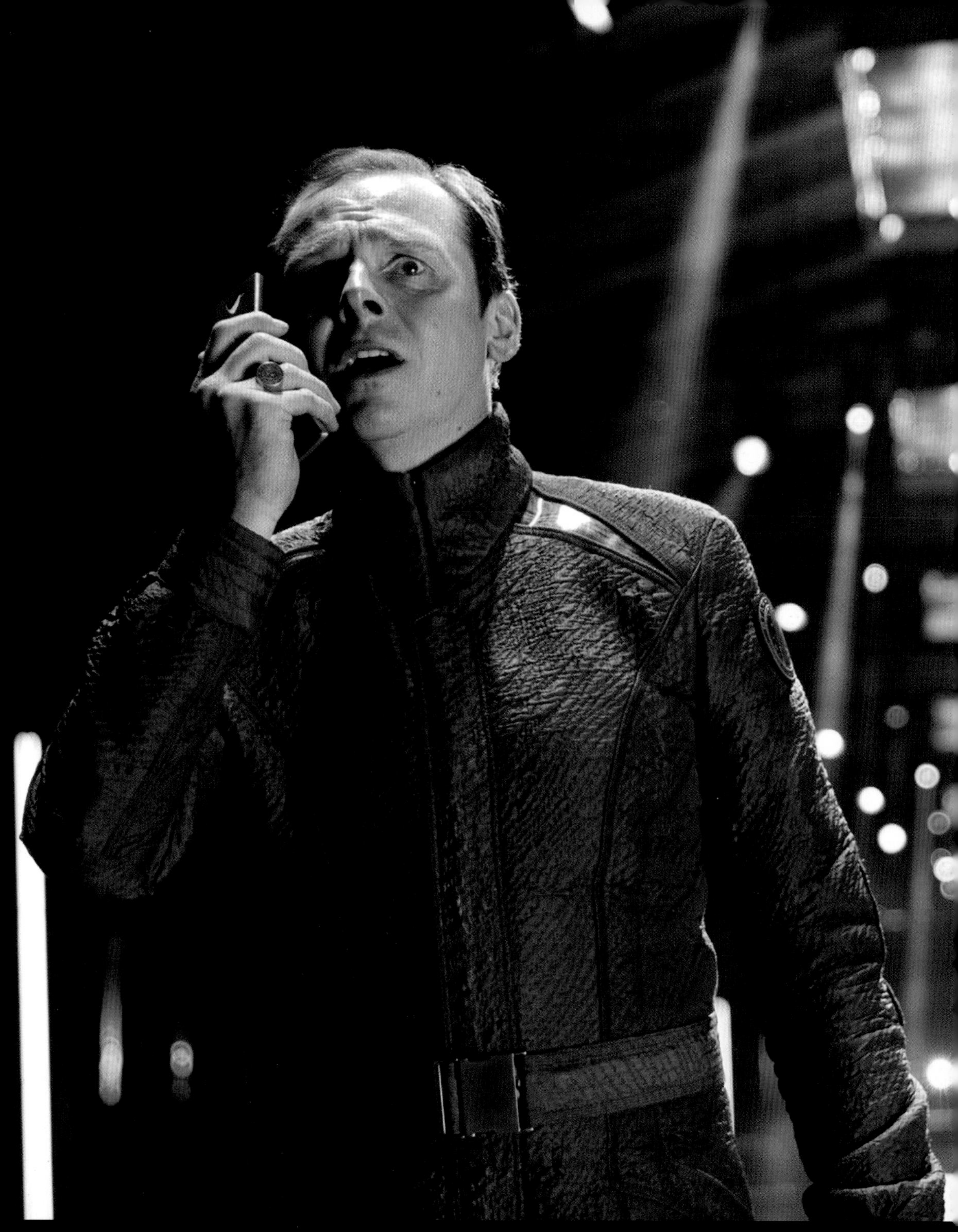

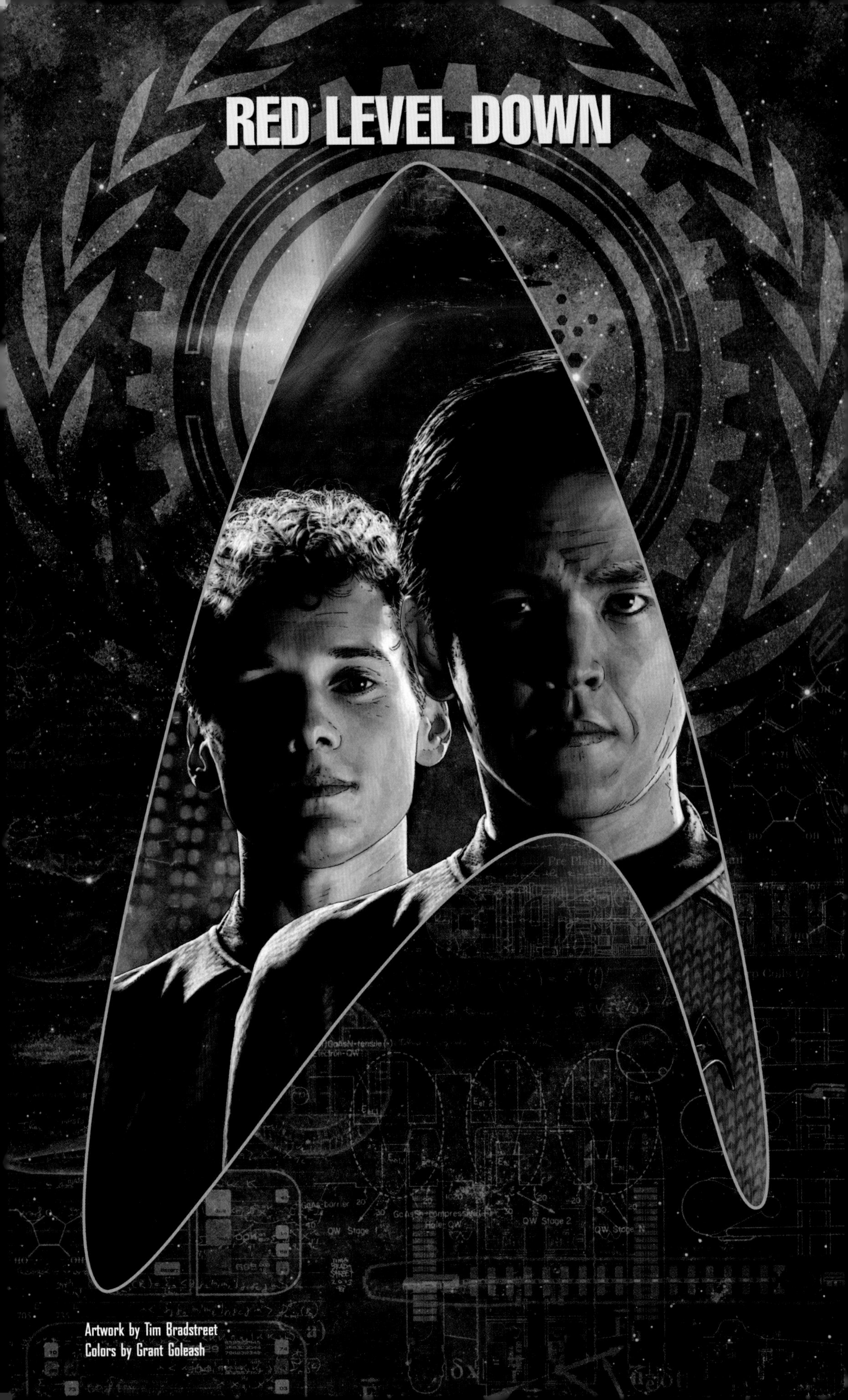
RED LEVEL DOWN
Artwork by Tim Bradstreet
Colors by Grant Goleash

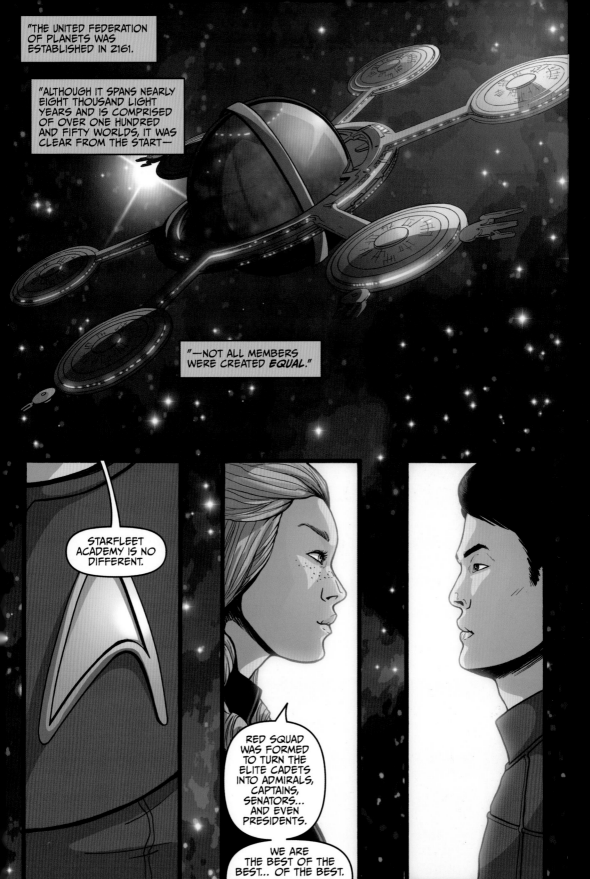

"THE UNITED FEDERATION OF PLANETS WAS ESTABLISHED IN 2161.

"ALTHOUGH IT SPANS NEARLY EIGHT THOUSAND LIGHT YEARS AND IS COMPRISED OF OVER ONE HUNDRED AND FIFTY WORLDS, IT WAS CLEAR FROM THE START—

"—NOT ALL MEMBERS WERE CREATED *EQUAL*."

STARFLEET ACADEMY IS NO DIFFERENT.

RED SQUAD WAS FORMED TO TURN THE ELITE CADETS INTO ADMIRALS, CAPTAINS, SENATORS... AND EVEN PRESIDENTS.

WE ARE THE BEST OF THE BEST... OF THE BEST.

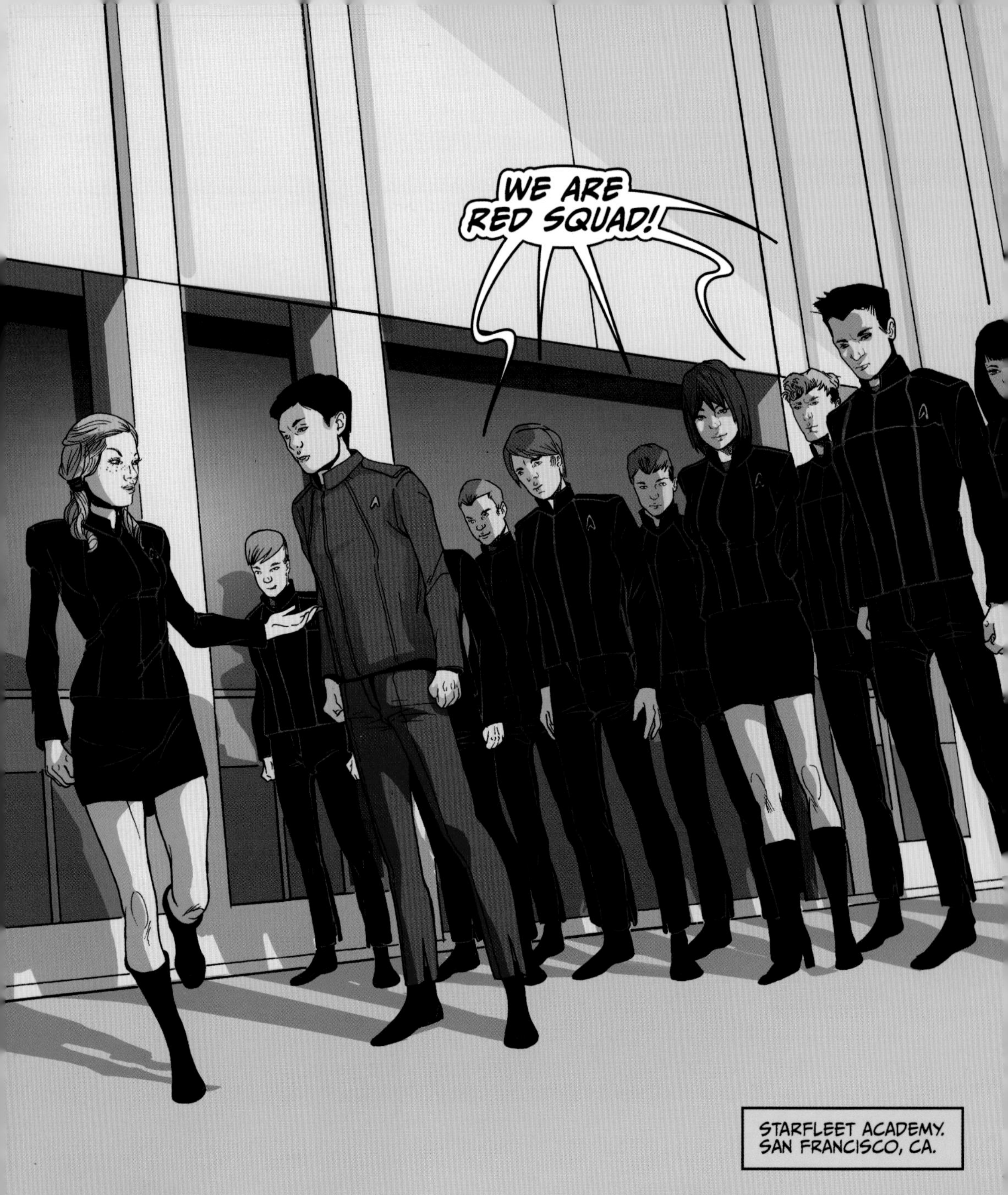
WE ARE RED SQUAD!
STARFLEET ACADEMY. SAN FRANCISCO, CA.

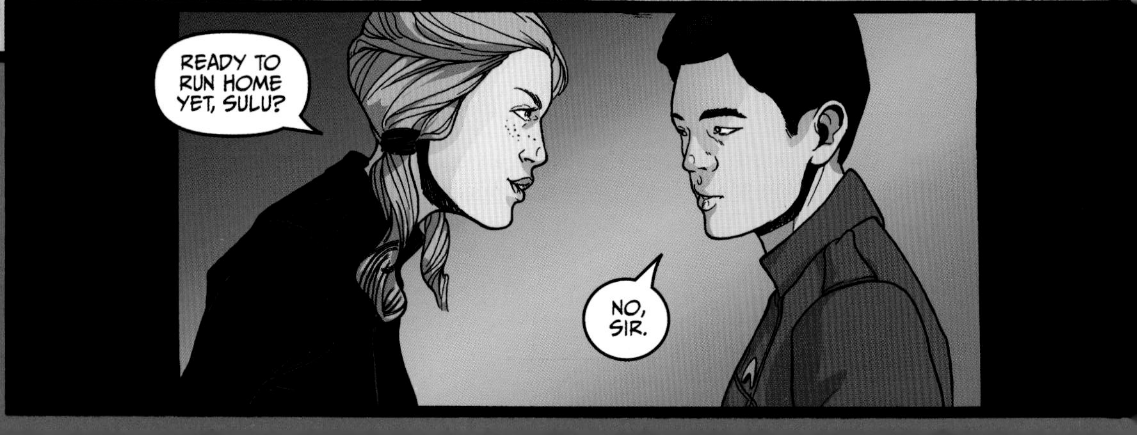
READY TO RUN HOME YET, SULU?
NO, SIR.

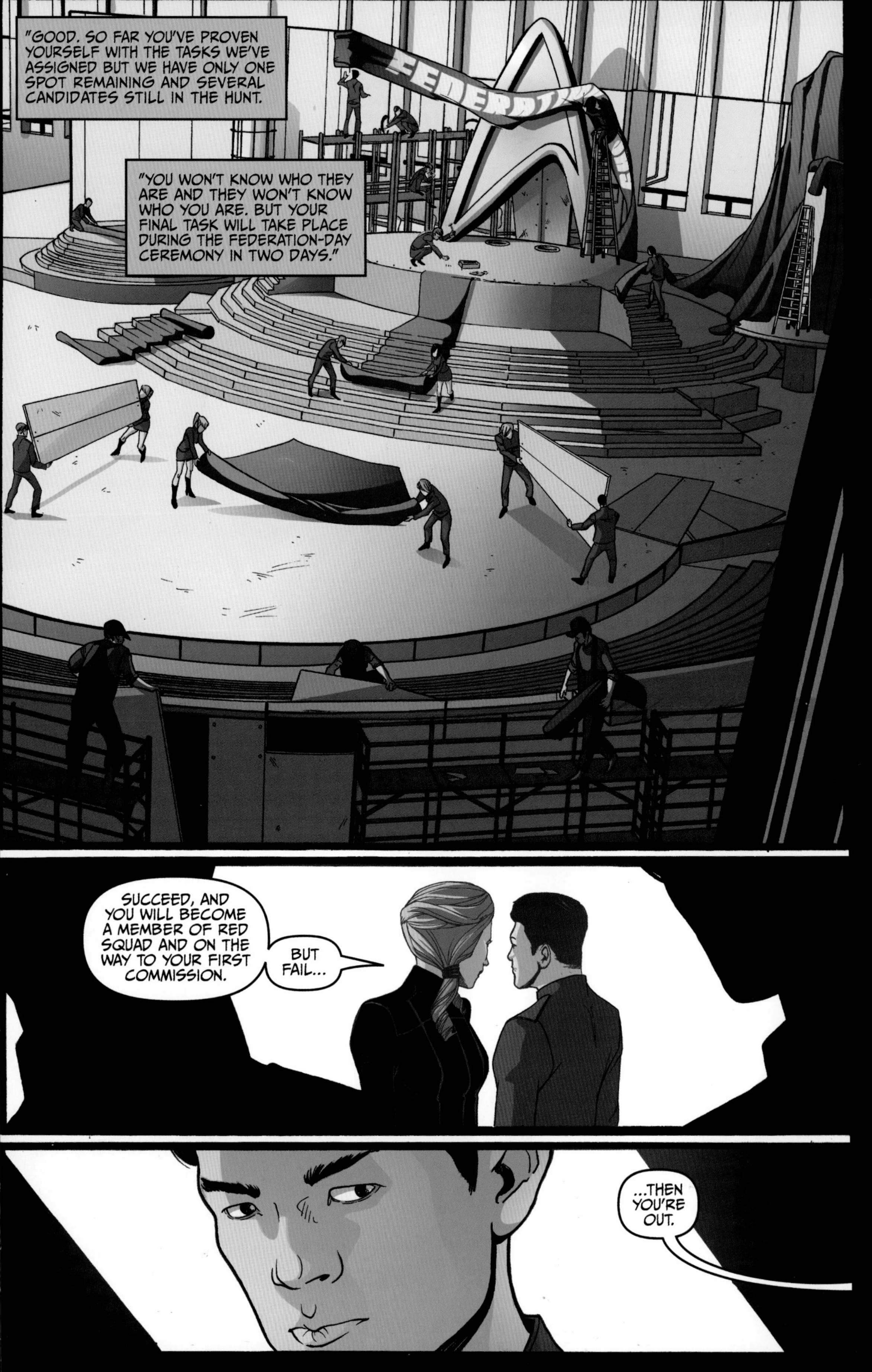
"GOOD. SO FAR YOU'VE PROVEN YOURSELF WITH THE TASKS WE'VE ASSIGNED BUT WE HAVE ONLY ONE SPOT REMAINING AND SEVERAL CANDIDATES STILL IN THE HUNT.
"YOU WON'T KNOW WHO THEY ARE AND THEY WON'T KNOW WHO YOU ARE. BUT YOUR FINAL TASK WILL TAKE PLACE DURING THE FEDERATION-DAY CEREMONY IN TWO DAYS."
SUCCEED, AND YOU WILL BECOME A MEMBER OF RED SQUAD AND ON THE WAY TO YOUR FIRST COMMISSION.
BUT FAIL...
...THEN YOU'RE OUT.

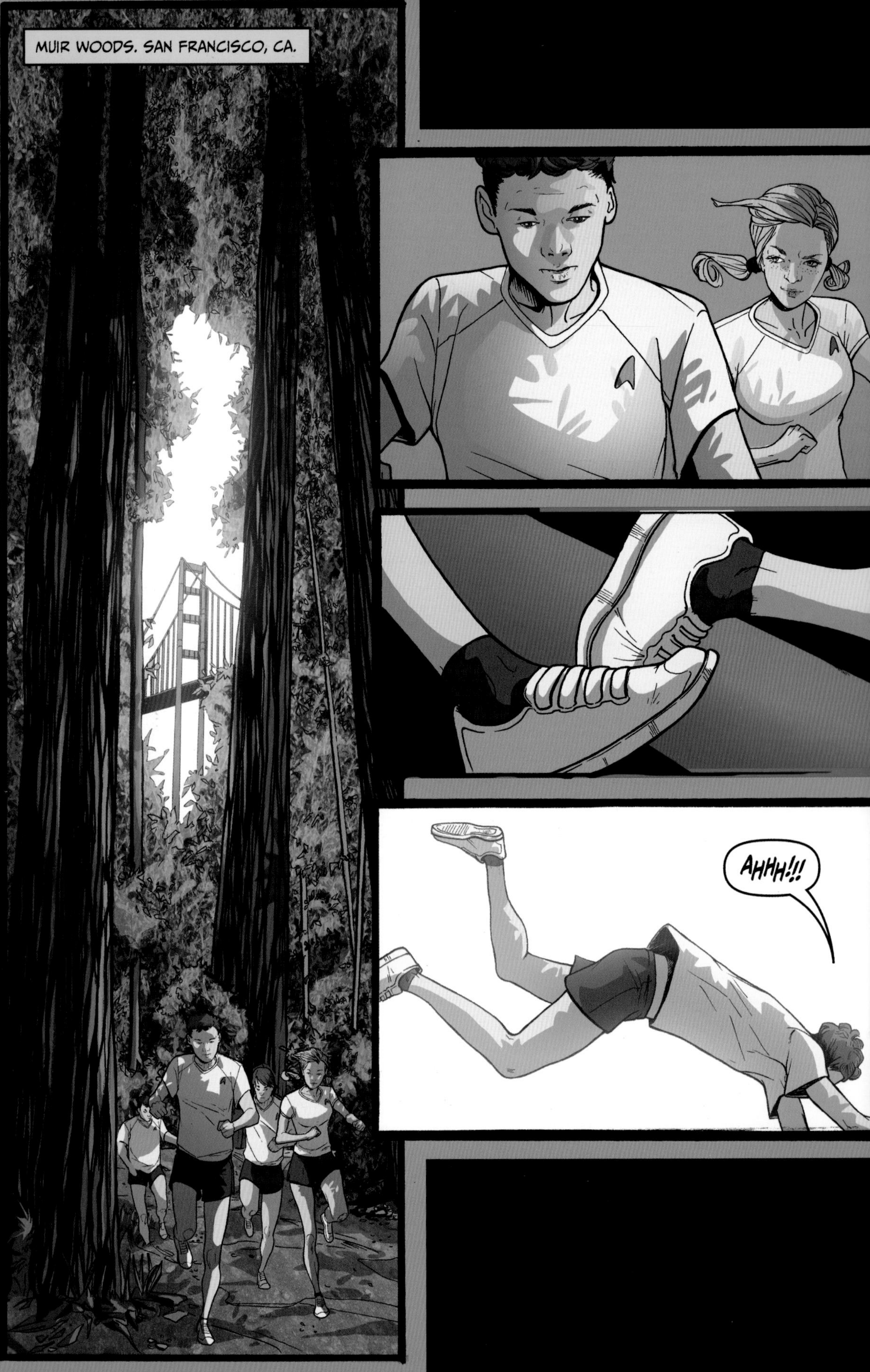
MUIR WOODS. SAN FRANCISCO, CA.
AHHH!!!

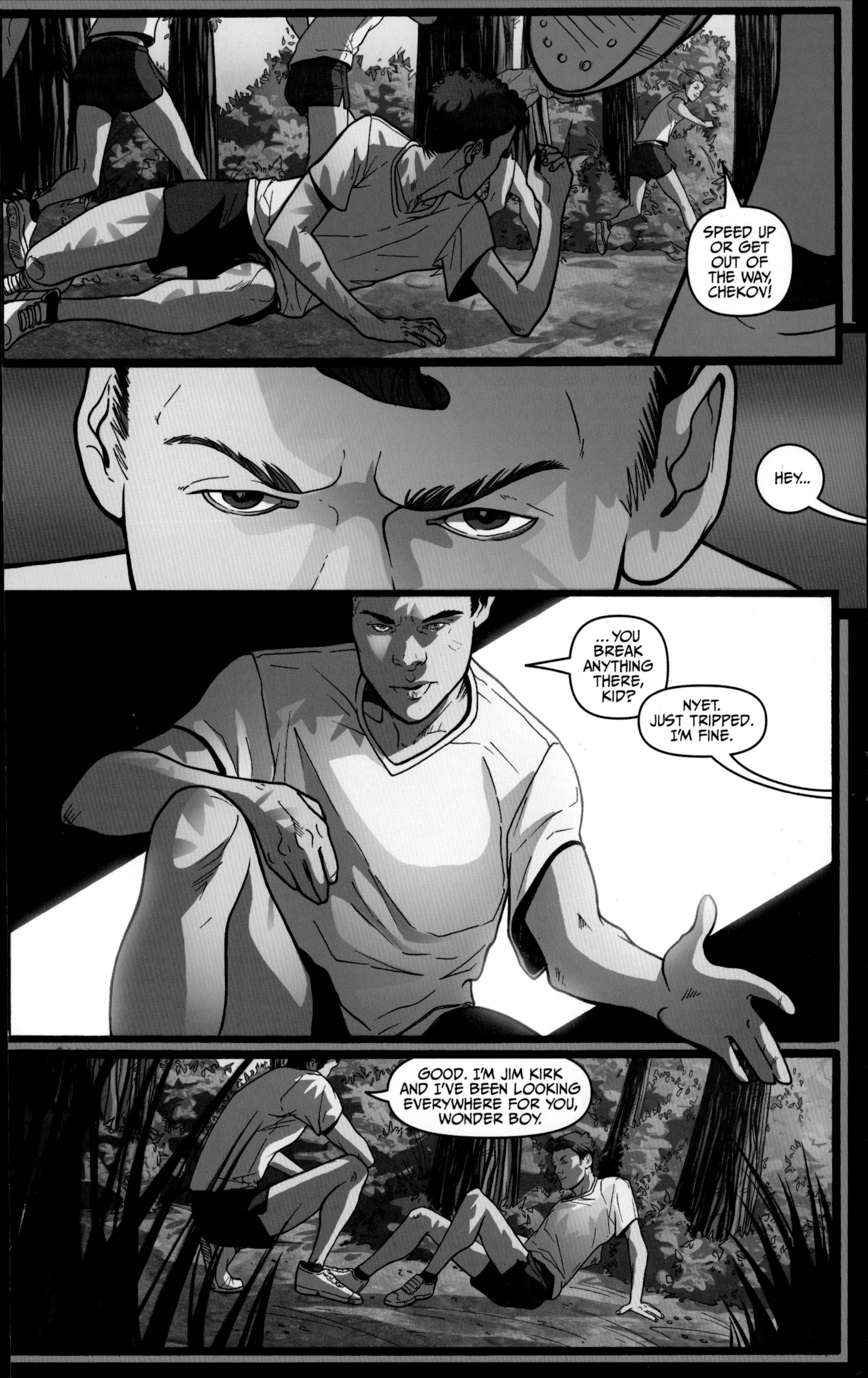
SPEED UP OR GET OUT OF THE WAY, CHEKOV!
HEY...
...YOU BREAK ANYTHING THERE, KID?
NYET. JUST TRIPPED. I'M FINE.
GOOD. I'M JIM KIRK AND I'VE BEEN LOOKING EVERYWHERE FOR YOU, WONDER BOY.

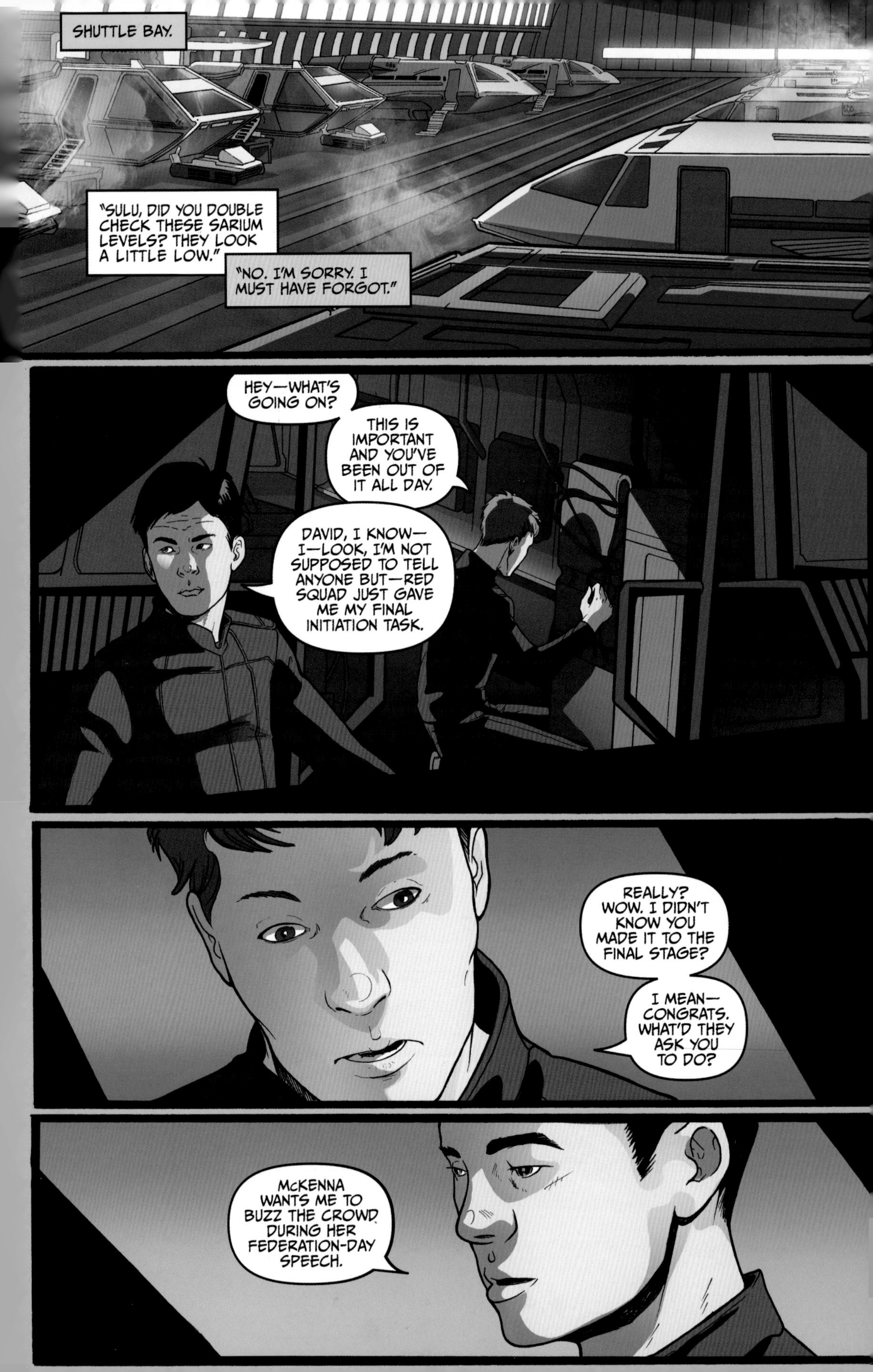
SHUTTLE BAY.
"SULU, DID YOU DOUBLE CHECK THESE SARIUM LEVELS? THEY LOOK A LITTLE LOW."
"NO. I'M SORRY. I MUST HAVE FORGOT."
HEY—WHAT'S GOING ON?
THIS IS IMPORTANT AND YOU'VE BEEN OUT OF IT ALL DAY.
DAVID, I KNOW— I—LOOK, I'M NOT SUPPOSED TO TELL ANYONE BUT—RED SQUAD JUST GAVE ME MY FINAL INITIATION TASK.
REALLY? WOW. I DIDN'T KNOW YOU MADE IT TO THE FINAL STAGE?
I MEAN— CONGRATS. WHAT'D THEY ASK YOU TO DO?
McKENNA WANTS ME TO BUZZ THE CROWD DURING HER FEDERATION-DAY SPEECH.

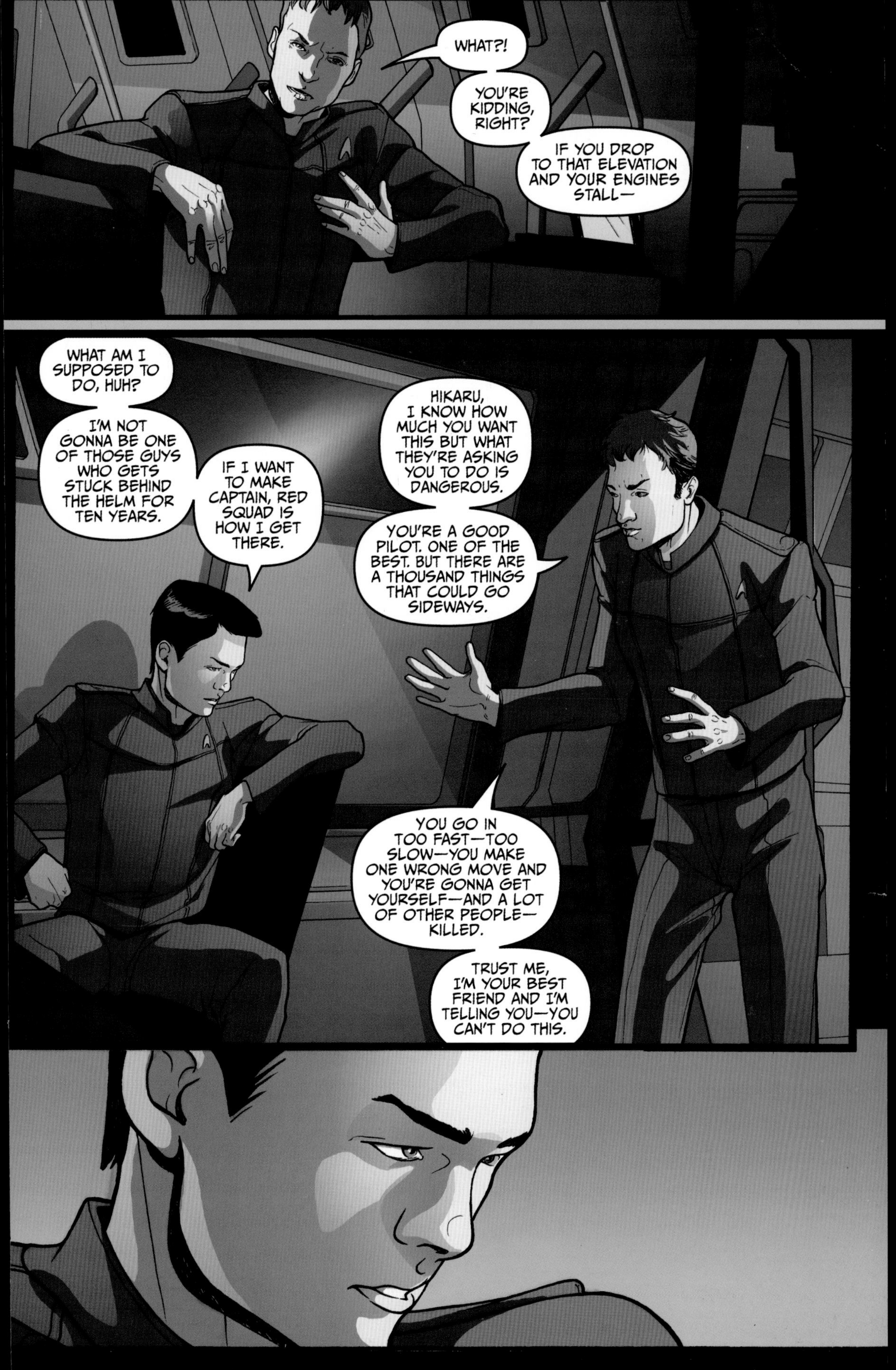
WHAT?!
YOU'RE KIDDING, RIGHT?
IF YOU DROP TO THAT ELEVATION AND YOUR ENGINES STALL—
WHAT AM I SUPPOSED TO DO, HUH?
I'M NOT GONNA BE ONE OF THOSE GUYS WHO GETS STUCK BEHIND THE HELM FOR TEN YEARS.
IF I WANT TO MAKE CAPTAIN, RED SQUAD IS HOW I GET THERE.
HIKARU, I KNOW HOW MUCH YOU WANT THIS BUT WHAT THEY'RE ASKING YOU TO DO IS DANGEROUS.
YOU'RE A GOOD PILOT. ONE OF THE BEST. BUT THERE ARE A THOUSAND THINGS THAT COULD GO SIDEWAYS.
YOU GO IN TOO FAST—TOO SLOW—YOU MAKE ONE WRONG MOVE AND YOU'RE GONNA GET YOURSELF—AND A LOT OF OTHER PEOPLE—KILLED.
TRUST ME, I'M YOUR BEST FRIEND AND I'M TELLING YOU—YOU CAN'T DO THIS.

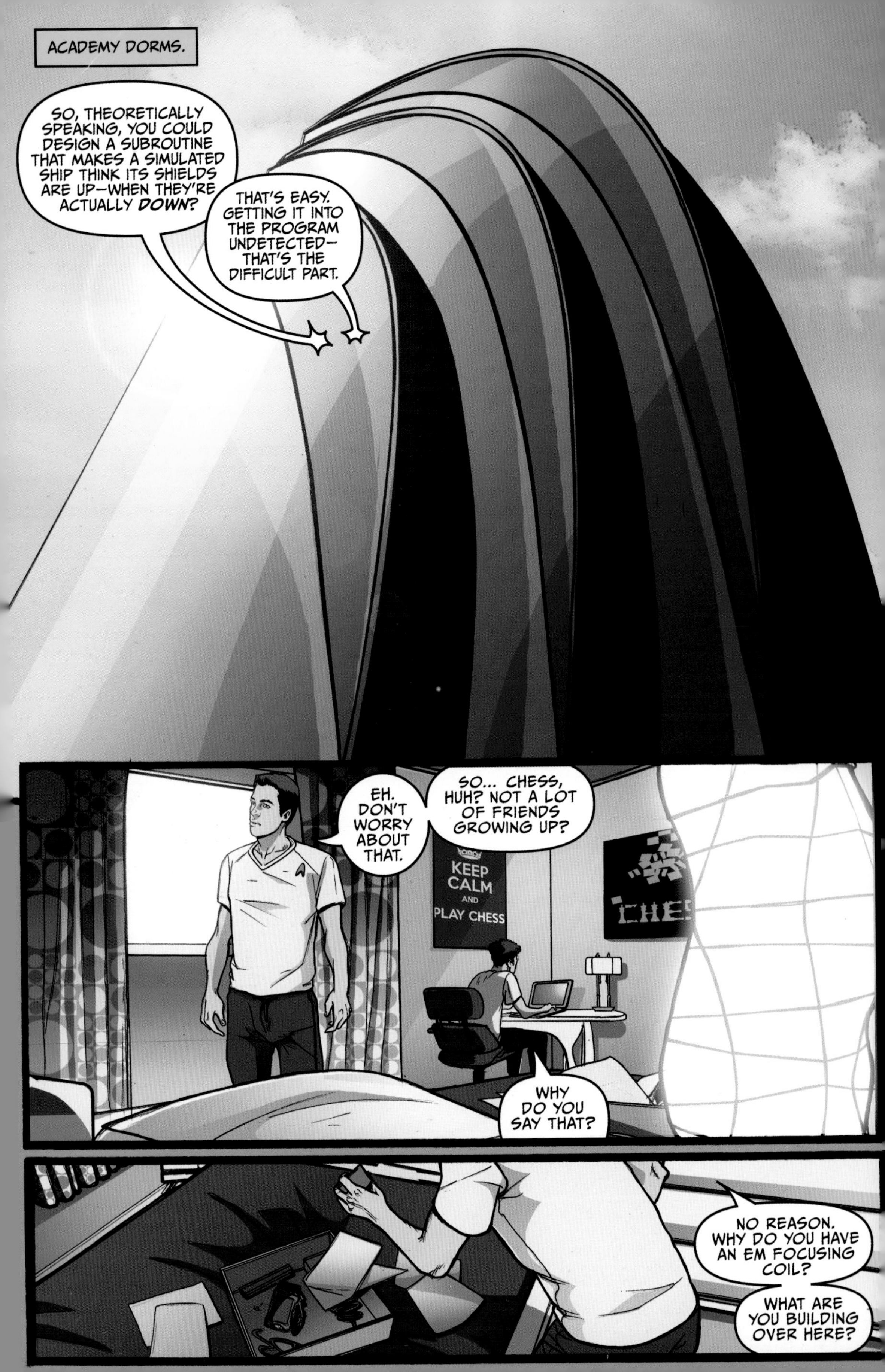
ACADEMY DORMS.
SO, THEORETICALLY SPEAKING, YOU COULD DESIGN A SUBROUTINE THAT MAKES A SIMULATED SHIP THINK ITS SHIELDS ARE UP—WHEN THEY'RE ACTUALLY *DOWN*?
THAT'S EASY. GETTING IT INTO THE PROGRAM UNDETECTED—THAT'S THE DIFFICULT PART.
SO... CHESS, HUH? NOT A LOT OF FRIENDS GROWING UP?
EH. DON'T WORRY ABOUT THAT.
KEEP CALM AND PLAY CHESS
WHY DO YOU SAY THAT?
NO REASON. WHY DO YOU HAVE AN EM FOCUSING COIL?
WHAT ARE YOU BUILDING OVER HERE?

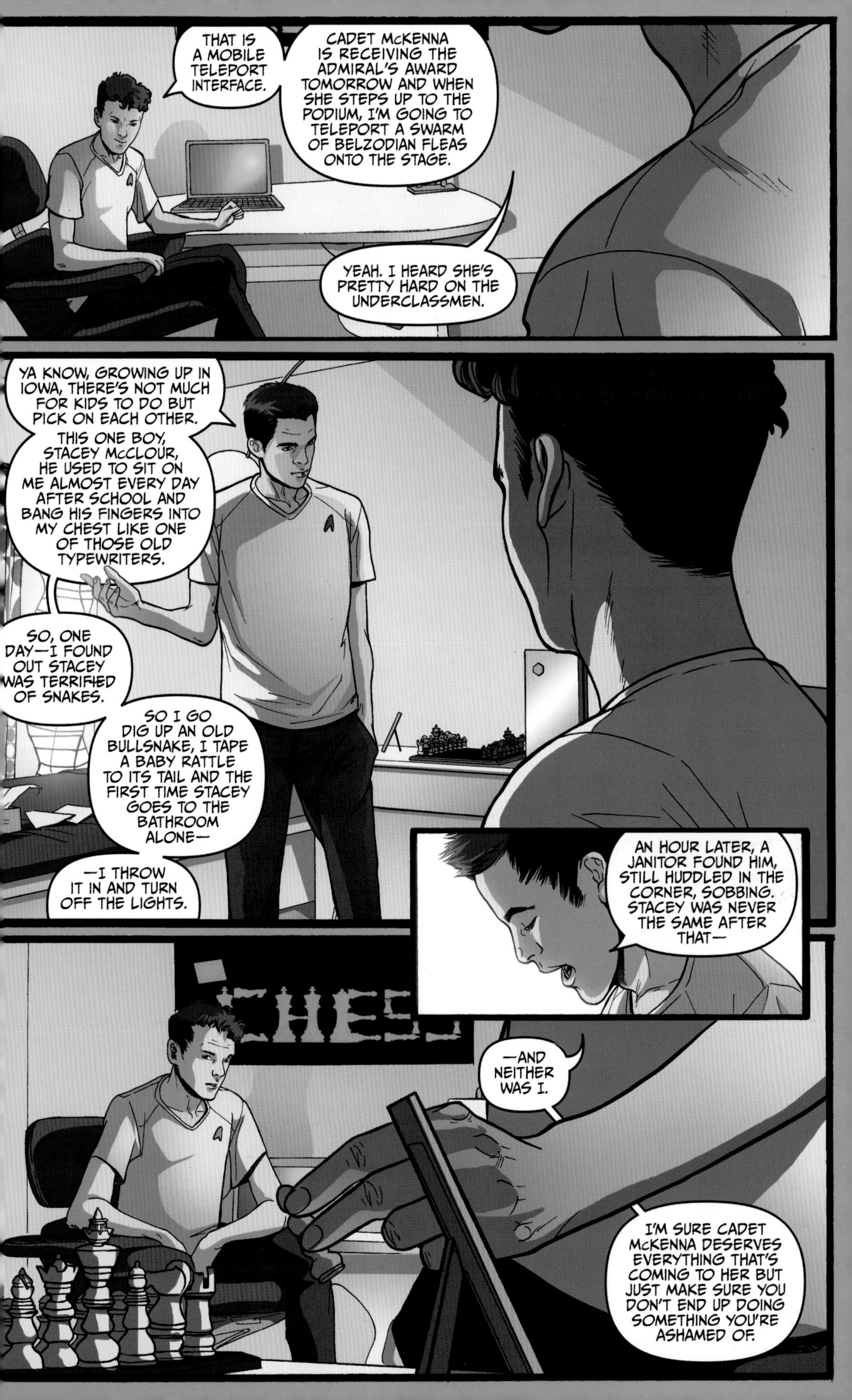
THAT IS A MOBILE TELEPORT INTERFACE.
CADET McKENNA IS RECEIVING THE ADMIRAL'S AWARD TOMORROW AND WHEN SHE STEPS UP TO THE PODIUM, I'M GOING TO TELEPORT A SWARM OF BELZODIAN FLEAS ONTO THE STAGE.
YEAH. I HEARD SHE'S PRETTY HARD ON THE UNDERCLASSMEN.
YA KNOW, GROWING UP IN IOWA, THERE'S NOT MUCH FOR KIDS TO DO BUT PICK ON EACH OTHER.
THIS ONE BOY, STACEY McCLOUR, HE USED TO SIT ON ME ALMOST EVERY DAY AFTER SCHOOL AND BANG HIS FINGERS INTO MY CHEST LIKE ONE OF THOSE OLD TYPEWRITERS.
SO, ONE DAY—I FOUND OUT STACEY WAS TERRIFIED OF SNAKES.
SO I GO DIG UP AN OLD BULLSNAKE, I TAPE A BABY RATTLE TO ITS TAIL AND THE FIRST TIME STACEY GOES TO THE BATHROOM ALONE—
—I THROW IT IN AND TURN OFF THE LIGHTS.
AN HOUR LATER, A JANITOR FOUND HIM, STILL HUDDLED IN THE CORNER, SOBBING. STACEY WAS NEVER THE SAME AFTER THAT—
—AND NEITHER WAS I.
I'M SURE CADET McKENNA DESERVES EVERYTHING THAT'S COMING TO HER BUT JUST MAKE SURE YOU DON'T END UP DOING SOMETHING YOU'RE ASHAMED OF.

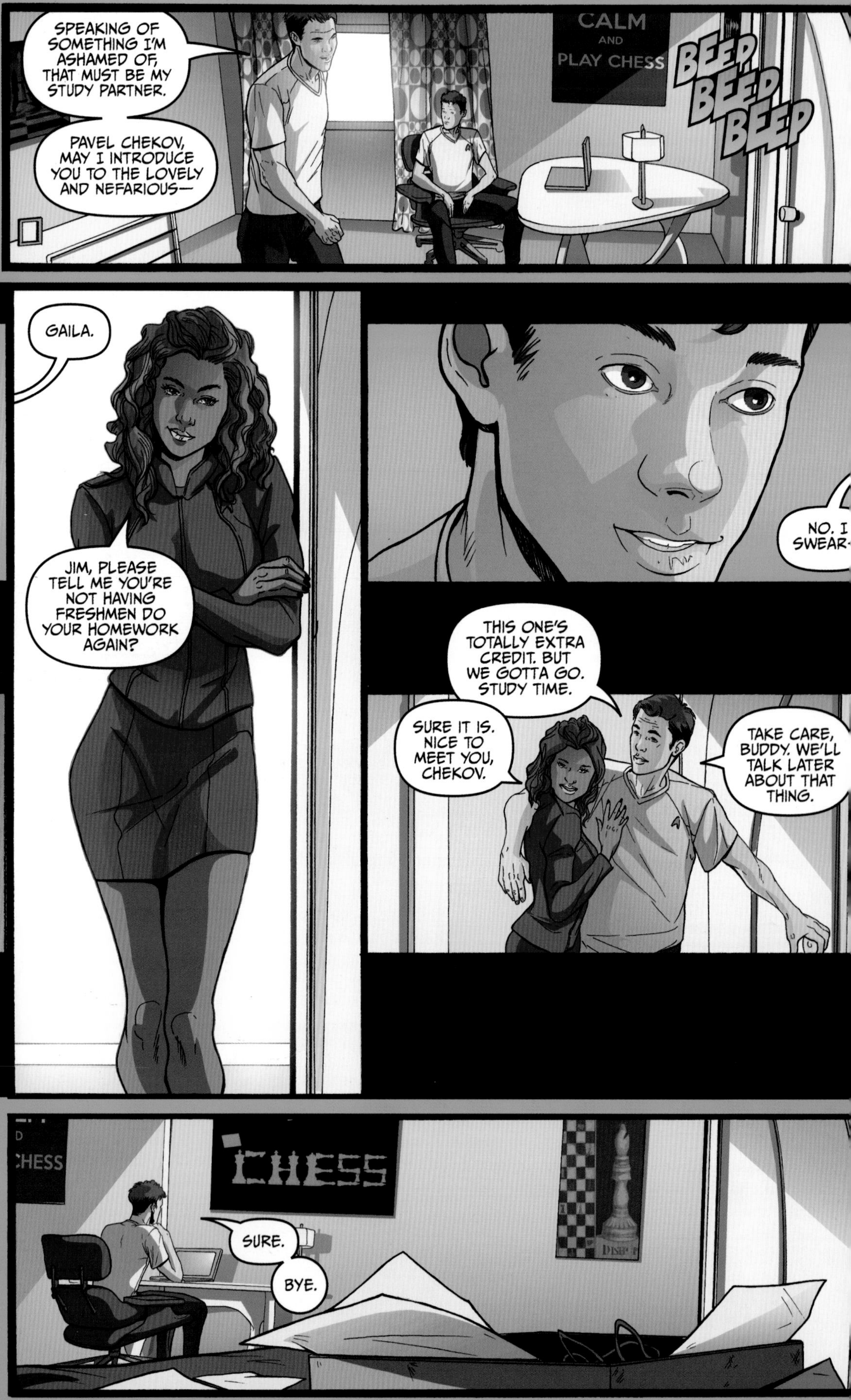
SPEAKING OF SOMETHING I'M ASHAMED OF, THAT MUST BE MY STUDY PARTNER.
PAVEL CHEKOV, MAY I INTRODUCE YOU TO THE LOVELY AND NEFARIOUS—
CALM AND PLAY CHESS
BEEP BEEP BEEP
GAILA.
JIM, PLEASE TELL ME YOU'RE NOT HAVING FRESHMEN DO YOUR HOMEWORK AGAIN?
NO. I SWEAR-
THIS ONE'S TOTALLY EXTRA CREDIT. BUT WE GOTTA GO. STUDY TIME.
SURE IT IS. NICE TO MEET YOU, CHEKOV.
TAKE CARE, BUDDY. WE'LL TALK LATER ABOUT THAT THING.
CHESS
SURE.
BYE.

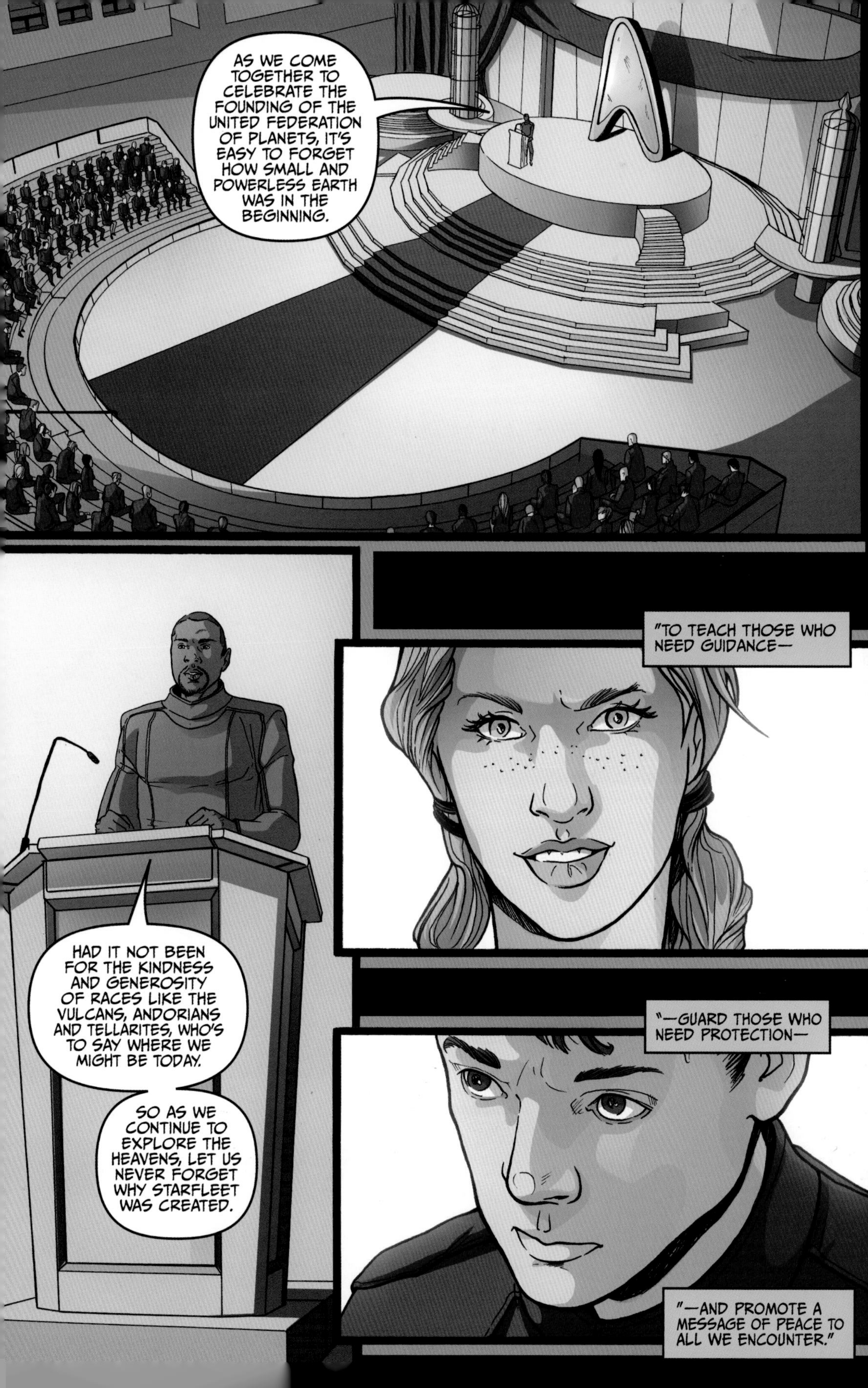
AS WE COME TOGETHER TO CELEBRATE THE FOUNDING OF THE UNITED FEDERATION OF PLANETS, IT'S EASY TO FORGET HOW SMALL AND POWERLESS EARTH WAS IN THE BEGINNING.
HAD IT NOT BEEN FOR THE KINDNESS AND GENEROSITY OF RACES LIKE THE VULCANS, ANDORIANS AND TELLARITES, WHO'S TO SAY WHERE WE MIGHT BE TODAY.
SO AS WE CONTINUE TO EXPLORE THE HEAVENS, LET US NEVER FORGET WHY STARFLEET WAS CREATED.
"TO TEACH THOSE WHO NEED GUIDANCE—
"—GUARD THOSE WHO NEED PROTECTION—
"—AND PROMOTE A MESSAGE OF PEACE TO ALL WE ENCOUNTER."

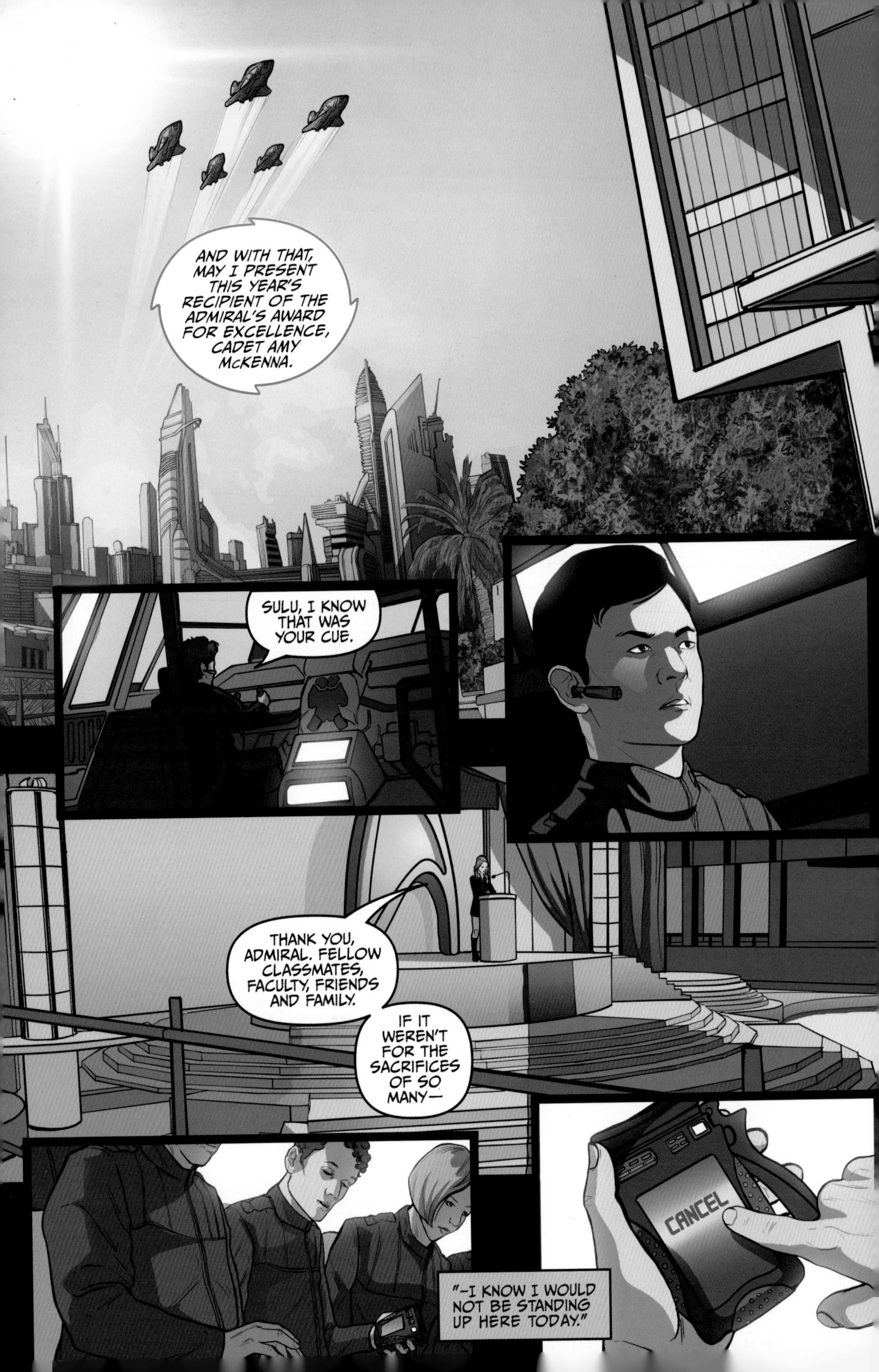
AND WITH THAT, MAY I PRESENT THIS YEAR'S RECIPIENT OF THE ADMIRAL'S AWARD FOR EXCELLENCE, CADET AMY McKENNA.
SULU, I KNOW THAT WAS YOUR CUE.
THANK YOU, ADMIRAL. FELLOW CLASSMATES, FACULTY, FRIENDS AND FAMILY.
IF IT WEREN'T FOR THE SACRIFICES OF SO MANY—
CANCEL
"—I KNOW I WOULD NOT BE STANDING UP HERE TODAY."

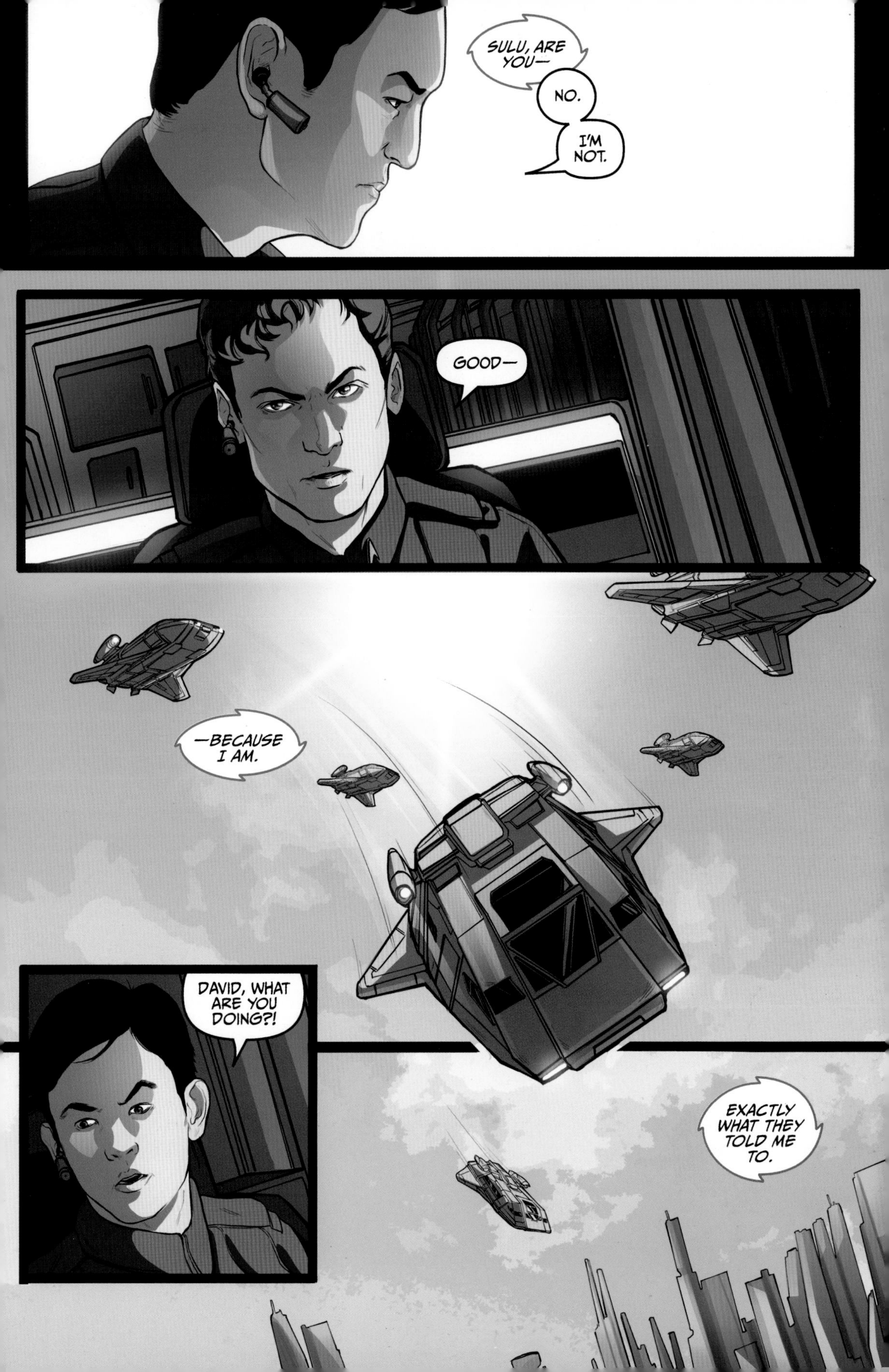
SULU, ARE YOU—
NO.
I'M NOT.
GOOD—
—BECAUSE I AM.
DAVID, WHAT ARE YOU DOING?!
EXACTLY WHAT THEY TOLD ME TO.

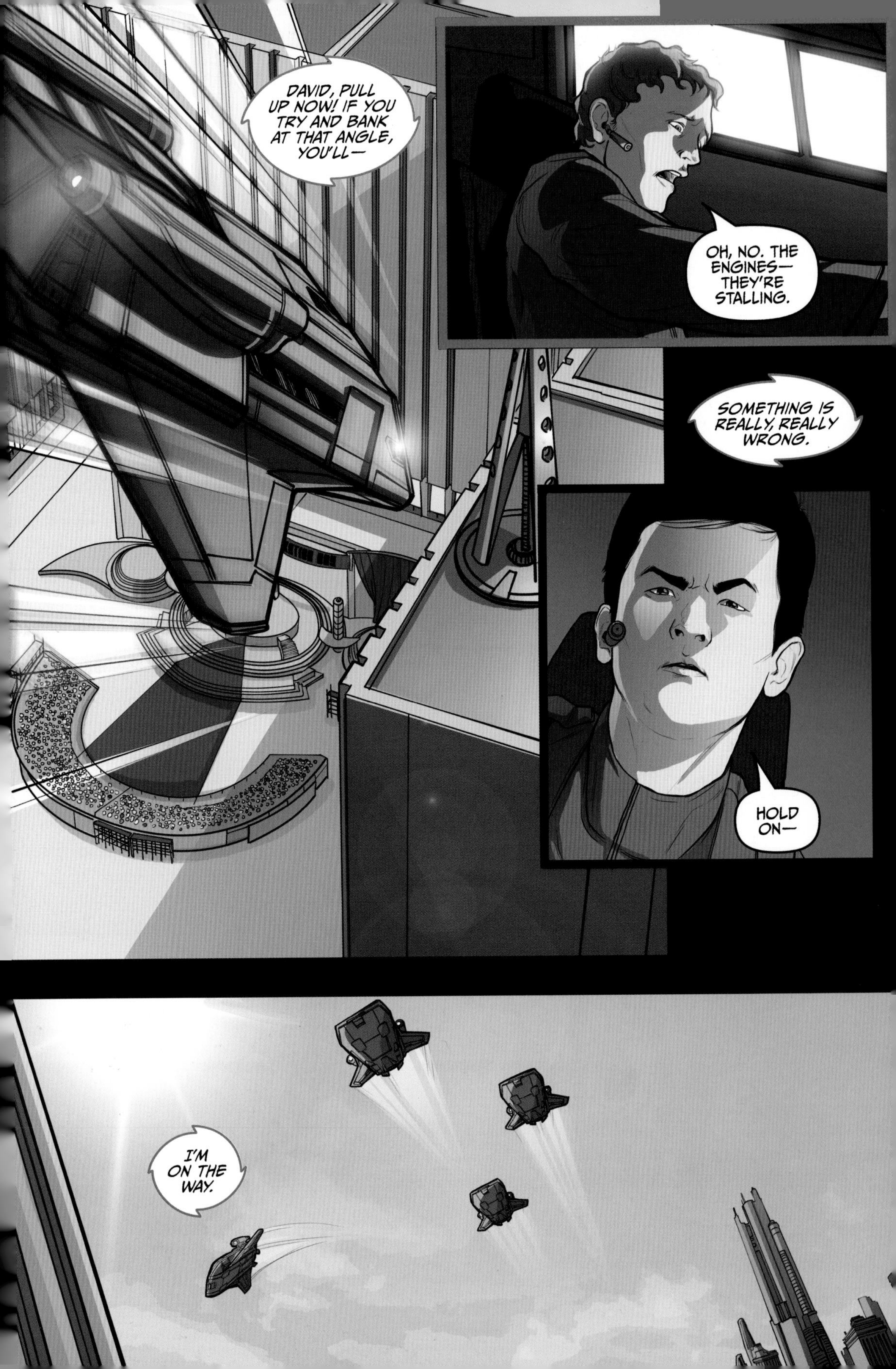
DAVID, PULL UP NOW! IF YOU TRY AND BANK AT THAT ANGLE, YOU'LL—
OH, NO. THE ENGINES— THEY'RE STALLING.
SOMETHING IS REALLY, REALLY WRONG.
HOLD ON—
I'M ON THE WAY.

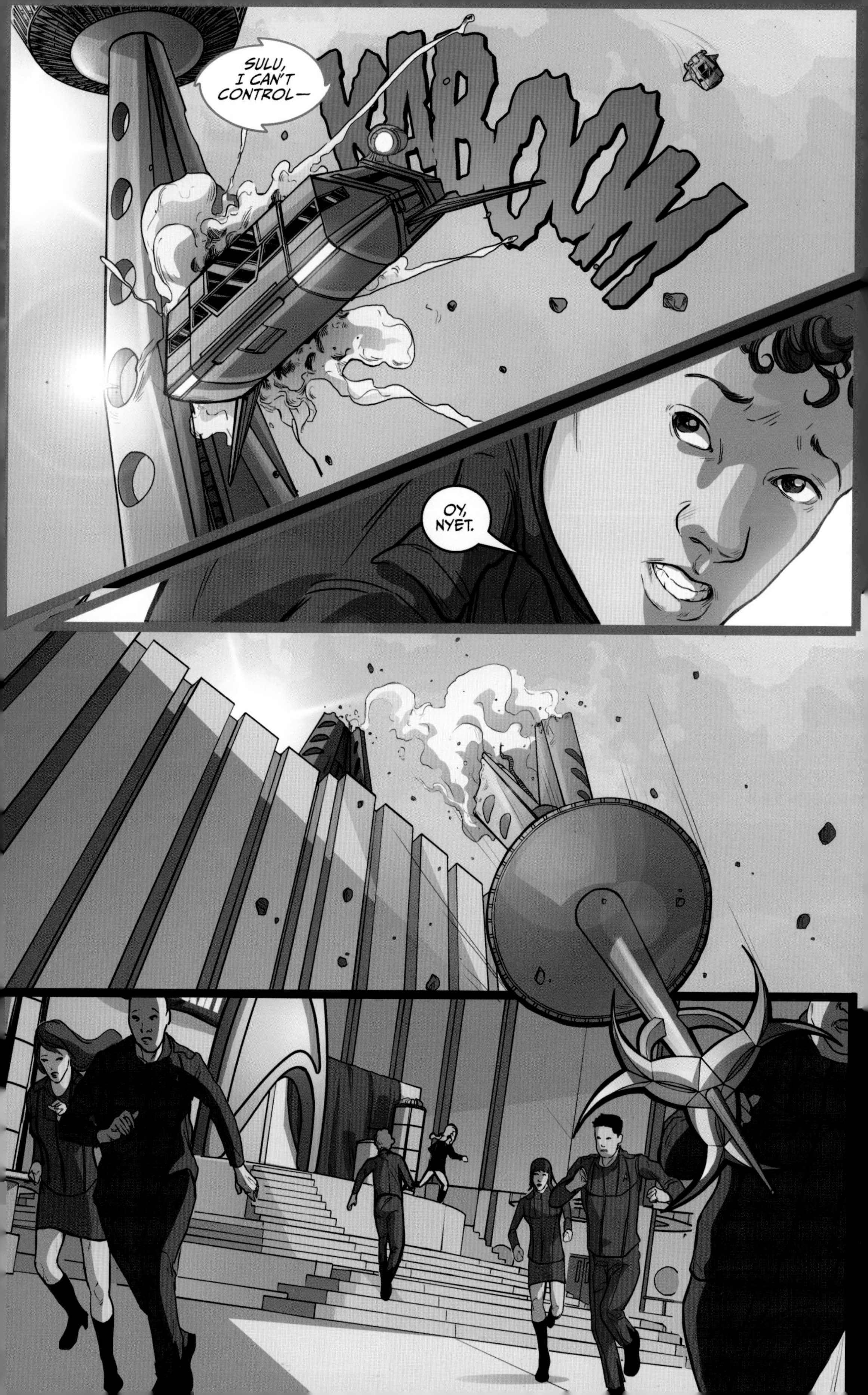
SULU, I CAN'T CONTROL—
KABOOM
OY, NYET.

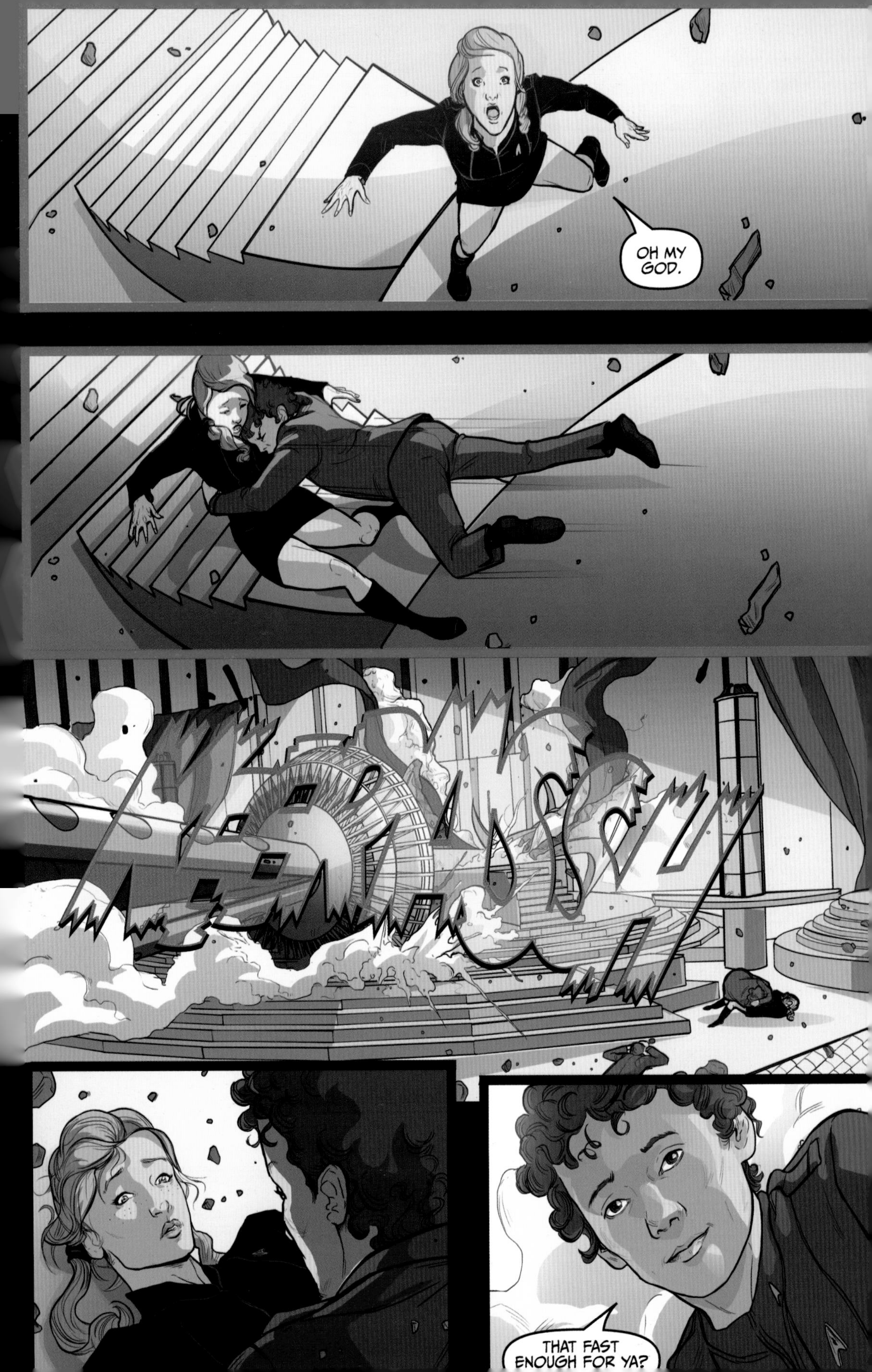
OH MY GOD.
THAT FAST ENOUGH FOR YA?

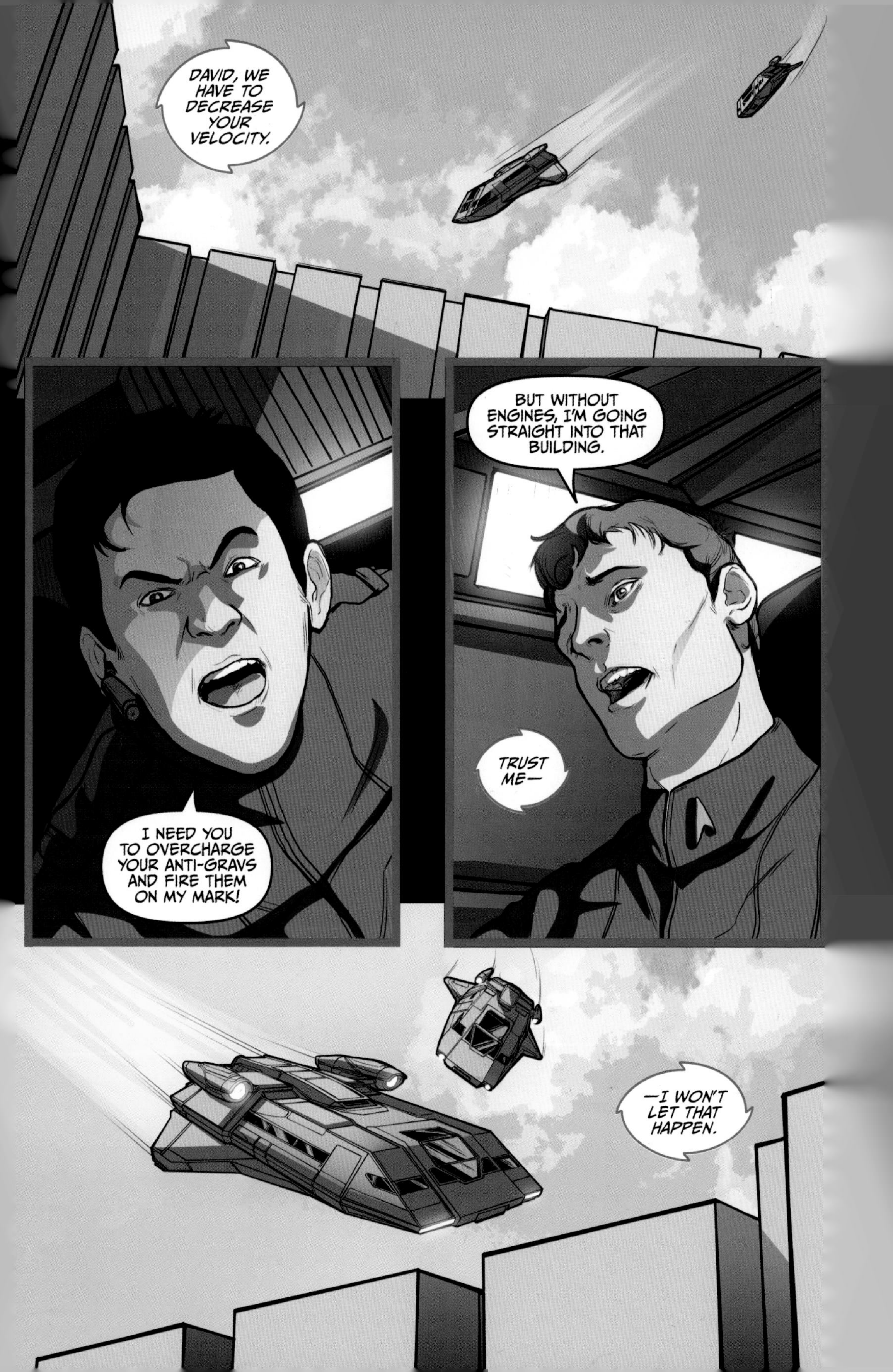
DAVID, WE HAVE TO DECREASE YOUR VELOCITY.
I NEED YOU TO OVERCHARGE YOUR ANTI-GRAVS AND FIRE THEM ON MY MARK!
BUT WITHOUT ENGINES, I'M GOING STRAIGHT INTO THAT BUILDING.
TRUST ME—
—I WON'T LET THAT HAPPEN.

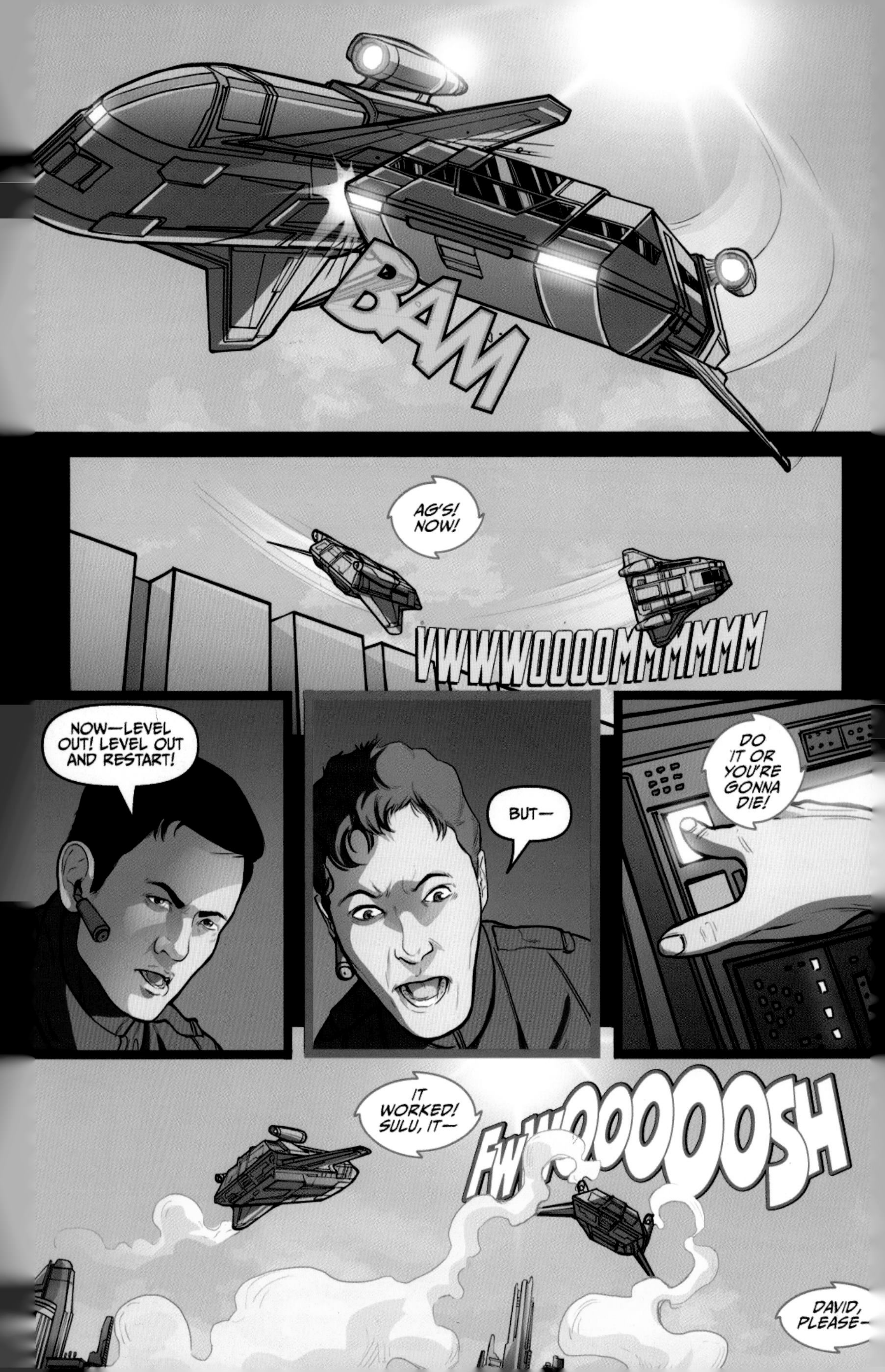
BAM
AG'S! NOW!
VWWWOOOOMMMMMM
NOW—LEVEL OUT! LEVEL OUT AND RESTART!
BUT—
DO IT OR YOU'RE GONNA DIE!
IT WORKED! SULU, IT—
FWOOOOOOSH
DAVID, PLEASE—

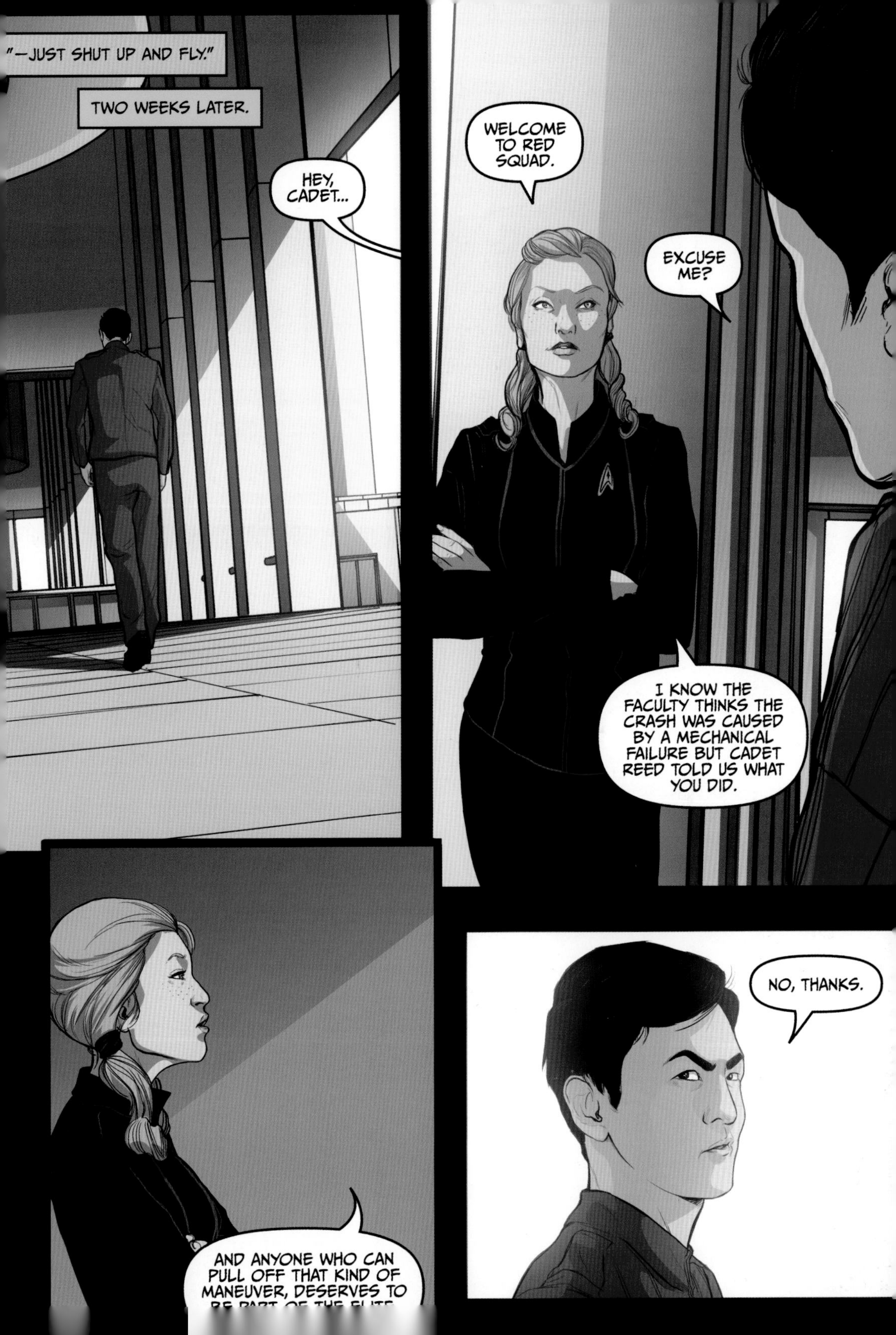
"—JUST SHUT UP AND FLY."
TWO WEEKS LATER.
HEY, CADET...
WELCOME TO RED SQUAD.
EXCUSE ME?
I KNOW THE FACULTY THINKS THE CRASH WAS CAUSED BY A MECHANICAL FAILURE BUT CADET REED TOLD US WHAT YOU DID.
AND ANYONE WHO CAN PULL OFF THAT KIND OF MANEUVER, DESERVES TO
NO, THANKS.

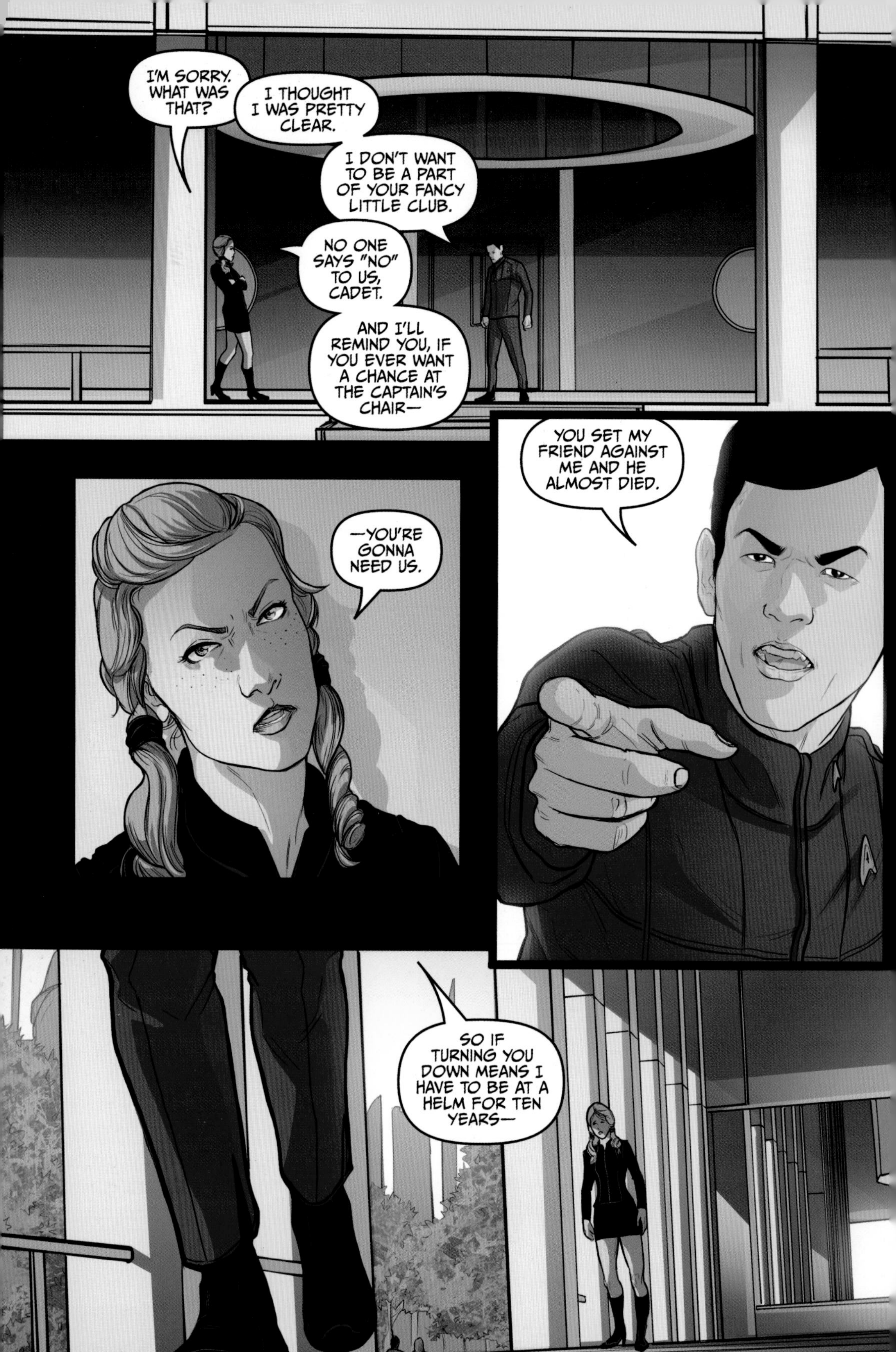
I'M SORRY. WHAT WAS THAT?
I THOUGHT I WAS PRETTY CLEAR.
I DON'T WANT TO BE A PART OF YOUR FANCY LITTLE CLUB.
NO ONE SAYS "NO" TO US, CADET.
AND I'LL REMIND YOU, IF YOU EVER WANT A CHANCE AT THE CAPTAIN'S CHAIR—
—YOU'RE GONNA NEED US.
YOU SET MY FRIEND AGAINST ME AND HE ALMOST DIED.
SO IF TURNING YOU DOWN MEANS I HAVE TO BE AT A HELM FOR TEN YEARS—

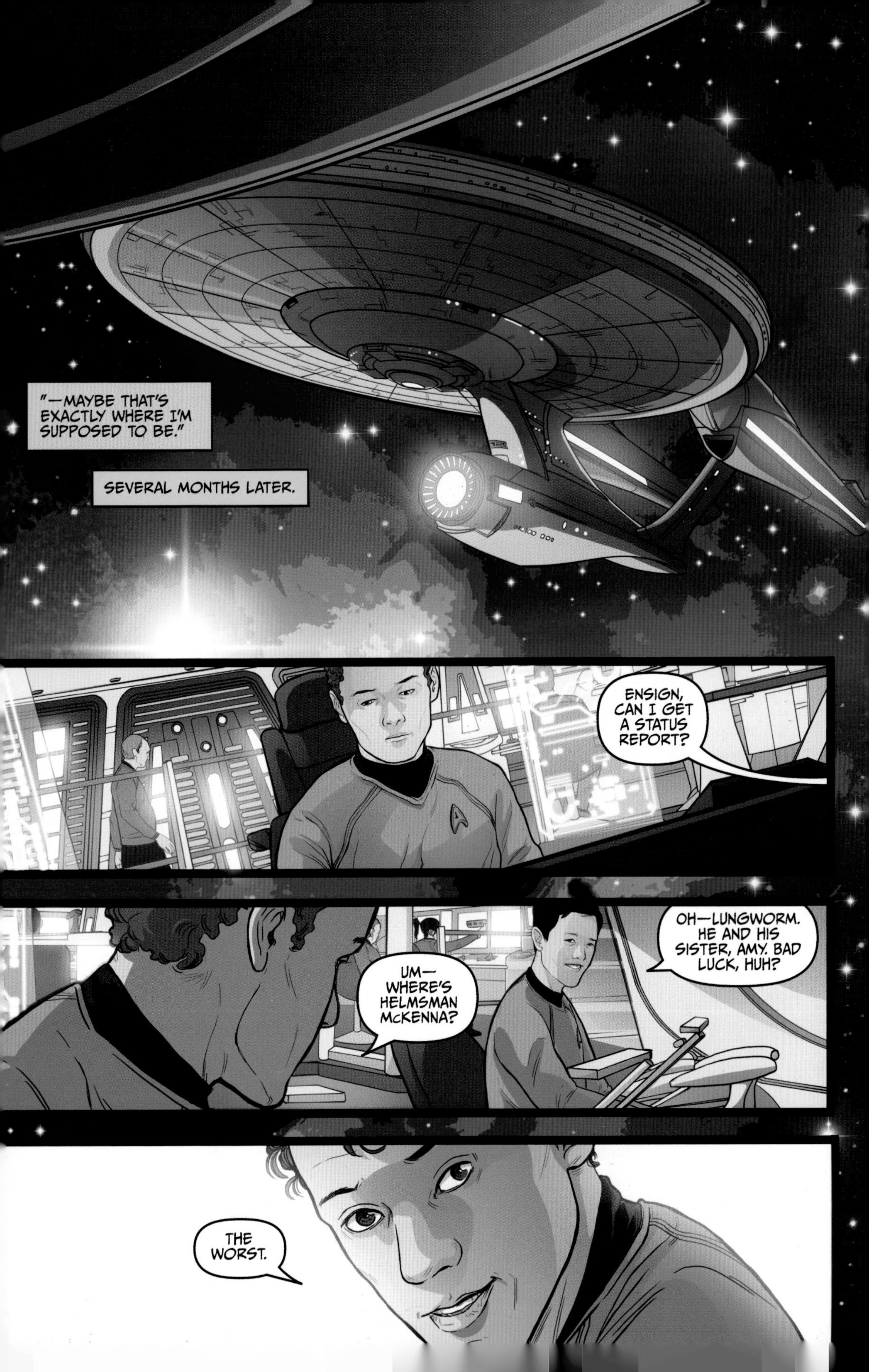
"—MAYBE THAT'S EXACTLY WHERE I'M SUPPOSED TO BE."
SEVERAL MONTHS LATER.
ENSIGN, CAN I GET A STATUS REPORT?
UM—WHERE'S HELMSMAN McKENNA?
OH—LUNGWORM. HE AND HIS SISTER, AMY. BAD LUCK, HUH?
THE WORST.

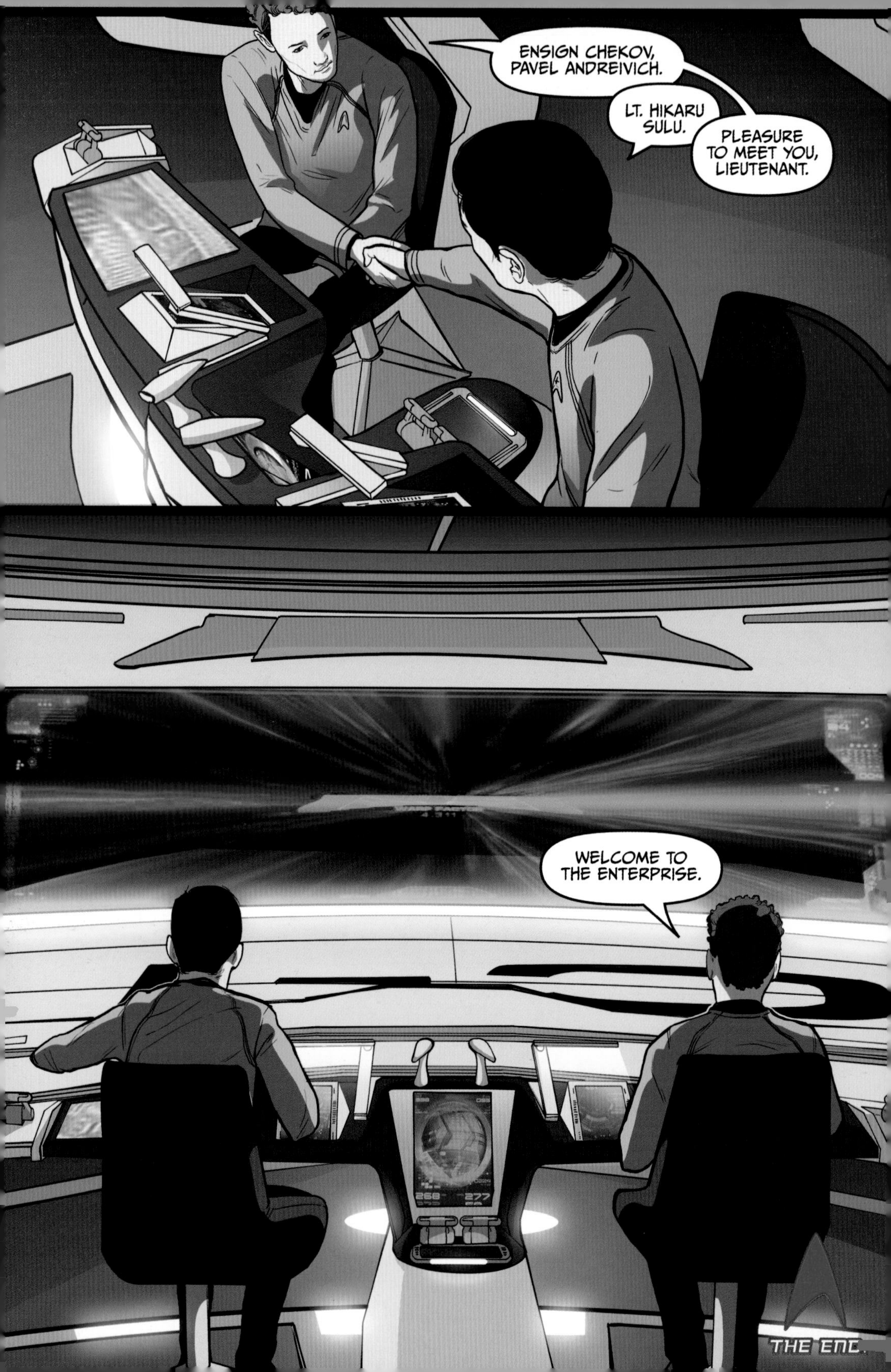
ENSIGN CHEKOV, PAVEL ANDREIVICH.
LT. HIKARU SULU.
PLEASURE TO MEET YOU, LIEUTENANT.
WELCOME TO THE ENTERPRISE.
THE END.

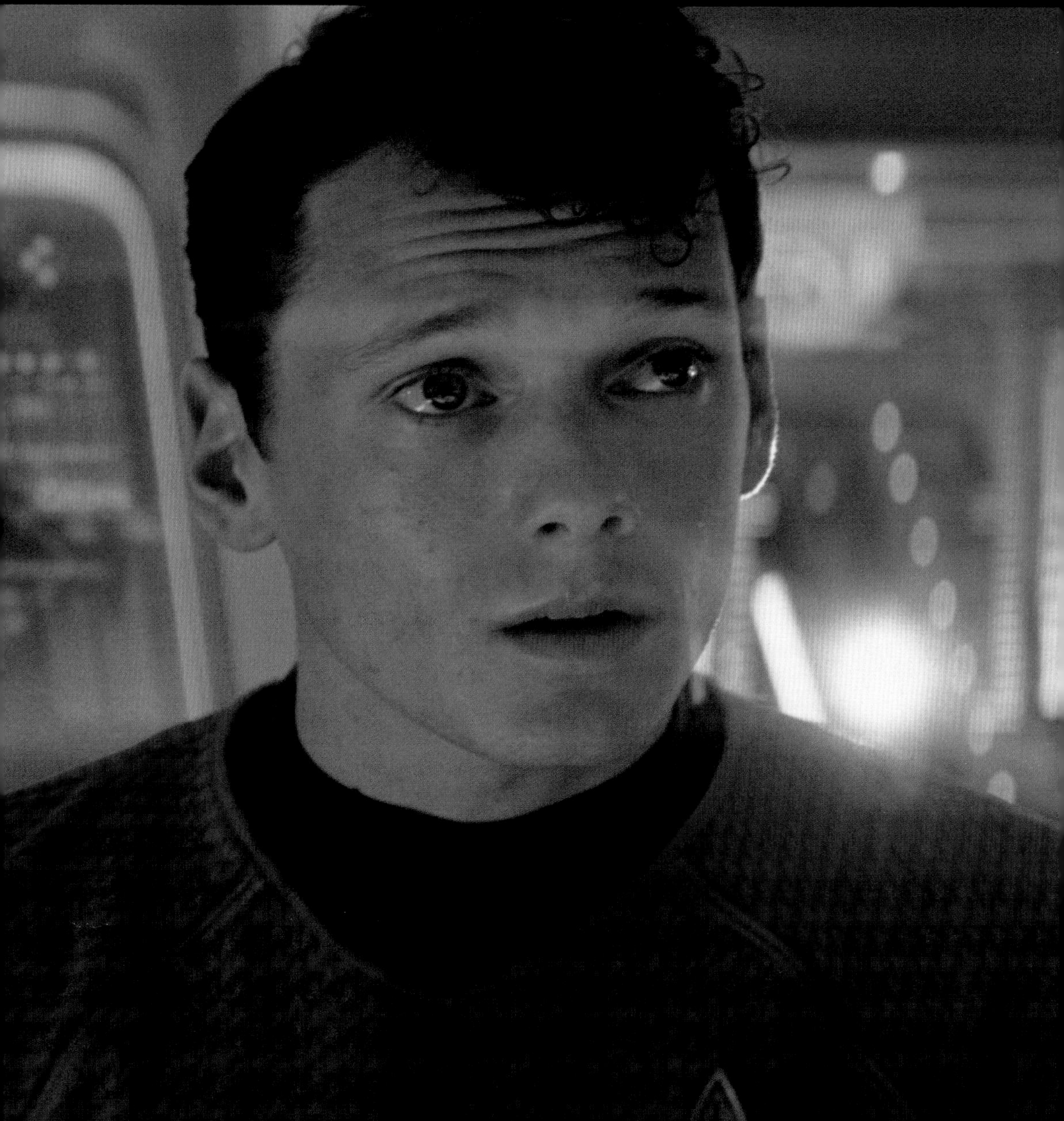

Artwork by
Tim Bradstreet

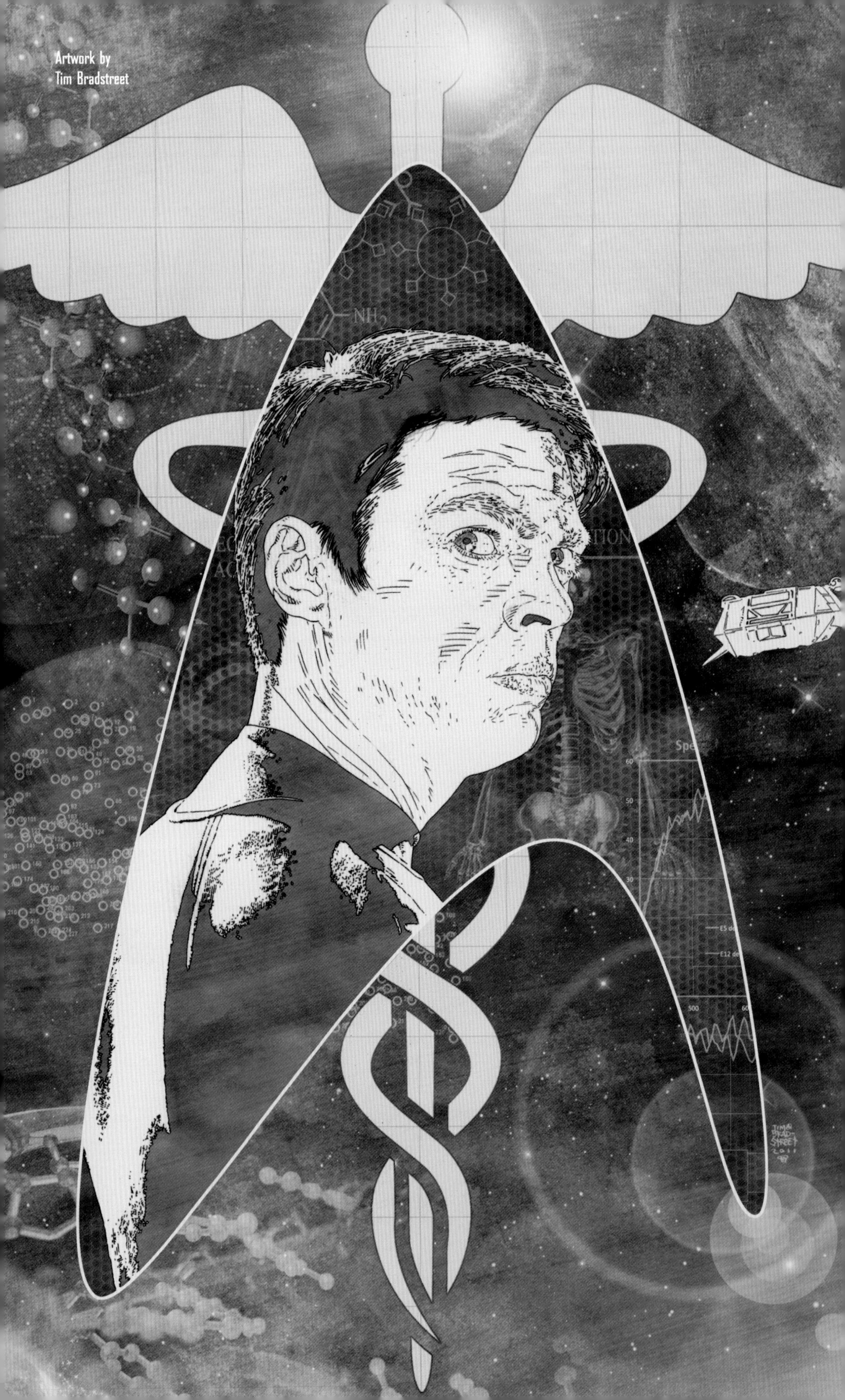
NH2
TIM BRADSTREET 2011

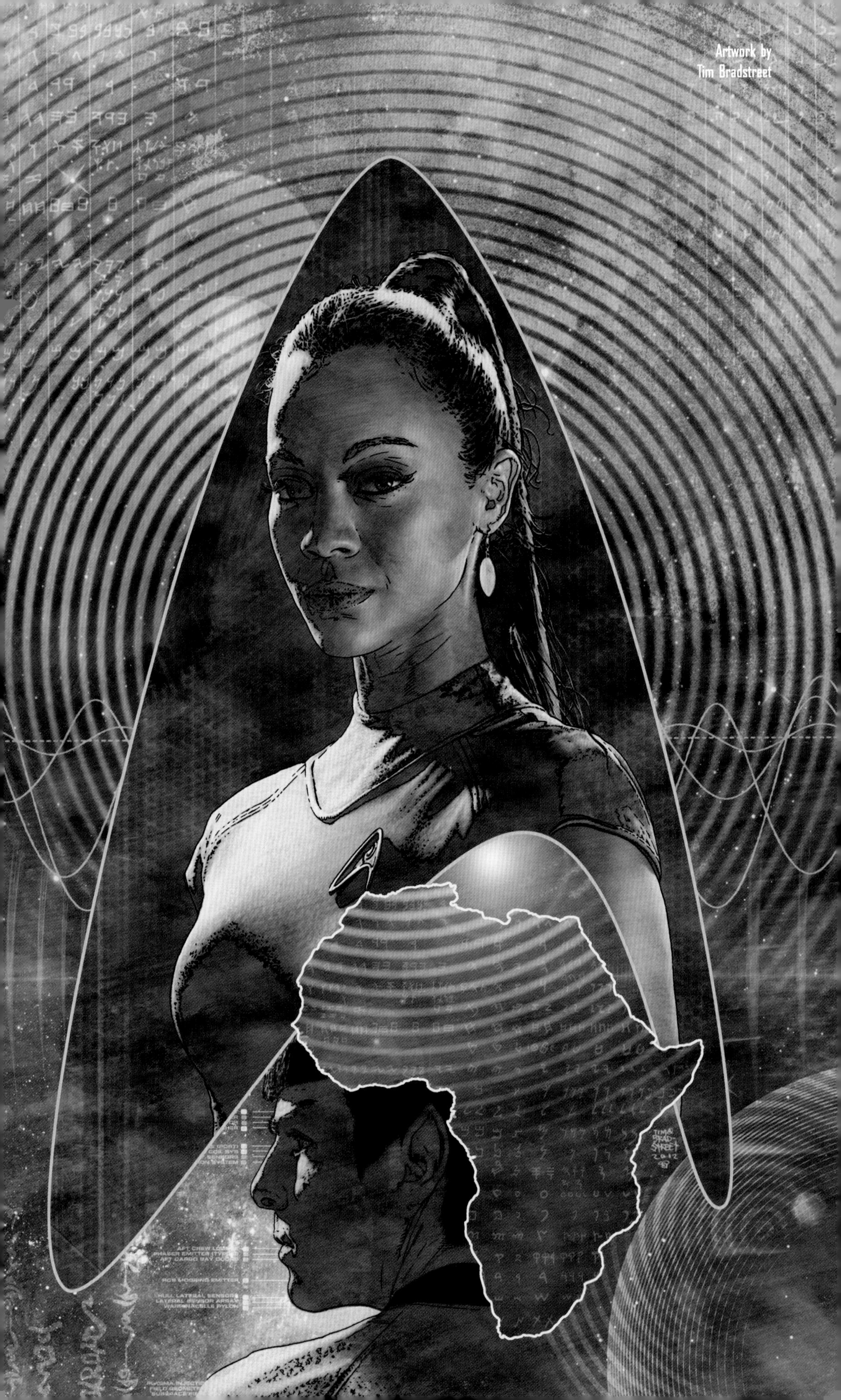

Artwork by
Tim Bradstreet

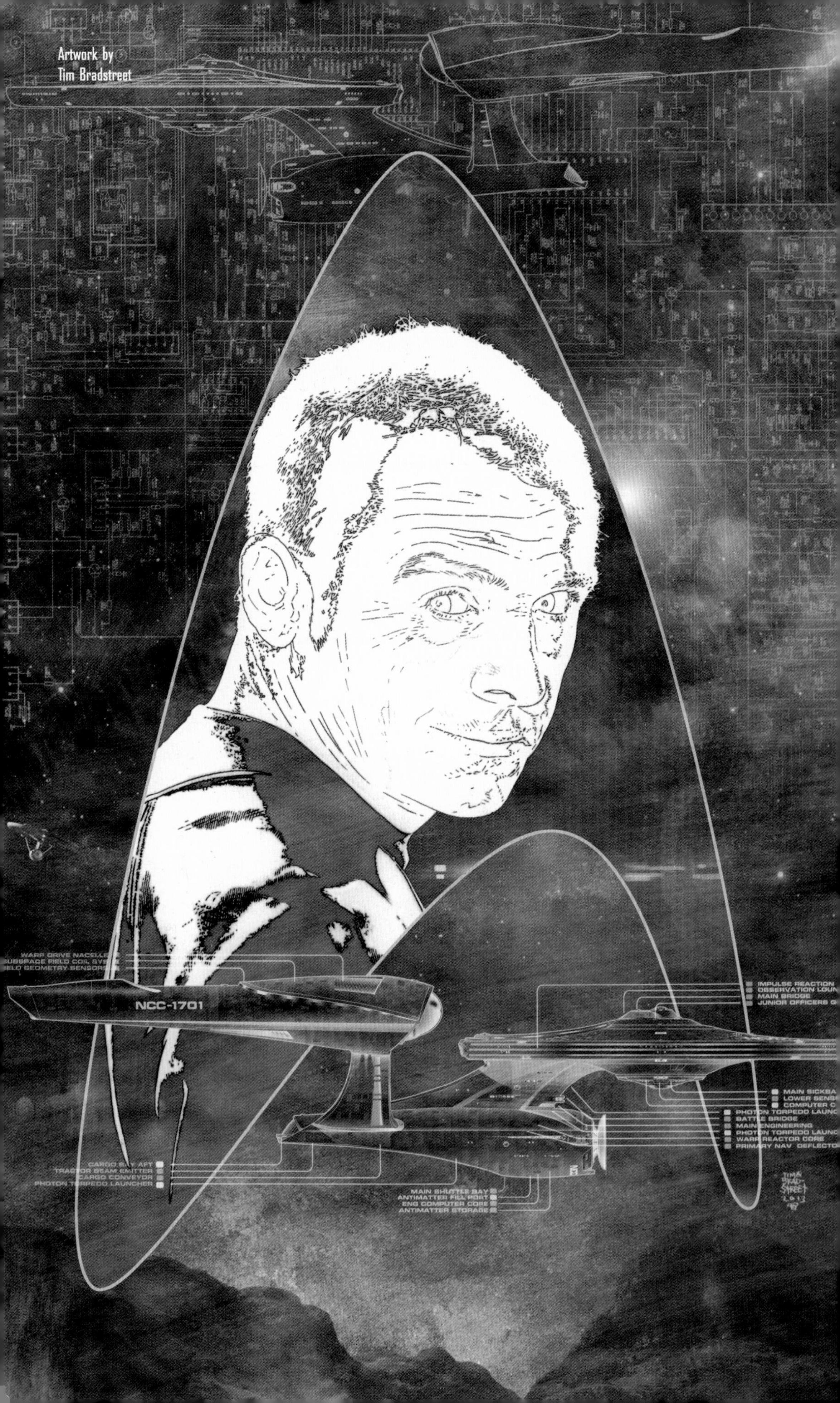

Artwork by
Tim Bradstreet
WARP DRIVE NACELLE
NCC-1701
IMPULSE REACTION
OBSERVATION LOUN
MAIN BRIDGE
JUNIOR OFFICERS Q
MAIN SICKBA
LOWER SENS
COMPUTER C
PHOTON TORPEDO LAUNC
BATTLE BRIDGE
MAIN ENGINEERING
PHOTON TORPEDO LAUNC
WARP REACTOR CORE
PRIMARY NAV DEFLECTO
CARGO BAY AFT
TRACTOR BEAM EMITTER
CARGO CONVEYOR
PHOTON TORPEDO LAUNCHER
MAIN SHUTTLE BAY
ANTIMATTER FILL PORT
ENG COMPUTER CORE
ANTIMATTER STORAGE

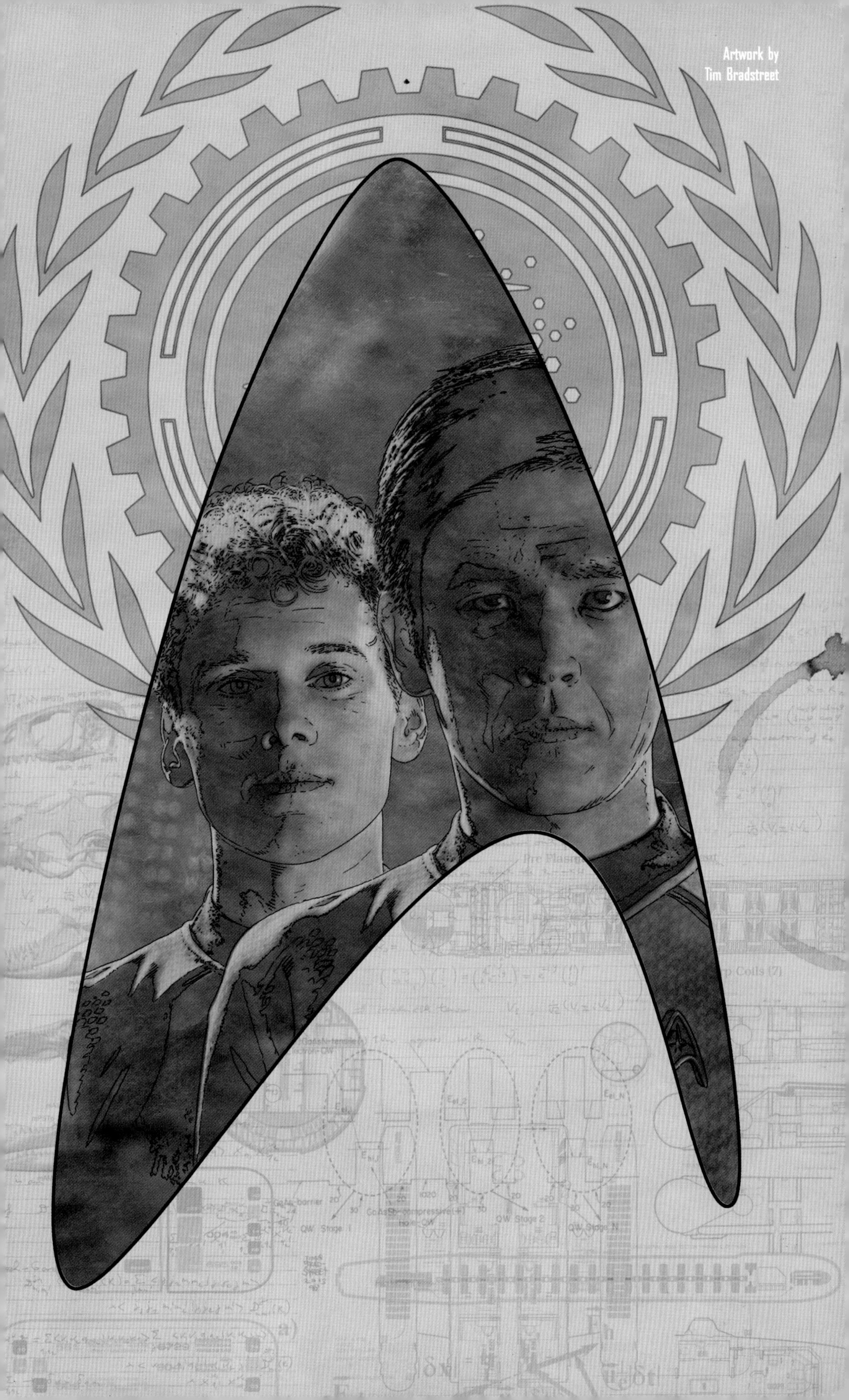
Artwork by
Tim Bradstreet